The Lucky Gods of Otsu

of

Otsu

An Akitada Novel

I. J. Parker

I•J•P
2021

Published 2021 by I.J.Parker and I·J·P Books
3229 Morningside Drive, Chesapeake VA 23321
http://www.ijparker.com
Cover design by I. J. Parker.
Cover image by Chikanobu
Back cover image of Ebisu by Utagawa
Publisher's Note: This is a work of fiction. Names, characters, places, and
incidents are a product of the author's imagination.

The Lucky Gods of Otsu, 1st edition, 2021
ISBN 9798493315848

Praise for I. J. Parker and the Akitada Series

"Elegant and entertaining . . . Parker has created a wonderful protagonist in Akitada. . . . She puts us at ease in a Japan of one thousand years ago." *The Boston Globe*

"You couldn't ask for a more gracious introduction to the exotic world of Imperial Japan than the stately historical novels of I. J. Parker." *The New York Times*

"Akitada is as rich a character as Robert Van Gulik's intriguing detective, Judge Dee." *The Dallas Morning News*

"Readers will be enchanted by Akitada." *Publishers Weekly* Starred Review

"Terrifically imaginative" *The Wall Street Journal*

"A brisk and well-plotted mystery with a cast of regulars who become more fully developed with every episode." *Kirkus*

"More than just a mystery novel, (*THE CONVICT'S SWORD*) is a superb piece of literature set against the backdrop of 11th-cntury Kyoto." *The Japan Times*

Characters

Japanese family names precede proper names

Main characters:

Sugawara Akitada   nobleman, official
Sadako   his wife
Yasuko   his daughter
Minamoto Michiyasu   her suitor
Akiko   Akitada's sister
Tora, Genba, Saburo   his retainers
Nakatoshi   his friend
Fujiwara Morozane   minister, his superior
(also: the prime minister and assorted officials)

Characters associated with the case of government corruption:

Fujiwara Sanenari   governor of Omi Province
Fujiwara Yoshinaro   Markets Office director
Minamoto Norisuke   provincial chief
Master Cricket   hermit
Kai, Masashi   young boys, brothers
(also: beggars, laborers, street children, and the lucky gods of Otsu)

1

Characters associated with the murder of a former police official:

Kobe	former police superintendent
Heishiro	his son
Hayashi	his servant
Haruko	another servant
Nagaie	a pharmacist
Kojima	an overseer

(also: local police, a learned physician, and an abbot)

Characters connected with the disappearance of a noblewoman:

Fujiwara Yukiko	Akitada's former wife
Fujiwara Kosehira	her father, Akitada's friend
Fujiwara Arihito	her brother
Lord Okura	her former lover

(also: a servant couple).

1

Friends and Enemies

Sometimes bad news arrives when the world is new and full of hope.

It was spring again. Almost overnight, the young leaves had appeared on the willow trees that lined the canal. The sky was blue and a pair of courting ducks waddled along the canal below the veranda of the wine shop.

Two officials sat there. They were lifelong friends and had enjoyed their weekly get-together here for more than five years now. The place was near the *Daidairi* where both worked but had somehow escaped the attention of most other officials in spite of its excellent wine.

The taller of the two was Sugawara Akitada, senior secretary in the Ministry of Justice. The other was Ono Nakatoshi, junior assistant minister of Ceremonial. Both had served their government all their lives and grown gray in the service.

Nakatoshi glanced at Akitada and said, "It's a beautiful morning. Why are you so glum today?"

"I'm getting old and I'm still a poor man and that grieves me for the first time."

Nakatoshi chuckled. "What are a few more gray hairs? Look at me! I've lost most of mine. And you're not a poor man."

"I didn't think so, but now my daughter has a suitor."

"My best wishes. Lady Yasuko is a beauty and must be eighteen by now. It's high time she was married and gave you grandchildren. Or has she set herself against your wishes?"

Akitada smiled a little. "Not at all. She's quite eager to leave her home."

His friend raised his brows. "The groom won't move in? He has his own establishment then? He must be a prosperous man."

"He is. That's the problem. There is the matter of the dowry." When Nakatoshi still looked blank, Akitada added, "Her suitor is Minamoto Michiyasu."

"Michiyasu? But that's excellent. Don't worry. He's a very nice young man and much sought after. But yes, his family is wealthy. Is he unaware of your position?"

Akitada sighed. "I have no idea. Yasuko met him when she was invited to court. That was my sister's doing. Since then it seems he's been a secret visitor to my home. My wife told me of the affair and I was about to put an end to it when his friend Fujiwara Akimitsu arrived on his behalf to offer marriage." He grimaced. "Mind you, I could see that Akimitsu was uncomfortable, but when I was blunt about my circumstances, he said that Michiyasu was deeply enamored and quite determined. He actually cast up his eyes. It was embarrassing."

"Oh, dear. What will you do?"

"Nothing for the time being. Perhaps Akimitsu will talk him out of it. But it brought home to me my responsibilities to my children. And I was passed over for promotion again this year."

"Such a marriage is sure to bring you good fortune in the future. Michiyasu's father will see to it that your name is on the promotion rolls."

"I'd be ashamed to owe it to my daughter's husband rather than my own work. It's not who I am or ever can be. No, I fear Yasuko will be very disappointed when she finds out she isn't wanted after all."

Nakatoshi said, "Surely there may still be hope? If the young man is truly in love . . ."

Akitada smiled a little sadly. "You're an incurable romantic, Nakatoshi."

Silence fell, while the two men watched the ducks foraging among the weeds. The female was quite busy, while the male hovered protectively, watching for danger.

After a while, Nakatoshi said, "I'm afraid my own news isn't very good either."

"Why? More wars?"

"Not precisely, though the monks on Mount Hiei are starting new quarrels. No, your minister may be replaced."

"What? There have been no complaints. I thought everything was running smoothly."

Nakatoshi nodded. "Thanks to your hard work. I know very well that you've carried the load for many years now. And so do they."

"Kaneie is not a bad official. And I've had a lot of help from the staff. But tell me what's going on!"

"They say Fujiwara Morozane has expressed an interest in the position."

"Morozane?" Akitada frowned.

"Yes. He's a toady who'll use his power to further the interests of our prime minister."

"Oh. But surely the Ministry of Justice isn't the best place to do that." Akitada paused and swallowed. "Unless . . ."

"Indeed. They plan to pass new laws to enrich their cronies."

"Well, that settles my fate then. And Yasuko's. I shall have to resign." Akitada rose abruptly, causing the ducks to fly away with a clatter of wings. "I'd better get back to work."

Nakatoshi said quickly, "Don't do anything rash, Akitada. Things at court change daily."

Akitada nodded. "Don't worry. Let's hope there's better news next time we meet."

Akitada returned to his office and sat behind his desk. He stared with unseeing eyes at the documents that lay spread out on it. What was he to do? He wished Kosehira were home, but his other longtime friend had taken on another governorship and was presently in Izumo Province.

It was true that young Michiyasa had a surprisingly good reputation among the imperial offspring. He was one of the grandsons of Emperor Go-Ichijo. Michiyasa's father had accepted the Minamoto name and resigned his claim to the succession. But even as a commoner, Michiyasa was still part of the highest-ranking elite in the government with all the opportunities and wealth that entailed. Such a man could expect a rich dowry with each wife.

Akitada had just passed into his fifty-second year. He had grown gray laboring over dusty documents in this ministry. He had suffered wounds and bore the scars of his service elsewhere. And he had little to show for it. Or at least not much more than had fallen to him as his father's heir. He had failed to enrich himself as others did when they were promoted. And now his daughter would be bitterly disappointed in him.

The thought brought tears to his eyes. He buried his head in his hands and groaned.

"Sir?"

Startled, Akitada dropped his hands and looked up at his clerk, ashamed to be caught in a fit of self-pity. "What?" he snapped.

The clerk's eyes widened. "There's s-someone to s-see you, sir," he stammered.. "I'm very sorry f-for the interruption, but I thought it was important."

Akitada said, "I left word that I was too busy to see people."

The clerk retreated a few steps. "I . . . I didn't know, sir." He fell to his knees and touched his head to the floor.

The man's hair was nearly white and had grown quite thin.

Akitada gulped. "Oh, get up!" he said, dabbing his eyes with his sleeve. "I shouldn't have spoken to you like that. My mind was elsewhere. I'm sorry. Who wants to see me?"

The man scrambled up painfully. He was even older than Akitada and had also spent his life in this ministry, taking abuse from his superiors. Akitada resolved to be kinder to him and to the others from now on.

Then the clerk said, "It's a Lord Okura, sir."

Akitada thought he had not heard correctly. "Who?"

"Lord Okura. I believe he currently serves as director of the Bureau of Horses. I did not think I should turn him away, sir."

"No. But why . . ." Akitada was at a loss to explain this visit. What could have brought his ex-wife's lover to visit him? All these years they had carefully avoided a meeting. First the problem with the dowry and the likelihood of his resignation and now his ex-wife's lover at his door!

The clerk shifted from foot to foot. "What should I do?" he asked timidly.

"Show him in!"

The clerk walked out and Akitada got to his feet, brushing a hand over his hair and arranging his robe. He felt a mild curiosity to see the man who had seduced his young wife and left her pregnant. And had not bothered to offer her marriage after Akitada had divorced her!

The man who came in was both much younger than Akitada. He was tall, broad in the shoulder, straight-backed, and slightly tanned as if he enjoyed outdoor pursuits. His thick hair was neatly tied and he had a well-trimmed beard and mustache. But his face was too fleshy, and his body showed signs of becoming portly in the future. Still, he was impressive in appearance and manner, his robe and trousers were of the finest brocade and silk and the colors were unexpectedly tasteful for someone who spent his days at court seducing impressionable young females.

They bowed to each other.

Okura smiled and said pleasantly, "It is very good of you to see me, Akitada. I know you must be very busy.

Akitada said coldly, "Indeed. In what way may I assist you, my lord?"

Okura flushed a little. He had used Akitada's proper name, as was customary among equals, but Akitada had insisted on the distance between officials of different ranks. Okura was one rank below him.

His visitor became flustered and glanced about the room. "It concerns the Lady Yukiko," he said, sounding a little desperate.

"Then you have come to the wrong place. I have no contact with my former wife."

For a moment it looked as though Okura would leave without another word. But he bit his lip and said, "I'm worried about her and there is no one else. Her father's house stands empty. Believe me, I would not have come here if I could have gone elsewhere." He made a perfunctory bow and turned.

Akitada recalled the unfortunate clerk. He cleared his throat. "Wait! I regret my lack of courtesy. Please sit down and tell me what the problem is."

Okura hesitated for a moment, then returned and sat down. "I think she's ill," he said. "And now she seems to have disappeared."

"Ill? How ill?"

Okura looked embarrassed. "I'm afraid I don't know. We haven't kept in touch."

Akitada could feel the old resentment returning. "Then what makes you think she needs your help now?"

Okura flushed again. "I don't think there is anybody else." He paused, then said defensively, "She has

7

refused to see me. I finally gave up. But now . . ." He stopped.

Discussing the relationship between Yukiko and her ex-lover was utterly repugnant, but Akitada asked, "What has happened to cause you such concern?"

"Someone has seen her and reported that she is deathly ill. When I tried to find her, no one knew where she was."

"Where and when did this person see her last?"

"A week ago. He paid a visit to her house in the eastern hills. But when I went there, I found the house abandoned and empty."

Akitada, who did not know Yukiko had a house in the eastern hills, a house where male visitors were apparently welcome, decided to end the conversation. He said, "I regret that Lady Yukiko is not well, but I think you must bring the matter to the attention of her family. Lord Kosehira should be notified."

Okura hung his head. "It will take weeks. He's in Izumo," he said dully.

"You may try her brother Arihito. He is, I believe, at the family estate outside Otsu."

Okura got up. "I didn't know that. Yes, I shall go immediately. Thank you. My apologies for this, um, awkward intrusion."

He bowed and fled, leaving behind a whiff of the expensive sandalwood incense used to perfume his robes and a bemused Akitada.

2

Trouble at the Ministry

Okura's news that Yukiko was seriously ill troubled Akitada enough that he went to speak to his sister Akiko who was a frequent visitor at court and would surely have heard some gossip if it was true. He doubted the tale because his ex-wife had always been of robust health and was only thirty-six years old.

Akiko was only a few years younger than he, but she dressed well and carried herself with considerable elegance. She waved him to a cushion and asked, "Well, have you signed the marriage contracts?"

His personal worries instantly returned. "No. I see no way to satisfy their expectations. That's not why I'm here."

Akiko sighed. "A pity. Such a fine match and Michiyasu is such a nice man. I suppose it cannot be.

I've tried to tell you to make more of an effort." She saw her brother's face. "Oh, I'm sorry. I didn't mean that. Forgive me."

"No, you're right. I blame myself, but still I know I couldn't have done the things that would have given me the sort of wealth that is required. The match is simply too uneven."

"Well. Yasuko will get over it. What brings you then?"

"I had a visit from Okura yesterday."

Her eyebrows rose. "Do tell!"

"Yes. I was stunned and rather rude to him, I'm afraid. He wanted to find Yukiko."

"No!" Akiko, rarely surprised by court scandals, gasped. "He comes to you to find her?"

"Yes. He says she's ill and must be found. I sent him to Arihito, but the story seemed so unlikely I thought I'd ask you about it."

"She hasn't been at court lately. Come to think of it, I haven't heard her mentioned this year at all. She could be paying a visit to Kosehira. He's raising her child, isn't he?"

"Yes, he's adopted the little girl. But Okura says she was staying at her own place only a week ago."

"Then perhaps she's gone on a pilgrimage? Or she's gone to live with another man."

"The latter seems most likely," Akitada said dryly. "So you've heard nothing about an illness?"

"Not a word."

Akitada got up. "Well, Okura's been misinformed then. I expect Arihito will reassure him."

"But how odd!" Akiko said. "I thought that affair was over years ago."

Akitada did not want to pursue the subject. "I don't care one way or another. And I'd better get back to the office. The minister wants to see me today."

The minister of justice, Kaneie, was busy sorting documents into boxes with the help of several clerks. Akitada stopped just inside the door, surprised.

Kaneie looked up. "Ah, there you are! I'm getting out. Taking my personal papers. Don't want those falling in the wrong hands."

"What happened?" Akitada got along well with Kaneie. Over the years they had come to appreciate each other's qualities. Kaneie knew little about the intricacies of the law, but he was an easy-going man who had friends on many levels and of all ranks. He appreciated Akitada's expertise and had left decisions to him.

Kaneie grimaced. "Have been reassigned. Kyushu, I'm afraid. You know the place, I think."

Akitada had served briefly as governor in one of the provinces in Kyushu. It had been a tragic assignment because he had lost his first wife and a child while he was there. He nodded and recalled Nakatoshi's news. Things were happening too quickly. "But why now? Such assignments are usually made for the New Year."

"I have no idea. I've been told my successor is Fujiwara Morozane."

So it was true. And he was quite unprepared to deal with it. He looked around Kaneie's office in sudden desperation. Morozane would be a hard man to work for.

Kaneie guessed Akitada's thoughts. He said in a kindly tone, "Don't look so worried, Akitada. The man would have to be an idiot not to recognize that you've been running the place for years."

11

That was generous. Akitada said quickly, "Not at all, Kaneie. But we've worked well together. It grieves me to see you leave."

Kaneie turned back to his boxes. "Yes, well, it can't be helped. I don't relish leaving."

Akitada hesitated, then asked, "May we not share a meal or a cup of wine before you go?"

Kaneie closed a lid and came to him. "Of course we may. I'm too depressed to go on with this. Let's go!" He told the clerks to finish up and have the boxes taken to his house, and then walked out of the ministry with Akitada.

They headed for the same wine shop where Akitada had met with Nakatoshi earlier. The owner greeted them with a broad grin, probably convinced that Akitada had developed a chronic thirst.

The hour they spent together did nothing to cheer up either, though the springlike weather still prevailed. Akitada shared some of his experiences in Kyushu, and Kaneie revealed that his assignment, while ostensibly a promotion, was most likely a form of punishment because he had expressed reservations about some changes in existing laws.

He said, looking doleful, "I had meant to consult you about this, but now it doesn't matter."

"What did it concern?"

"Oh, the transport system from the eastern provinces. You know there have been many complaints recently. Well, someone wants fewer restrictions on the local officials. I refused."

"Fewer? Those complaints were mostly about the officials, as I recall."

"Indeed. I pointed this out. I'm afraid my comments were not well received."

"But who wants those illegalities to continue?"

Kaneie gave him a pitying look. "Sometimes, Akitada, I wonder about your good sense. Clearly somebody is making a lot of money in places like Otsu and Yamazaki."

Akitada flushed a little. Kaneie was right. He should have known this. But it had been a terrible day for upsetting news. And now Kaneie was leaving, and that meant that very soon he would have to cope with a new minister and one who might expect him to bend the rules and rewrite the laws.

"I shall have to resign," he said.

"Don't be ridiculous. What would you do? No, we all submit to whatever men are in power and hope we can subdue our consciences."

"You didn't," Akitada pointed out.

"Do you plan to join me in Kyushu? Or perhaps they'll find an even more hopeless and remote place for you."

They stared at each other, and Akitada realized that he would miss Kaneie not only as an understanding and fair superior but as a friend. Too late now. They would probably not see each other again.

Akitada said, "Can you refuse to go? Is there nothing else you can do?"

Kaneie drained his cup. "No, my dear Akitada. I fear for you. You are too good an official to fare well in the present government. Will you write me an occasional letter?"

"Yes. Will you come back for a visit?"

"If my fortune permits it." Kaneie smiled. "If I do, we'll come back to this place. The wine is excellent.

13

But now I must go home and make my preparations for the journey."

They left together and walked back to the ministry where they embraced, much to the consternation of the clerks, and then parted.

Akitada spent the rest of the day clearing the paperwork on his desk and getting ready to receive the new minister. He knew little of Fujiwara Morozane's ability because the man had spent most of his time serving in various provinces and had only recently returned. The New Year's appointments had listed him as one of the lucky men who had been promoted in rank. Perhaps he was an efficient administrator.

But he did not believe that they would get along, not after Nakatoshi's warning and Kaneie's comments. Nakatoshi had called the man a toady and said he was the prime minister's choice.

Morozane had been given the position because the prime minister, or someone close to him, wanted changes in current laws. And now Kaneie had confirmed it. Akitada suspected that he would be opposed to these changes and foresaw serious problems.

Akitada stared bleakly around his tidy office. Night had fallen and the ministry had grown silent. Kaneie was gone, along with the rest of the staff.

Tomorrow was a day of rest, and the coming week could wait.

3

Only a Servant

Sadako was waiting in her husband's study. As always his heart lifted when he saw her. Sadako was his third wife. She had been a companion to his daughter Yasuko after his first wife had died in childbirth and his second had left him. They had been married now for five years, the happiest of his life even though they had lost two unborn children early in her pregnancies and she still grieved that she had not given him a child. He, for his part, was relieved because he had not wanted more children. Besides, given his present worries about his daughter's future, he could have ill afforded them.

Sadako bowed formally to her returning husband and murmured, "I hope you've had a good day, Akitada."

"Thank you. Let's not talk about it. How are you, my love?"

"I am very well now that you're home." She studied his face anxiously. "Would you like the evening rice now?"

"Later. Will you have a cup of wine with me first?"

As soon as she had poured and he had taken his first sip, he said, "Kaneie is leaving."

Sadako smiled. "Oh, is that all? Where is he going?"

"Transferred to Kyushu."

"Oh!" She grasped the implications and her shock hung between them in the heavy silence.

Akitada sighed and added, "Fujiwara Morozane will take over from him."

"A difficult man?"

"More than likely."

"What will it mean for you?"

"I suppose I'll wait and see." To take her mind off the dangers lurking in their future, he said next, "Lord Okura paid me a visit today."

Sadako looked puzzled. "But isn't he . . .?"

"Yes. The likely father of Yukiko's daughter."

"How strange! Why did he come to you?"

"Concern for Yukiko. He cannot find her."

"He cannot find her and comes to you to look for her?"

"Exactly."

She laughed, and after a moment he joined her and felt a little better.

"He must be a very silly man," Sadako said, still giggling. "I wonder what she saw in him."

"Well, he's much younger than I and very handsome."

She gave him an adoring look. "He cannot be more handsome than you."

Akitada took her hand and kissed it.

She smiled. "You've had a very exciting day."

He nodded. "And you?"

"Well, not so much, though there was a rumor about the superintendent."

"Kobe? What rumor?"

"They say someone broke into his house and attacked his servant."

Akitada frowned. "I worry about him. He's getting frail. I think I'll ride out to see him tomorrow."

Neither thought the situation dire yet and turned to more pleasant matters.

The next day was one of rest for officials. Akitada started it with his usual sword practice with Tora. They had both been out of practice and become aware of it. Their days of fighting were long since over, but age and a sense of inadequacy had crept in, and the daily sword practice served to keep both at bay.

Afterwards, Akitada saddled his horse and rode out to the Kadono district where Kobe's small farm was. When he arrived, he found Kobe safe though very shaken. His servant had not fared as well. He was, like his master, an old man, and a blow to his head had proved fatal. The district police had come and taken Hayashi's body away with them. Kobe sat outside his house, white-faced and looking ill. When Akitada greeted him, he alternately wept and shook with impotent fury.

"Who would do such a thing, I ask you?" he said. "Hayashi was as weak as a bird. The thief could've

17

just pushed him aside and helped himself to whatever he wanted. But he was a monster, a devil who enjoys destroying people. They must find him and kill him."

Akitada tried to soothe his anger. "They will, my friend. Give them time!"

Kobe glared at him. "Time? There's not enough of that for any of us. We've grown old like poor Hayashi. Look at me! I'm a useless wreck."

The words "we" and "us" struck Akitada forcibly. Kobe was a decade older than he, but they had both reached a point in their lives where hope for the future dimmed along with their physical stamina. He bit his lip and started asking questions.

Kobe had been on a visit to the nearby Saga temple. Like most people, he had become more devout with age. While he was gone, a robber had apparently entered his house in search of money and had been met by Hayashi. The intruder had made quick work of the old servant and then had taken his time searching and destroying the contents of Kobe's house. Kobe had returned that evening and found Hayashi dead among the debris.

The inside of the house looked terrible. Everywhere there was wanton destruction. The robber had taken an axe to furnishings, scattered books and papers, broken open chests and trunks and rifled through them, leaving the contents strewn across the floor. In the kitchen area, every bowl was smashed and the sacks of beans and rice slashed, spilling their content across the stone slabs.

Akitada shook his head at it. "Are you sure this was just one thief?"

Kobe pointed to tracks. "He stepped in some rice flour. I saw only one size of footprints. He was wearing boots."

Akitada went to look. "Did you notice that one of the boots is missing a bit from the sole? The left one, I think."

Kobe revived a little and came to inspect the tracks. "Right," he said. "It will be proof. If they find him, that is. But he's long gone by now. I wish I hadn't left Hayashi to face the bastard alone." He swayed for a moment and held on to one of the beams that supported the roof.

Akitada said, "You might be dead also. We'll find him. Are you feeling ill? Is there some wine? Or water?"

Kobe gulped. "No. Don't bother. I can't keep anything down."

Akitada did not like his friend's condition, but he asked, "What did he take?"

"I don't know and I don't care." He added in a broken voice, "It's Hayashi I've lost. I loved that old man. There's nothing left for me now. I don't want to live any longer." Kobe covered his face.

Akitada thought such grief seemed excessive. He said firmly, "Hayashi was old and he was only a servant. There are other servants." As soon as he said it, Akitada realized his mistake. "I'm sorry. I didn't mean it like that."

But Kobe had already turned away from him. "Go home, Akitada. There's nothing you can do here."

"You're coming with me. You cannot stay here by yourself."

"I'm staying." Kobe staggered away, stopped, and looked blankly around at the destruction.

Akitada said sadly, "It grieves me, my old friend, that you will not accept my offer."

There was a moment's silence. Then Kobe seemed to give himself a little shake. "Oh, well, in that case, let's go."

On the way, they stopped at the police station for the district. Kobe looked gray and sagged in the saddle, but the sergeant and the local pharmacist who had looked at Hayashi's body came out to talk to them.

The pharmacist was a nervous little man, made all the more so when confronting a high-ranking official and the retired superintendent of the capital police. He bowed repeatedly and stated in a high voice, "The subject died as the result of a deep wound to his head. It seems he lived only a short time after receiving this wound."

Kobe stared down at him. "He lived a while? How long?"

The pharmacist twisted his hands. "Impossible to say, sir."

Kobe glared. "What? Don't you know your job? How many bodies have you seen like his?"

The pharmacist cringed. "Not so many, sir. I'm sorry, sir."

Kobe muttered a curse and looked at the sergeant. "We found tracks. Did you see them?"

The sergeant shot a glance of commiseration at the coroner. "Yes, sir. One person's prints. A man, I think. A large man. Inside the house only. Nothing outside."

It had been dry weather, so Akitada was not surprised that nothing had been found outside. Kobe was not so easily assured. "No horse tracks?" he demanded.

The sergeant said, "There could have been, but you, sir, also returned on a horse."

Kobe nodded. "Well, what are you doing?"

"Sir, we think the murderer came to attack you."

Kobe became agitated again. "No. Why would he do that? I wasn't home. No, he wanted to steal and Hayashi caught him. Round up all the known villains and question them."

The sergeant looked uncomfortable. "We don't have anyone like that here. He must have come from the city. You know only farmers live around here. They're all honest."

Akitada doubted this claim, but he knew well enough that the sort of violence he had seen was not the work of an ordinary thief. He asked Kobe, "Do you keep anything in your house that might have brought this person to your place? An ordinary thief would not have stayed when confronted by a servant. Whoever it was wasn't deterred by Hayashi and he spent a good deal of time and effort searching through your belongings after he had knocked him out."

The sergeant nodded eagerly. "Yes, sir. This was personal. The mess he made. This was an angry man, sir."

Kobe was silent for a moment. Then he shook his head. "Nonsense. It's what any lout would do after not finding gold. I had no gold and precious little silver."

The sergeant said, "Well, are you sure there isn't someone who had a reason to hurt you? Someone from your time in the police, I mean? Some criminal who escaped from jail or came back from some prison camp?"

Kobe shook his head again. "It's not likely. It's been too long since I left my position. And why kill my poor Hayashi if he wanted me?"

The sergeant had no answer. "We'll keep looking, sir. Will you let us know if you remember someone who might bear a grudge?"

Kobe sighed. He looked exhausted. "I'll be staying with Lord Sugawara. Keep me informed. And tell the monks, I want a good funeral for Hayashi. I'll pay for it."

As they turned the horses to leave, Kobe would have fallen off if Akitada had not caught him. He asked, "Do you feel able to ride?"

"Yes. Don't fuss. I just get a little light-headed sometimes. Haven't eaten much lately."

Akitada did not find this reassuring, but they managed to return to the capital without incidents. After Kobe dismounted, he clung to his saddle. With Genba's help, Akitada got him into the house and to the room next to his study. Sadako came and called for maids who spread bedding. Kobe protested weakly, but in the end he lay down and closed his eyes. They left him.

Akitada sent for a doctor. Then he told his wife what he had found at Kobe's house. "The sergeant was right," he said. "This was personal. The intruder was searching for something but he was also very angry. He destroyed everything he saw."

Sadako said softly, "He killed the servant."

"Yes. Kobe was extremely distraught. He must have been fond of the man."

"It's natural. They were two old men who had no one but each other."

Akitada looked surprised. "But Hayashi was only a servant. They had nothing in common."

"We cannot know that, Akitada. Remember Kobe's companion Sachi."

Yes, there was that.

Kobe, a man who was well-born, had briefly attended the university in his youth and later married well and raised a family. Then, when he was almost sixty, he had suddenly taken a blind shampoo girl from the willow quarter as his fourth wife. Since she had also been a murder suspect at the time, the scandal had cost him his post and his family. He and Sachi had moved to the farm, leaving the rest of his property to his other family. Their affair had been very moving because they had been so utterly devoted to each other, but Sachi had become ill and had died. Kobe had not returned to his former family, who had treated him and Sachi with angry disdain. Since then, he had lived alone, except for Hayashi.

Akitada thought of the past and felt the old guilt again. He had been preoccupied with his own problems and all too often he had forgotten Kobe on his remote farm. The fact was, he too had been scandalized by Kobe's behavior. He noted that Sadako had referred to Sachi as his "companion" rather than his wife, and yet Kobe had treated her as a wife, as a favorite wife, which she could never be in the real world. Therein lay the scandal and the reason why his family had rejected him.

"Poor man," Sadako said into the long silence.

Akitada had never thought of Kobe with pity. In the early years, Kobe had been a hard-driving policeman who had frequently irritated him. Kobe's background was different from his own. Though he came from a good background, his people had gradually sunk in the hierarchy of families and had sent their only son into the military. But Kobe was intelligent and well-read and those facts brought him to the attention of those in power who thought he might do well in the capital police. He worked his way up to become superintendent. He was not as malleable as they had hoped, but conditions improved in the city and around the *Daidairi* thanks to his rigorous prosecution of criminals and so he stayed in his position.

But the current Kobe was a broken man. The love affair with Sachi had caused the break with his family and Kobe had been deeply hurt when his adult children had rejected and mocked him. Sachi's death had done the rest. And then he had been alone.

"He was quite strong when I saw him last," Akitada said defensively.

"Do you think he's seriously ill?"

"I hope not. He grieves for Hayashi, blames himself."

"You will investigate the murder, won't you?"

Akitada was dismayed. "The police are doing that. It's not my business."

"He's your friend."

"Yes, but Hayashi was a servant and even older than Kobe. It was probably an accident that the blow killed him."

Sadako looked severe as she got up. "I think, Akitada, that you must become involved. A friend would expect it. I'm going to bed."

Akitada sat for a long time by himself, trying to make sense of the events of the last two days, hoping to find ways to deal with all his new troubles.

24

4

The New Minister

When Akitada arrived at his office the next morning, an unnatural quiet seemed to have fallen on the building. The Ministry of Justice employed a number of senior students from the university to work in its archives. He had himself started his professional career there and knew well enough that youngsters found the archives incredibly dull and used every chance to leave, chasing each other down the corridors and pretending to be on some urgent mission if caught.

Now the corridors lay empty and the doors were all closed. Perhaps, he thought, they had been given the day off as the ministry servants prepared for the arrival of a new minister.

His own room was empty. Neither of his two clerks had arrived. He heaved a sigh of relief. A quiet morning was what he had hoped for.

Then he saw the documents on his desk. His desk had been clean the night before. They did not look at all familiar. Where had they come from? He had plenty to occupy himself and Kaneie had left. So who could have decided to add to his assignments?

He approached the documents much as a man might approach a poisonous snake and was just extending a cautious finger to lift the top cover, when the door opened behind him.

"Sugawara?"

Akitada jumped and turned around. In the doorway stood a short man with a large belly and a round face. He looked irritated as he stared at him without introducing himself or explaining his improper and sudden arrival. Akitada had never seen him before. The man wore the black robe of most officials but he was a stranger.

Akitada said, "Yes. And you are?"

The fat man waddled in and closed the door. "I would have thought you might have called on me when you got the news."

"What news?"

The fat man cast up his eyes in exasperation. "Of my appointment, of course. If you had bothered to attend the formal meetings called by the prime minister, you might have known who I am."

An awful suspicion dawned. "Lord Morozane?"

"Correct. You might bow. Clearly you lack even the most basic manners. They did say you are an odd character."

Resentment rose in Akitada. "Did they? I'm not surprised. I'm afraid they neglected to keep me apprised of your arrival." He decided to ignore the comment about missed meetings and bowed belatedly.

"Allow me to welcome you to the ministry, Lord Morozane. I'm at your service."

Morozane came farther into the room and looked around. "You've been given extravagant accommodations. A veranda and a private courtyard? And two desks for clerks?"

Akitada said mildly, "I've served here for many years and I *am* the senior secretary."

"In my view it's not a good thing when officials become too comfortable in their positions."

Akitada bit his lip. "I've also served as governor a few times."

But Morozane had lost interest in Akitada's career. He went to the desk and pointed at the documents with a pudgy and accusing hand. "You don't seem in any hurry to start working." Then he turned on his heel and waddled out.

Akitada found his hands and knees were shaking with suppressed anger. He went to sit down. This was as bad a start to working with the new minister as could be imagined. It was almost as if Morozane had come purposely to declare war. Everything the man had said pointed to an animosity that was very strange, given that they had never met. He had no idea what was behind it, but it was clear his life was about to become very difficult.

With a sigh, he turned to the documents. He found they concerned complaints against several local officials in Omi Province. The complaints were by an abbot and by several men who were living and working in the capital. One was a ranking member of the court. The others were merchants and officials in the city administration. The complaints contained charges of malfeasance by local landowners and notables, as well as

27

depredations by gangs of transport workers of various types.

He was mildly shocked by the number of incidents and the details. Such problems had existed for a long time, but not until now had they become quite so serious. In the past, complaints had usually proved to be minor squabbles over rights the government had given certain individuals to collect fees in return for supervising the smooth transfer of goods between the provinces and the capital. The local people had resented interference in what they considered their domain and they had carried on small wars of retaliation. Usually, a strong letter of warning had stopped them. But in these complaints there were charges not only of thefts amounting to whole shipments of goods, but also of armed conflicts that had resulted in people dying.

Akitada made some notes about the more serious incidents in preparation for his report to Morozane. He was in the midst of this, when a servant announced Lord Okura.

Okura came in almost shyly. "Forgive me," he said. "You must be very busy. I understand your new superior has arrived."

Akitada did not hide his irritation. "That is so," he said. "What do you want this time?"

Okura took a couple of steps toward him and paused. "I've been to Otsu. To her brother's house. They wouldn't speak to me. The servants said they haven't seen her or heard from her for weeks. I'm worried."

So Arihito had refused to receive Okura. He shared Akitada's outrage at the man who had seduced his sister. This pleased Akitada. He said more calmly,

"It's still none of my business. And as you say, I'm very busy."

The other man looked at him reproachfully. "How can you be so hard? You must have loved her once. Don't you care at all what happens to her?"

Angry again, Akitada got to his feet. "Don't be ridiculous. I expect my former wife has shared her opinion of me while you were lovers."

Okura had the grace to blush. He murmured, "She was very young. And very disappointed. You mustn't blame her. She wept bitter tears."

So he had been right. Yukiko had mocked him behind his back to her lover. Akitada said bitterly, "Yukiko betrayed me with you and probably with other men at court while I served in a distant province. She refused to join me or to live with me as my wife in my home. When she found herself pregnant and abandoned, I offered to acknowledge her child, but she refused again. I had no choice but to divorce her. And now you, her lover, and probably the father of her child, come to *me* for help?"

Okura hung his head. "Yes. Because there is no one else and because I thought you had a heart." He paused. "This is not about the past. This is about now."

The other man's persistence was surprising. And he had not denied being the father of Yukiko's child. Akitada felt a grudging admiration and a sudden curiosity to understand this man. "Why did you abandon her all those years ago? It seems to me that you had an obligation to acknowledge your child. Besides, it was very much in your interest. Yukiko is well-born and her father is an influential and wealthy man in the government. Kosehira dotes on his eldest daughter and would have done his utmost to promote your future interests. Furthermore, you seem far more suited to each other in your ages and tastes than she and I were. You could have taken her to wife before the child was born. I would not have stopped her."

Okura smiled sadly. "She wouldn't have me. She was like one obsessed, ranting against you, but pushing me away. I tried to convince her that she must ask you for a divorce. She refused and left me to return to her family. I was twenty and a fool and I gave up."

Akitada thought about this. The man who had stolen his wife years ago had only been a year older than Yukiko. They had both been mere children caught in the intrigues and affairs of the court. He sighed and shook his head.

Okura shuffled his feet. "I'll go," he said. "But she always loved you. I thought you might have some thought for her even now."

Akitada relented a little. "Your confidence deserves another. I don't believe Yukiko ever loved me. She thought she did at one time, but that soon changed to hate. I made the mistake of tying so young a woman to me when I had nothing to offer her but the dull existence as the wife of a midlevel official. I'm married again now, and I don't want to get involved in this. Yukiko is likely to cause me more trouble."

Okura nodded. "Yes. I can't blame you. I'm very sorry." And he left.

Akitada wondered if the apology had been for the intrusion or the seduction.

Shaking his head again, he bent over the reports and complaints and finished his notes.

It seemed clear that something serious was afoot in Otsu. He should have been aware of it earlier. Had Kaneie ignored the information, or perhaps suppressed it? Kaneie must have expected his reassignment for weeks now. Why had he kept the news to himself? It was all very puzzling. Akitada hated not having all the information he needed to discuss the case with Morozane, but he had no choice. Perhaps he might learn something in the process.

Feeling every year weighing down on his lean frame, he got up, gathered the documents and his notes, and went to see the new minister.

A servant posted at the minister's door admitted him. Morozane was busy dictating to a harassed-looking clerk. It sounded like instructions of some sort and was couched in threatening language. Two other clerks, both formerly serving Akitada, were bent over their desks, wielding their brushes with the utmost concentration. The atmosphere was charged with fear and resentment, and Morozane looked like a fat disgruntled Buddha with his fat cheeks, double chin, and rounded belly.

Morozane took no notice of Akitada, who decided to ignore the rudeness and sat down to wait.

Morozane's command of Chinese was execrable. The clerks blinked or twitched occasionally, but fear kept them writing. No doubt the resulting mistakes would be blamed on them. Akitada's initial gratification that his own learning was far better than Morozane's gradually turned to anger. The government was not served well by putting the incompetent in charge of the competent. Then he realized that his own position had probably rested entirely on the fact that he could correct the errors of his superiors. When Morozane finally stopped dictating and turned to him, Akitada was in a dangerous mood.

"I expected you several hours ago. What took you so long?" Morozane's tone and his heavy frown made it clear to his staff that the senior secretary was no better than the lowliest student assistant.

Akitada pointed to his stack of documents. "There is a great deal of information here. And some requires research into the contracts and laws that are involved. It will take time to unravel."

"Get people to help you. And you should know the laws. Or is that no longer expected of a university graduate?" The fat lips twitched into a mocking smile.

"It is certainly expected. As is competency in Chinese," Akitada said angrily.

One of the clerks snorted, then tried to hide the sound by coughing. Morozane flushed. "You are impertinent."

Akitada said nothing. He merely looked at the man.

"You have brought your report?"

"I am ready to discuss the situation, sir."

"Discuss? I have no time for that. Hand over your written report."

"I have only made notes to remind myself of the main points. I expected that we would talk about the matter. I have some questions."

"What? You have done nothing? I'll have you know I expect better work than this. And you have questions? You were to find the answers, not return with more questions." Having turned red with anger, Morozane reached for a tissue and dabbed his face. "Why do they expect me to work with a staff that is inept and lazy?"

Akitada stood up. "I suggest you question your own ability to handle your new position before you attack my character or the performance of the people who have worked in this ministry for years." He made a perfunctory bow and stalked out of the room leaving the documents and his notes behind.

In his own office, he stood for a moment, breathing hard and staring sightlessly around. Then he left it also and went home.

5

Family Matters

At home, Akitada checked on Kobe first. He found the physician, a former court physician and professor, waiting for him.

"He's resting now, sir," the old man told him. "I confess I don't like his condition. He's much too weak and he doesn't want to eat. No appetite. When I urged some broth on him, he said it would come back up."

"He's had a great shock. He found his favorite servant dead. I suppose that would turn anyone's stomach."

The physician looked doubtful. "Perhaps. Pao Tzu says that sorrow from grief is injurious. In any case, he sleeps now. We must hope for the best. I'll return tomorrow."

Akitada thanked him and went to peer in on Kobe. The superintendent looked more peaceful. He lay on his back and snored a little. Akitada felt sorry for what had happened to his friend, but his own troubles weighed more heavily on his mind at the moment.

His wife Sadako—his joy, his only joy these days, it seemed—was showing his daughter how to sew a piece of clothing. Their heads were bent together, and the spring colors of their silk robes and of the new costume flowed together around their graceful figures like the glowing blossoms in the garden outside.

Yasuko, a young woman now, had a charming blush of excitement on her face. She had become very beautiful. He should have known she would attract suitors. He should have been prepared.

They had not heard him approach on his stockinged feet and he heard his daughter say, "Oh, Sadako, he is wonderful. He is gentle and very clever and he loves me. I still cannot believe it. I cannot tell you how he makes me feel! I'm all giddy and get hot just thinking about him."

Sadako said matter-of-factly, "You're in love. It's a form of madness."

"It's not madness!" Yasuko protested and looked up in the fullness of her emotions. Then she saw her father and blushed. "Oh, father! You shouldn't creep up on us like that."

Perhaps she had seen the dismay on his face, because the joy left her own. He said awkwardly, "I'm sorry. I didn't mean to interrupt."

Sadako got up and came to greet him with a little bow as was proper in a wife, then searched his face with anxious eyes. Akitada glanced at his daughter and sighed. Yes, she was beautiful, he thought, with the beauty and sparkle only youth could give, but what did she know of love?

Or loss!

Sadako touched his sleeve. "What's wrong, Akitada?"

For a moment, he wanted to keep the bad news to himself. But they deserved to know. And they must know before things went any further. He would have done anything to spare Yasuko.

"It's been a . . . difficult day," he started.

Sadako took his hand and pulled him toward a cushion. "Please sit down. Would you like some wine? Or tea?"

"Nothing. Thank you."

"Tell us. What happened?"

Akitada started with his encounter with Morozane. "I'm afraid I shall have to resign," he concluded.

Sadako glanced at his daughter. "Is it really inevitable? And just now? Could you delay a little?"

He shook his head. "I'm sorry, Yasuko. I've wracked my brain how to come up with a dowry suitable for this marriage. I simply do not have enough. And now I shall also have to do without my annual income. I'm afraid it's just impossible."

Yasuko turned pale. Her eyes were wide with shock. "I cannot be Michiyasu's wife?" she asked in a small voice.

"I see no way to make this happen, child. Michiyasu is a very nice young man, but he comes of a better family than ours, and a much wealthier one. Your dowry must be commensurate to your groom's position and wealth, or you'll at best be ranked as a mere concubine and your children most likely would suffer in the future when your husband's senior wives produce sons. I could not allow my daughter to suffer this fate."

It was blunt and Yasuko understood. How could she not? She had been exposed to years of explanations of the system from her aunt Akiko. She dropped her hands in her lap, and wept, at first silently, then in heart-rending sobs. It broke Akitada's heart. He went to her and knelt to take her into his arms, but she pushed him away, got up, and ran out of the room.

In his pain, he turned to Sadako who held him, murmuring soothing words into his ear. He could not later recall what she had said, only that he had needed to hear them, had needed her arms around him, had needed to know that she did not reject him also.

Later they shared their evening rice, which he ate somewhat listlessly while he told her about the new minister in greater detail. She said, "I'll speak to Yasuko. She is young and loves Michiyasa, but she must learn that life can be hard. She has not had to worry about the future and this has come as a shock to her."

He nodded. "I should have spoken to her about our circumstances before, but she seemed happy and well-adjusted. I was glad she had put the desire to go to court from her mind and I did not want to make her unhappy. As always, I've made things worse."

"No, Akitada. You mustn't blame yourself. Who could have guessed that such an extraordinary young man would discover her?"

Akitada frowned. "Akiko took her to court. And I think Yasuko has grown quite pretty, hasn't she? I should have suspected."

"She is beautiful. But I think the young man loves her for her character. Yasuko has good sense and a sweet and happy disposition. I expect her mother must have been that way."

Akitada smiled and reached for her hand. "She was. But Yasuko also had your example to follow. Will she ever forgive me?"

"Of course. But you must give her time. It is very hard to lose your first love. She will grieve."

Akitada pushed the rest of his food away. "I must see what I can do about finding another position. We shall need the income."

The Sugawara household now held some twenty members beyond Akitada's immediate family. All of them needed to be paid and kept in clothes and shelter. The horses needed fodder. The house needed repairs.

When night fell, he knew he would not be able to sleep and walked out into the garden. It, too, reminded him of his neglect. He had spent too many hours in the ministry, doing the work of others, and too little time on his own life. Perhaps it was too late to change, but at the moment he was bitter enough to let the ministry sort out its own affairs. He would not go in to work in the morning but instead look after his household and Kobe's recovery.

A loud hammering at the front gate sent him hurrying around the house and into the courtyard. There Genba, already in his night clothes, was talking with a caller outside.

"Who is it, Genba?"

Genba turned. "A stranger, sir. He asks to speak to you."

"Well, let him in."

Genba hesitated. "I don't have my sword, sir."

Perhaps it was unwise to open one's gate at this late hour. The capital suffered much from crime. Gangs roamed its streets and even found their way into the palace enclosure. It seemed typical that the new minister was concerned about unrest in Otsu while the increasing dangers in the capital did not signify.

"Never mind. Let him in."

Genba opened the small gate and admitted a youngish man in the dark clothing of a clerk. Thinking him one of the people employed at the ministry, Akitada asked, "What brings you so late?"

"It's about my father, sir. At the farm they said he left with you."

Astonished, Akitada asked, "You're Kobe's son?"

The other man nodded and bowed. "I'm Kobe Heishiro. I expected him to be at his house. Can I speak to him?"

Akitada knew only too well the pain Kobe's children had caused their father over Sachi. "No," he said. "He's in no condition to be disturbed. The murder of his servant has shaken his health severely. What do you want from him?"

"Is he . . . is he dying?"

Perhaps it was the flickering light from the lantern Genba was holding toward the visitor, but Akitada thought there was a hint of unpleasant eagerness in the man's face. "No," he said. "He is ill and upset. We hope that good care is all he needs. Why do you care?"

The visitor was taken aback by this question. "Well, he *is* my father, though his behavior has caused a distance between him and his own family. Naturally, we care about him. I shall take him home with me."

Akitada did not believe this at all, and he was suddenly tired of the problems that seemed to invade his peace of mind. He said, "No. He stays here. You had no business disturbing him or my house at this hour. Go back to your family. Your father doesn't need you."

Kobe's son opened his mouth to protest, but Genba had already opened the small gate again and made a move toward the unwelcome visitor, who decided to give up. Making Akitada a small bow, he left.

Genba slammed the gate and shot the latch. "Can't say I liked his looks. Nothing like his father."

"No. Nothing like him, Genba. Good night."

The visit troubled Akitada. It was out of character after all the years Kobe's children had not spoken to him. Still, perhaps they had felt enough to want to know how he was. On this thought, Akitada went to his room and to bed. He was finally able to sleep.

6

Facing the Tiger

The next morning dawned gray with low clouds obscuring Mount Hiei to the north and casting an oppressive light over the capital. It seemed a fitting start to Akitada's day. He had done poorly at this morning's sword practice and felt old and useless.

He stood on his veranda, looking out over the garden when he heard the rustling of a woman's gown in the room behind him. Thinking it was Sadako, he turned eagerly, but it was his daughter.

She looked wan and strained, her eyes large and red-rimmed as they searched his face. "Father?" she asked timidly. "May I ask you something?"

"Yes, of course."

"Are you unalterably set against my marriage to Michiyasu?"

43

"I have nothing against Michiyasu. I liked him and I hear good things about him, but Yasuko, I'm a poor man when it comes to such connections. I regret it very much now that I see how it has affected you."

"Michiyasu doesn't need your money or any property. He has said so. He loves me. He has no wish for a dowry."

"That does him honor, but the reality of the situation is that I cannot allow you to go to your future husband like a beggar. You must see that it will affect your future and that of your children."

Tears filled her eyes. She cried passionately, "I'm willing to risk it. I'm willing to risk anything. I cannot go on living without him."

Akitada's heart twisted. So she was deeply in love—or deeply in an infatuation. He recalled the passion with which Yukiko had informed her father that she could not live without Akitada. It did not matter what his daughter's attachment was; it was about to destroy their relationship. He said nothing.

Her eyes widened. "I see. You won't change your mind." Her voice broke.

He nodded. "I cannot. It's for your benefit and it grieves me deeply."

She clenched her hands. "No! Don't lie. You don't care about us. You don't even care about Sadako. You will go and resign your position because you don't like the new minister. You always do whatever pleases you without regard to anyone else." With that she spun around and ran from the room.

Akitada turned back to the sad-looking garden under its oppressive clouds and considered her accusation. Yes, he supposed he had always made decisions for all of them and many, perhaps too many of them, had been governed by what he considered to be his duty to the emperor and by his concept of justice. Either way, it would not make any difference in the case of a marriage with Michiyasu, but Akitada decided not to hand in his resignation. He would try to work with Morozane, for without his position at the ministry, his family would suffer.

And perhaps his luck might turn.

His room at the ministry was still empty of clerks, but someone had left messages from the outside on his desk. These were a common occurrence as other ministries and bureaus tried to spread information. He took it as a sign that he had not been dismissed yet and quickly looked through them. Among them was a letter from the Ministry of Ceremonial. He opened it and found it was from Nakatoshi.

It was couched in the usual official language to disguise its personal subject matter. "This is to advise you," Nakatoshi wrote, "that some new appointments have been made." Akitada saw a number of names, each with a brief description of the position and the rank. They meant nothing to him until he reached the categories of "transport system of Omi Province" and "administration of the markets of the capital."

He read, "His Majesty has graciously confirmed Lord Minamoto Norisuke to serve as chief of the transport system in Otsu, comprising both land and water transport. A rank of *shorokuijo* (senior sixth, upper grade) accompanies the appointment. His Majesty has also confirmed a new director of the markets office, Lord Fujiwara Yoshinaro, with the rank of *jugoige* (junior fifth rank, lower grade)."

The communication ended with, "It is hoped that you accord these officials the usual respect and co-operation."

It was clear that Nakatoshi had sent Akitada this information about the new officials because his work would bring him in contact with both.

Akitada went to the archives to inform himself further about these two men. There he found the usual number of students who seemed to be cowering over their work or hiding among the books. When they saw Akitada, they relaxed a little and bowed. Akitada greet-ed them by name. This encouraged the boldest to say, "He's a regular dragon, that Morosuke."

Akitada agreed privately but issued a reprimand for speaking disrespectfully of the new minister. The boy—he was perhaps sixteen and recently graduated—grinned. "Never mind, sir! I'm not long for this work anyway. I'm joining the palace guards. It's the palace where all the girls are."

This, too, deserved a reprimand, but Akitada's heart was not in it. He had thought the same in his days in the archives though he had been more timid about announcing it. He just shook his head and asked for the documents he wished to consult. They appeared quick-ly—the youngsters liked Akitada—and he checked them for the newly appointed officials.

Minamoto Norisuke was forty-six years old and a provincial lord with holdings in Omi Province and in Izu Province. His appointment made sense. It was cus-tomary to call on men of importance to oversee local institutions and customs. But Akitada was suspicious, given the memo that had come from Nakatoshi and because the appointment coincided with that of Morosuke.

The same went for the markets office. Fujiwara Yoshinaro turned out to be a cousin of several Fujiwara lords who occupied positions closest to the emperor. He was in his early thirties and had no distinctions that might have brought him to the attention of anyone. Unlike Norisuke's, his appointment was somewhat surprising.

Both of these men had gained the power to affect trade and transport directly. Under normal circumstances their roles were supervisory, but they could interfere in the system by ordering changes and by suppressing criminal charges. There were plenty of charges to be dismissed, as he knew. More importantly, perhaps, they could extract direct payments in bribes from those engaged in regular trade. Minamoto Norisuke could also divert goods from their proper destinations, and Fujiwara Yoshinaro could arrange to sell them illegally in the markets. No doubt Morosuke, and perhaps others as yet unknown, planned to share in the rich proceeds. It would be a bold and very effective plan.

The documents told him nothing about the character of the two men. He thought that he might ask Nakatoshi, but that had to wait until later. He would have to try to make his peace with Morosuke first.

He went directly from the archives to the minister's office. The clerk who opened the door was clearly surprised to see him. He turned his head to announce, "Secretary Sugawara, Excellency."

Morosuke's voice snapped, "Well, let him in."

The new minister nodded to Akitada, who made his bow and wondered if Morosuke had forgotten his rudeness. To preempt another attack he asked,, "Have you had a chance to read my notes on the complaints from Omi, sir?"

47

To his surprise, Morosuke said, "Yes, I had a look at them. Mind you, I believe the charges are negligible. The Treasury Ministry has their usual worries about getting all their money and goods."

Akitada was relieved by this mild response. He said tentatively, "I thought it might be a good idea to look into one or two of the matters to satisfy them."

"Did you?" Morosuke pursed his lips. "Waste of time, but by all means send someone. Meanwhile draw up the proper response for the Treasury people. Assure them that we could find no truth in those outrageous allegations against honorable and loyal officials. You may suggest that in the future we'll be looking into slanderous statements against officials."

Akitada was appalled. Slander and false accusations carried severe penalties, including confiscation of property and exile. The Ministry of Justice had the power to bring such cases before the judges. But he swallowed down his objection, bowed again, and said, "In that case, I suggest that we make a show of clearing their names. Surely our cooperation will prevent future questions about our work."

Morosuke thought, then nodded. "Yes. Good point. See to it."

Akitada bowed. "I shall look into it myself, sir!"

Well, he had not been dismissed, though it was clear that he had merely delayed the fact. He had no intention of becoming Morosuke's tool in prosecuting honest officials in order to put more gains into the pockets of his corrupt colleagues and friends. His offer to take care of the matter himself would explain his absence from the ministry. He intended to go to Omi Province to investigate. This would remove him temporarily from Morosuke's ill will and might produce some evidence he could use against him. There was nothing to keep him in his office now that he had been deprived of his staff.

It was a more hopeful Akitada who returned to his family that evening. They seemed to be relieved that he had not resigned after all. He hoped it would not give false hopes to Yasuko but was glad to see that she was no longer angry with him. He was also glad to find Kobe looking better. He had been eating some of the special gruel that Sadako had prepared with soothing herbs and vegetables and had spent some time walking in the garden.

He told Kobe about his son's visit. Kobe grimaced and shook his head. "I don't want to see him," he said. "I don't want to see any of them."

That evening, after the evening rice, Akitada met with Tora and Saburo. He told them about the problems in Otsu. Both were eager to go. It seemed they took the trip as a welcome break from the boredom that had settled on the household over the past long winter. This, too, lifted Akitada's spirits.

7
Arihito

The rain had finally cleared, and they travelled pleasantly from the capital to Otsu. The road, however, was muddy and busy as always. It was the main road between the eastern and northern provinces and Heian-kyo and carried every sort of traffic. Many goods were brought to the city via the land route, both tax shipments and building materials which the great city absorbed at an astonishing rate even if fires were quite common with wooden buildings. In addition, farmers carried their produce to the markets daily. Travelers walked or rode, official messengers dashed by shouting warnings, and occasionally an important man passed with entourage, fore riders, and wagon trains carrying his family and property. These forced everyone but the messengers off the road to kneel or bow until the procession had passed. Governors journeyed in this manner to and from their duty stations.

But Akitada and his companions had left early enough to miss the heaviest traffic. The skies were blue, the mountains welcomed them, and ahead lay Lake Biwa. Akitada had fond memories of Otsu and Lake Biwa, among them his courtship of Yukiko. Never mind that their marriage had broken up with bitterness and recriminations. The weeks preceding their wedding had been among the most exhilarating in Akitada's life. Already near middle age and widowed, he had briefly found his youth again and fallen deeply and passionately in love with the beautiful eighteen-year-old daughter of his best friend. He saw it now as a form of insanity but nothing would erase the memory of those happy days when nobody in the wide world mattered but this young girl and the love she seemed to feel for him.

It was an older and wiser Akitada who returned to the site of his passion. And now he came, somewhat reluctantly, in hopes of finding her well and safe with her brother Arihito. For that had been the other purpose of his visit to Otsu.

The Fujiwara estate was in the foothills of the mountains and overlooked both the city below and the vast lake stretching away into blue distances of more mountains. It was a view that was both beautiful and busy. The lake served as another highway, carrying goods from the east and north to the capital. It was at Otsu that the ships unloaded and the cargo moved onward by land.

When they gained the point where the familiar view greeted them, Akitada paid fresh attention to the busy harbor. It struck him for the first time that it seemed larger and more varied, and therefore busier, than Naniwa where the big ships arrived from the western provinces. Many more people seemed to work here, and laborers moved about like so many ants on an anthill.

But first things first. They stopped at the gates to the Fujiwara house. It was past midday by now and the gates stood open. Servants came, bowed, and carried off the names of the guests. More servants rushed from the house, and Arihito himself followed, a little more slowly. In the absence of Kosehira, he was their master. He carried a little girl on his arm.

Akitada had lost track of Arihito's marriages. There had been several, and he had lost one wife already. Then, a few years ago, he had lost a young woman he had planned to take to wife to a ruthless assassin. But here he was, smiling, a little older but still handsome, carrying a toddler of about three years, the very image of a happy father.

He cried, "Welcome, Akitada! What a surprise! And Tora and Saburo, too. Come in and meet my family."

The cheerful greeting warmed Akitada's heart. He had become fond of Arihito while solving the murders of his betrothed and her family. Arihito had proved to be not only brave when the assassin struck, but determined and intelligent in the subsequent search for the killer.

The introduction to Arihito's wives—there were two—and five little children reminded him vividly of Kosehira's household so many years ago. There was a natural familiarity among all of them that was most unusual in noble houses. Akitada's own family was small, but even there formality reigned and his own children tended to avoid their parents.

They were made welcome and given rooms, and Akitada joined Arihito's family for the evening meal. Later, he and Arihito strolled through the garden.

Returning to the place where he had met Yukiko was deeply moving to Akitada. Not only had little changed in the rambling house and its several pavilions, but the large gardens still stretched around them. As he revisited his past, his mood imperceptibly changed. His animosity toward Yukiko lessened. He no longer saw just the haughty, mocking face of the woman she had become, but the laughing eyes of the young girl she had been. And with this change came the first real worries about her.

But Arihito had little to tell him about his sister. He had not seen her for several months and she had been well and full of energy then. She had hopes of regaining her influence at court which she had left two years earlier.

Surprised, Akitada asked, "Why did she leave? I thought she held the office of mistress of the wardrobe."

Arihito looked embarrassed. "A man. Some wild passion. She learned soon enough that he just toyed with her. Her past has made any more serious connection unlikely."

Akitada was also uncomfortable. Clearly, the society Yukiko aspired to had as little patience with her behavior as he when he was still her husband. And always in the back of his mind he ascribed part of the blame to the role he had played.

He said, "Okura came to see me."

Arihito was shocked. "Okura? What possessed the man? Did you quarrel?"

"No. Though I was cold. I wanted to be rid of him. I still do. But he had some troubling tale about Yukiko being ill and then disappearing. He says you wouldn't receive him."

Arihito ran his hands through his hair in frustration. "That's true. I had no intention of seeing him. He has shamed my family. But you listened to his nonsense? I admire your forbearance."

"Is it nonsense, Arihito?"

"Yes. Surely. I can't say I've spoken to my sister recently, but she's not the sort of person to disappear. Neither would she become ill without making a fuss." He grimaced.

So much for that. Akitada decided to turn the conversation to conditions in Otsu, specifically those involving the harbors.

Arihito became animated. "Yes, it's outrageous what goes on there. They are fishing dead people out of the lake almost every day. And the government turns a blind eye. Do you mean to say you are here finally to look into the matter?"

"Not officially. At least, I suspect that I'm intended to shore things up. Apparently all the complaints are causing unpleasant gossip."

"Oh!" Arihito left the comment hang there.

Akitada smiled. "You are disappointed?"

"Yes. And Father would feel the same way. They got him out of the way so they could plunder the local people and the honest traders at will."

"They got Kosehira out of the way? I thought he looked forward to being stationed in Izumo. "

"He likes Izumo, so that's all right, but he knew they wanted him out of the way. He'd started asking questions, you see."

55

"He didn't tell me. Who was behind sending him away?"

"The prime minister. It was one of the first things he did. Mind you, he made it look like a friendly gesture, an honor, a reward for years of service. But Father knew well enough that it was because of Otsu."

Kosehira had not lived in Otsu for years, preferring to remain in his residence in the capital, but Akitada knew that he would have felt an obligation to the people of a province he had once governed. And, since he had been a good governor to them, perhaps they had come to him for help. He would have tried his best, even though he had been ailing frequently after the grievous wound he had received in the attack at Shirakawa. Perhaps all those complaints that had been filed had been written on his urging.

Akitada asked, "How is your father? I haven't heard from him recently."

Arihito frowned. "He's well enough, but he's no longer young, you know."

Akitada winced. They were the same age. "I thought he was improving, that the climate in Izumo would benefit him."

"Oh, it does. But I cannot help worrying. And now there is this strange business about Yukiko. You know how fond he is of her."

"Yes."

"Don't mention this story to him yet."

"Of course not. There may be nothing to it. Okura seems to be the nervous type. It surprised me."

Arihito nodded, but he frowned. "It is very strange, this tale."

"Yes. Where exactly is her house? I didn't know she had a separate establishment." In fact he

knew nothing of Yukiko's life during the past five years
or so.

"It's hardly an establishment. She bought a
derelict summer house not far from here. I've seen it
and was shocked. It was in very poor condition, but
Yukiko said it would help her put the past behind her
and it was close to this place. Her little girl was staying
here in the summer."

"I see. When did you see your sister last?"

Arihito thought. "It was in the autumn. She
stopped by briefly before going up to her place. She
looked well."

Akitada sighed inwardly. More than six months
had passed since then. Anything could have happened
in the meantime. "Okura says she has not attended
court this year. Was she alone when you saw her?"

"She had her maid. The house has an old couple taking care of it, I think."

"We should go to talk to them."

Arihito nodded. "Tomorrow if you like."

Akitada decided that the next day Tora and
Saburo would ask some questions around the harbor of
Otsu, while he and Arihito rode up the mountain to
talk to Yukiko's servants.

8
Otsu

It was a clear day, and early, yet the town of Otsu was already very busy. They had taken their horses from the Fujiwara residence. Tora was no longer able to walk long distances since some hoodlums had broken his leg five years earlier, but it pleased Akitada that his friend was still quite handy with his weapons and that such exercise cheered him. They left the horses at the post
station stable and stopped in the market for their morning meal, which consisted of greasy but delicious fried fish, and now strolled contentedly along the shoreline of the lake, watching the boats and the milling, sweating workers.

The lake stretched away into a blue distance, water, sky, and distant mountains melding into each other in the morning sun. A convoy of square white sails was approaching Otsu from the north-east and small fishing boats dotted the water.

Tora, though taller than Saburo, had become heavier. This day, he wore an old robe that was patched here and there and he had tied up his gray hair with a bit of straw rope. Lean Saburo wore his hair loose and had borrowed a quilted jacket from the Fujiwara gardener. He had not bothered to disguise his scars and the people of Otsu averted their eyes from his disfigured face. They looked like two down-on-their-luck vagrants.

Neither spoke. Saburo occasionally glanced up the towering mountain range to the west. He could make out gilded spires and the curving roofs of pagodas. Mount Hiei was home to Enryakuji, a huge complex of many temples and monasteries, and Saburo had spent his youth here. He had lived among Enryakuji's monks and had come to know their political aspirations well. Now there was talk that new troubles were brewing as the factions on Mount Hiei confronted their low-land rivals. Saburo had suffered his disfigurement in one of the conflicts between his own temple and an enemy monastery when he had worked as a spy and been caught. He knew what cruelties monks were capable of in the service of their faith. The experience had destroyed his own faith and thrown him among the vagrant beggars of the land until Akitada had recognized his ability and employed him. Akitada had been reluctant at first, because he hated spies and had little love for power-hungry monks, but over the years he had come to appreciate Saburo's skills, especially his skill with the brush.

Tora had also been here before, but he took a greater interest in the activity at the wharves. All types of laborers were at work loading and unloading carts and boats, handling the oxen and horses that pulled the heavily laden wagons, and maneuvering boats and ships to landing places.

The wharf was cluttered with huge piles of lumber, trees cut in far distant forests and carried down by road and water to be used in the great buildings of the capital or by the always expanding temple complexes. Farther along, there were mountains of rice bales and wine and oil barrels. One boat unloaded mostly cloth, hemp and silk woven by the women of the north and east. Even horses had been shipped across the water, perhaps to avoid having them injured on the roads.

Tora and Saburo spent a good portion of the day wandering about, looking at ships and the piles of cargo sitting on the ground. Many of the goods would continue by land, making their way to the capital, where they were destined for the government warehouses, or for the private compounds of noble families, or for one of the two markets.

Tora pointed out a corpulent man in a green robe and tall black hat. "There's the harbor master."

Saburo nodded. The man's status was clear from the fact that people approached him with papers and wooden tokens in their hands, which he studied before entering something on a tablet he carried. Saburo's attention was on the line of half-naked men who were carrying bales down the gang plank of one of the ships tied up at the quay, its huge sails folded and its tall mast swaying slightly on the waves.

Tora sniffed the air. "Pleasant work for once. You see anything illegal going on?"

"No. It's too early. Look at the number of constables and guards around. I doubt we'll see anything interesting until dark."

Tora nodded, then narrowed his eyes. "Something odd about those imperial guards over there. The peach-colored tunics are right, but those insignia look strange."

Saburo looked. "Never paid much attention to their uniforms. Why bother? They are what they are. Most are drunks who beat their women. Nothing unusual in that."

But Tora had already drifted closer to a pair of guardsmen who were watching the unloading of the ship. They looked bored.

"Nice day," Tora said to the older of the two. "Are those tribute goods for His Majesty?"

The man glanced at him. "Move along. Nothing to see here!" he growled.

Tora nodded toward the line of workers carrying boxes, bales, and crates from the ship. "Looks like treasure," he said. "Fine silks for His ladies, I bet. And dainty cups for them to sip from. And gold from the mines on Sado Island for the emperor's chests."

The guard put his hand to the hilt of his sword and started toward him. "Did you hear me, scum? Move!"

Tora backed away. "No offense, Officer," he said, grinning. "Nothing but admiration for His Majesty's brave soldiers." He rejoined Saburo. "Those uniforms are fakes. Bet they're thieves."

"How do you know?" Saburo asked, eyeing them. "Those patches?"

"Them and the weapons. The patches aren't sewn properly. Threads are hanging loose. And they

don't have the same swords. Yuki's sword is different."
Tora's son served in the outer palace guard.

"You think they are stealing the cargo off that ship?"

Tora looked back. He saw the guard officer talking to some men in the red jackets of the police and pointing toward Tora.

"I don't know, but I think we'd better move. Looks like they're setting the harbor guard on us." They started to walk away, but then they heard a whistle and saw the red coats rushing after them.

Saburo cursed. "Run!" cried. Tora hesitated as moment, then followed, limping awkwardly. They dove into a narrow alley way between houses and waited. Tora was gasping.

Saburo said, "You shouldn't have talked to those two men in imperial uniforms when you knew they were crooks."

"And you shouldn't have run! What could they have done to us? Now we look like thieves."

They peered out after a while and saw no red coats.

"It's well past time for the midday rice, and I need a drink," Tora announced.

Saburo protested, "We won't get anything done if you start drinking now. Besides, we aren't dressed for it. They'll put us in a dark corner and give us sour swill."

Tora peered at a ragged curtain with faded lettering. Rich odors of frying food came from inside. "That looks like a good place," he said and strode off.

Muttering, Saburo followed.

A good place it was not. It was dark, dirty, and nearly empty. A few smoking oil lights shone on ragged pieces of *tatami* that served as seats for customers. An old hag with one eye waddled toward them, bowing and greeting them with a toothless grin. "Welcome, welcome!" she rasped. "Fine wine here. And cheap. You won't regret it. Fried eels and shrimp to eat. Delicious!"

Tora scanned the room and saw only one other guest, a white-haired, bearded fellow who seemed to doze leaning against a pillar. "Bring us your best, my beauty," he said cheerfully. "A large pitcher. And a platter of food."

She eyed their clothes. "It'll be twenty coppers apiece," she said, torn between greed and caution.

"Pay her, Saburo," Tora said grandly, sitting down on one of the mats.

Saburo shot him an angry glance. "Twenty coppers is too much," he said. "I'll pay ten." Saburo was tight with money and cringed at spending even ten.

The woman opened her mouth to protest, and Tora snorted. "Dammit, pay her what she asks. You're a skinflint."

Saburo scowled and counted out forty coppers so slowly that it was clear he hated to part with each one. The woman snatched them up, bowed again, and bustled off. "You're pretty quick spending my money," Saburo said resentfully.

Tora laughed. "I'm teaching you a lesson, brother. Getting too attached to money is bad for your character. People will think you can be bought."

Saburo clenched his fists. "That's a lie!"

Suddenly a deep voice said, "It is wrong to spend money like water."

They looked at the white-beard who had woken and eyed them with disapproval.

Saburo nodded. "Exactly!"

"Still, it's the way of the world. Even Emma can be bribed," said the old man.

"Yes, even the judge in hell takes money," Tora agreed. "Money opens doors. Everybody knows that."

The old man chuckled. "You believe in the lucky gods? Money is everything. They say a man has a face like Ebisu when asking for a loan, and a face like Emma when repaying it."

Saburo glowered. "That's because things borrowed are forgotten, but people never forget what you owe them."

Tora waved a finger at Saburo. "It shows a lack of trust between friends. And who says I'm borrowing?" He turned to the old man. "We share what we have, though my friend does look like that angry judge of hell when asked to part with a copper."

The old man nodded. "Never borrow from a friend because you'll lose him."

The exchange of wise sayings might have gone on, but the old woman arrived with wine and a platter of fried eels and shrimp. Saburo simmered down and Tora invited the old man to join them. "You from around here?" he asked him.

The old man lowered himself carefully onto a mat and held out his cup. "Born and raised," he said. "You fellows from the capital?"

"There and elsewhere," Saburo said quickly. "We like travel. What's happening here?"

The old man studied him. "Interesting," he said thoughtfully.

Tora munched and passed the food around. He asked, "So tell us. We like a bit of excitement."

The old man took his eyes from Saburo's scarred face and helped himself to a piece of eel. "You look like a soldier, but I can't make out your friend. It's

65

clear he's seen some action, but he looks like a schoolmaster."

Saburo refused to comment. The old man was asking all the questions and giving nothing away. Tora decided to tell the truth. "We're here to look into some irregularities at the harbor. You know of anything like that?"

"Irregularities? A fine word. What sort of irregularities? Theft? Murder? Rape? Fights? Depends on what you're looking for. Who sent you?" He waited expectantly.

Saburo said stiffly, "Crimes are crimes regardless of who sent us. Unless you think we're crooks."

The old man chuckled again. "I suppose that answers my question. What exactly do you want to know?"

Tora passed the food again and refilled the cups. He asked, "What about the harbor? Have there been murders?"

The old man nodded. "Yes, there are those. And not just there, though bodies tend to float up to the shore after a while." He stroked his beard.

"So? Who gets killed and who does the killing?"

Their guest shook his head. "Ah! You'll have to ask the police that question."

"The police? But you must have an idea. People talk. What are they saying?"

"They say, 'Ask the police!'"

Saburo looked disgusted. "It sounds like there's no law and order. Who's the governor these days? We should've kept up."

The old man chuckled. "Yes. Diligence pays off." He held out his cup. Tora refilled it and said,

"Well, it's not Lord Kosehira any longer. He's in Izumo Province now."

"Good man, for a Fujiwara," said the old man, then added, "We have Lord Sanenari now."

A brief silence fell. The food was gone. After a moment Saburo asked, "So who gets killed?"

The old man finished his wine and wiped his mouth with his hand. "Anybody who's careless and asks too many questions." He rose. "My advice is, be on your guard!"

For an old man, he walked out quickly, leaving Tora and Saburo to stare after him.

Tora growled, "What did he mean by that?"

Saburo shook his head. "You wasted food and wine on him. That old man's in his dotage. He would say anything for a cup of wine."

Before Tora could answer, the one-eyed woman came to collect the dishes. Tora asked her, "Who was that old man?"

"He's Master Cricket. You're lucky he talked to you."

"Lucky?" Saburo glowered. "He ate our food and drank our wine and left without saying thanks."

"He doesn't bother with most people. If he talked to you, you're honored."

Saburo snorted again and started for the door. Tora hung back. "What's his real name and where does he live?"

"Everybody just calls him Master Cricket. He lives in the street behind Miidera temple. But he's a hermit. He doesn't like to be bothered."

Tora thanked her. Outside he caught up with Saburo.

The sun was already setting. Lights flickered on here and there. People had lit paper lanterns outside

67

shops and eating places, and oil lamps glimmered inside. The lanterns people carried in the streets glowed like fireflies here and there. It was cloudy, but the lake beyond the houses shimmered with the reflection of the last daylight in the sky above.

"We've wasted too much time. I'm going back to the waterfront," said Saburo. "Whatever's happening there will happen at night."

9

Yukiko's House

They set out early for the mountain. Arihito seemed more troubled this morning. He was clearly anxious to see for himself what had become of his sister.

It was a beautiful spring morning, their horses were fresh, and so was the air up in the foothills. From the narrow road that climbed the side of the mountain range to the temples high above them, they had a view of the great lake as it stretched into a blue distance. Akitada had always loved Lake Biwa, though he knew there were many beautiful sights in their country. As always, his heart swelled with pride that the gods had so generously bestowed this land on them.

"What made your sister come all the way up here?" he asked. "It's a long way from you and from everything else."

"I expect that's why. She didn't want any of us berating her for her behavior."

Akitada winced. "I wish you hadn't. Our failed marriage was my fault as much as hers."

Arihito nodded. "Perhaps, but Father didn't see it that way. He was crushed by what she did. But it wasn't just that. It was also how she acted later. She turned her back on her daughter, and when my parents reminded her of her child, she got angry. We saw very little of her during those years. Father disapproved of her life at court."

So she must have misbehaved with men, for surely they did not object to her position as lady of the wardrobe.

Arihito went on, "Yukiko bought the property from one of the temples. Mother thought perhaps she wanted to be near the holy sites, but I doubt it. Yukiko was never religious."

Akitada nodded. "Yes, it seems unlike her."

They fell silent after that.

When they reached the place chosen by Yukiko for her retreat, Akitada saw the land was wooded, rocky, and unproductive, but it allowed glimpses of the lake and the world below. There was a modest house with a stable for a horse and a smaller place for two servants. It was a good hideaway to entertain a secret lover. He felt a twinge of pity for Okura.

Arihito said, "I haven't been here for a while. My sister never was very welcoming."

This did not surprise Akitada, considering that Arihito and her family blamed her for her behavior.

70

They were greeted by a small woman in her fifties, plain-faced, and dressed in blue cotton, her head covered with a cloth. She came to them from the small house, bowed, and said, "Welcome, my Lord. My lady is not here."

She looked placid enough as she said this, but her lack of concern struck Akitada as ominous.

Arihito said, "Kimi, this is Lord Sugawara. We were told that my sister has disappeared. We are concerned about her and came to take a look and find out what you know."

She bowed to Akitada, then told Arihito, "My lady must be visiting. There was also another gentleman. He asked many questions."

Akitada asked, "Lord Okura?"

"That's his name. A very handsome lord!" She chuckled. "And in love with my lady, I think."

"Nonsense!" Arihito frowned. "He's just an acquaintance. And don't be saying things like that. When did my sister leave?"

She looked vague. "A week has passed, I think. Maybe a bit more."

Akitada said, "Lord Okura had heard she was ill."

The woman looked uneasy. "Maybe. I made food, but she ate very little. I think she was fasting for Buddha. To be pure."

This was a surprise. Yukiko had never been religious, but years had passed. She might well have changed. No doubt she had a great deal to regret.

Arihito clearly did not believe it. "So she left to visit one the temples?"

Kimi looked vague again. "I think so. We go down to the market every week. To buy vegetables and fish. When we got back, she was gone."

71

It almost sounded as if Yukiko had not wanted witnesses to her departure. Akitada asked, "Do you always go on the same day?"

She nodded. "Tatsuo and me. Every day of the rabbit. It takes both of us to carry back the food."

Arihito said, "Tatsuo is her husband. They share the work."

It was possible that the servants knew nothing. Akitada felt a little sorry for the pair. He said, "Let's have a look inside."

The main house, though modest, was well-built of sturdy beams and had a thick thatch roof. A pretty veranda surrounded it. They walked up the steps to the door, Kimi joining them to open it.

"I keep it clean for her," she said, pointing proudly at the shining floor.

There was only one large room, but it was appointed with thick *tatami* mats and silk pillows. Two painted screens surrounded the sitting area with its lamps and braziers, its musical instruments and its bamboo rack with books. Yukiko had not done without the luxuries she had become accustomed to at court.

There were also lacquered trunks for her clothes and for bedding, lacquered boxes for her writing utensils and games, lacquered trays and bowls for her food. In one corner was a small altar with an exquisitely carved and gilded Buddha figure.

Akitada looked at these things and then asked the woman, "Did Lady Yukiko receive guests here?" Her brother would not like the subject, but under the circumstances it was necessary to know who had come and gone.

Kimi gave Arihito an anxious look and said, "My lady came here to be alone."

It was an evasion. Akitada pressed her, "We are concerned about Lady Yukiko's wellbeing. She is said to have been very ill, and now she's disappeared without telling anyone where she has gone. She may be visiting one of her friends. We must know who has come here."

Arihito added bleakly, "Both men and women, Kimi."

Kimi hesitated. Clearly she was becoming nervous. "There was someone. My lady is very beautiful and much loved. But I don't know his name and it was night. I didn't see him well. I think now she's only gone to pray to the Buddha."

Akitada asked, "Is her horse gone?"

"Yes, yes. She took the horse."

The woman was obviously afraid she would be blamed, but if Yukiko had not gone far, why was she still away? More than a week was a long time for a visit to a temple.

"Which of the temples would she go to?"

But Kimi did not know. She mentioned either Enryakuji, which was high on the mountain above, or Miidera in the city below. And it could be any of a number of smaller temples connected with the two big ones. It was too large an area to search.

Arihito had found his sister's writing box and was sorting through her papers. "She used to keep a diary," he said.

The thought of perusing his ex-wife's diary made Akitada cringe, but she might indeed have left a clue to where she had gone. He started to look through her books.

Yukiko's reading had been, predictably, mostly courtly romances. She had the entire *Prince Genji* by Lady Murasaki, illustrated books that must have cost a great deal of money. But there were also two famous diaries with poems, and two poetry collections. Only one book of Buddhist writings was in the collection. To his surprise, he found also an old document in one of the books. It was from the time when he had served as governor of Mikasa Province. He stared at it, wondering how she had managed to get hold of it. It was a report about the destruction wreaked by a great storm. As he looked more closely, he realized it was a draft in his own hand. Presumably it had later been copied by a clerk and the draft discarded. Why had she kept it? It held nothing of interest to a woman who read romances. It was written in the dry, bureaucratic language of such official reports. And in Chinese! Yukiko probably knew some Chinese. Her father had seen to a good education for his favorite daughter, but she was hardly adept at it.

Akitada was still pondering this puzzle, when he heard Arihito exclaim, "Look at this!"

He turned and saw that Arihito had moved the box containing Yukiko's papers and was bending over the *tatami* mat. When he joined him, he saw several irregular dark brown stains.

They looked like dried blood.

10

Looking for Trouble

Tora and Saburo walked quickly. Dusk was falling when they reached the harbor. Lights came on at shops, houses, and warehouses like a golden chain of fire flies along the curving shore. The lake beyond turned dark, but the moon's reflection bobbed and shimmered on the water.

Tora paused to look. The loading and unloading had slowed, but there still seemed to be a lot of people about. They clustered in front of wine shops or gathered in small groups here and there all along the harbor. Some lights blinked also on the anchored boats.

"Looks peaceful enough," Tora commented. "What did you make of that Master Cricket?"

75

"What a name! He was senile. The kind children mock in the street."

"I don't know. He sounded wise. Like he knows more than he wants to say." He pointed toward the town. "Let's go see what they're serving over there. I'm still thirsty."

Saburo frowned. "You drink too much. I think I'll look around a bit longer. It's too early to give up."

Stung, Tora growled, "Who's giving up? I can learn more while I'm drinking than you can wandering about in the dark. Give a man enough wine and he'll share his deepest secrets."

"All right. Let's split up and see what we come up with. We'll meet back at the stables after the hour of the boar. That should give us more than two hours." And with that, Saburo walked off.

Tora had not planned on spending that much time drinking. He had looked forward to his comfortable bed in Lord Arihito's house long before then. But it was true that they had accomplished little beyond confirming that the transfer of goods in the harbor should be investigated and that a crazy old man thought snooping was dangerous.

Shaking his head, Tora entered a busy and well-lit wine shop. The atmosphere was steamy, fishy, smoky, and raucous. Someone was cooking over an open hearth in the back of the room. Men were sitting in groups or perching on raised platforms, drinking, eating, talking loudly, and shouting at each other. Even with his long years of exploring wine shops and eating places all over the country, Tora had not encountered quite such a mass of unruly humanity. They were mostly dockyard workers who had finished their day and were still half naked, wearing only their loin cloths, their bodies shining with sweat from the warmth, the wine, and the food.

Prominent on a pillar the center of the room was a carved figure of the god Ebisu, carrying a huge sea bream and a fishing rod. Fishing was a big industry on the lake and the god brought luck to fishermen and those who sold and consumed fish.

Tora found a seat near a large group of customers, but the stench of their sweat caused him to move away a little. The next group was also sweaty, but they wore clothing. It was rough and dirty, but at least they did not look like slippery eels and they smelled marginally better. What was more, they made room for him in a comradely fashion and offered him some wine. He accepted, drank, and nearly choked on the rough brew. As soon as he had passed on the cup, he found that he was expected to pay for the next pitcher. He did so with good grace, laughed at someone's joke, and told one of his own.

They wanted to know where he worked. He said he had just come to town and was looking for work. It was an inspired ploy. It seemed they worked for a man who owned the wagons carrying goods from Otsu to the capital.

Tora asked, "Is the money good?"

"Pretty good," said the man next to him, "but you've got to be strong." He cast a dubious eye at Tora's physique. "And young," he added.

Tora said, "I can work. I've worked all my life. And what's more, older workers work smarter."

There was some amusement at this. Tora decided it was not the time to pick a fight and joined in the laughter. "Come on!" he said when things were friendly again, "tell me about the job."

They did. In fact, they were quite outspoken. They had little respect for their bosses and spoke quite freely of the ones who helped themselves to some of the goods entrusted to them. Life was hard and violent. They were overworked and beaten, and they and their cargo encountered robbers on the road who thought nothing of killing them.

Tora listened and readily paid for refills to keep the conversation going. Once or twice he became a little uneasy. He had a strange feeling that eyes were drilling holes in his back, but whenever he turned to look, nobody was watching him. They all looked busy with their own concerns.

He listened for the cries of the watchman, and when the time came to meet Saburo, he parted from his companions and left.

Outside, things had become quiet. There were fewer lights. Here and there, a solitary figure moved in the shadows, but most of the harbor's business had stopped. The men had gone to their homes and beds, or to a wine shop, or perhaps to find a prostitute.

Tora was content with what he had learned. He walked through the dark city, trying to make out landmarks that would take him back to the post station where they had left their horses. Now and then he saw another shadowy walker with a lantern, and once there was a footfall behind him. He passed a small shrine to Ebisu, one of many in Otsu, crossed a bridge over a small stream, and turned the corner into a residential quarter. Here it was mostly dark and quiet. Behind the tall bamboo fences, an occasional tree was in bloom and he smelled its fragrance in the air. Humming a happy tune, he thought of the soft bed that awaited him.

The residential quarter gave way to an open field. Warehouses lay ahead, large dark shapes against the lighter water of the lake, and he knew he was getting close to the stables.

He was also no longer alone on the road. Steps were following him. Quick steps . . . of more than one person.

Tora turned, but he was too late. Three or four dark figures came for him as he reached for the short sword under his jacket. They wore dark cloths around their faces. He saw their eyes glittering and heard their sharp breaths as they reached him.

"Stand back or you're dead," he shouted, raising his sword.

One of them cursed, then they attacked from all sides. He slashed and twisted and cut, heard shouts and screams, felt blows from cudgels, and fought on, until he collapsed.

When he came to, he lay on the road in a puddle of blood. His face felt wet and he had to wipe his eyes to see. He was alone, except for one man who had fallen down some distance away. His other attackers had taken to their heels.

Tora did not bother to check the one left behind. One glancing cudgel blow had opened his scalp and he was bleeding badly. He staggered to his feet and made his way to the station as quickly as he could.

The groom stared at him in horror. Feeling sick and dizzy, Tora washed some of the blood off at the trough and asked about the time. It was well past the hour when they were to meet and Saburo had not returned.

Saburo had spent some of the time after parting from Tora in watching the ship they had noted earlier, but he kept his distance from the guards in their spurious imperial uniforms. The goods had all been loaded onto carts and the carts were ready to depart. A well-dressed man arrived with two companions who carried bags. He stopped to speak to the guards, and they in turn set the line of carts into motion. As soon as the carts had gone, the well-dressed man shouted at the waiting workers to line up. His companions opened the bags. The guards drew closer. Then they had begun to pay off the men in the loincloths who took their money and immediately dispersed.

When the space in front of the docked ship was empty, the well-dressed man, his companions, and the guards also departed.

Saburo followed them at a distance.

They left the harbor behind and went inland. After passing through streets that were still busy with men seeking food, wine, or companionship after their workday, they entered a quiet neighborhood of private homes behind fences and walls. Here Saburo had to hang back farther to avoid being noticed. They did not seem to suspect anything, however, and eventually he saw them heading for a large private compound behind tall stone walls. It clearly belonged to someone of wealth and power. Banners with the paulownia crest flew above the massive gates and many roofs rose beyond the tall walls. The men he had been following walked in. The gate remained open, but Saburo could not risk being seen. He walked back to the shrine of the god Ebisu he had seen in passing. There were always a few beggars at shrines.

He found an old man with a crippled leg and two small boys. The boys kept their distance from the old man, who threatened them with his cane from time to time. Saburo ignored the boys' cries for pennies and approached the old man, who grinned at him toothlessly and extended his open hand.

"Evening, grandfather," Saburo greeted him. "I see you've sought the protection of the god."

The old man nodded. "Ebisu protects fishermen. I pray he gives you a soft heart, master, because I'm hungry." He raised his hand a little.

He looked well nourished, so Saburo ignored that. "What happened to your leg?"

"Oh, it was terrible. I was working on a fishing boat. A rope jerked me off my feet and wrapped itself around my leg, and then the wind caught the sails and the ship turned, and the rope went tight. I screamed and screamed, hanging there by my leg, and blood running all over. They got me down after a while, but my leg was twisted and half the flesh ripped off. They thought I'd had it and were gonna throw me overboard, but the gods saved me. Only I couldn't work, so I sit here, hoping the gods will make people kind." The hand waved again.

Saburo said, "Hmm," and studied the mangled limb. The gory colors were well done.

The old man waited. After a while he said, "You don't look too good yourself. What happened to your face?"

"Monks."

"Monks?"

"They don't pray to any lucky gods and I have to earn my own food."

The old man was becoming angry. "What do you want?"

"Information."

Hope returned to the wrinkled face. "Ask. I know many things."

81

"Who lives in the big house?" Saburo pointed in the direction he had come from.

The cripple grinned. "What's it worth?"

Saburo glared at him. "Nothing. I could ask those boys."

A pause. Then the old man said, "His Excellency Bloody Norisuke lives there."

"Bloody?"

That got Saburo a cackle. The gnarled hand shot out. "Pay me or I'll tell them you've been asking questions and you'll find out about 'Bloody'."

Saburo resisted a moment longer, then laboriously detached a single copper from his string and put it into the beggar's hand. "Tell me more."

"Pah!" The old man spat and put the coin away. "Talk to the boys."

Saburo peeled off another coin. This also had no results. He had to part with five more before the old man said, "He's a thief and a murderer, but he's got many soldiers. The police won't touch him."

Saburo nodded. "I thought so." He walked over to the boys, who watched him with cautious expectation. The older was perhaps eleven, the younger eight. They wore rags, and their unkempt hair stood up stiffly with dirt and bits of straw and twigs in it. They clearly lived on the streets. Reluctantly, he parted with another coin. "Who can show me how to get into Lord Norisuke's place?"

They looked at each other. The older boy said, "We both can. It'll cost you." After payment of several more coins, they set off together. The boys led him to a gnarled cedar that grew in the back of the huge compound. Saburo glowered at them.

"What's this? I need a door to get in."

They shook their heads in unison. The bigger of the two said, "Locked. Besides they'll kill you if they catch you."

Saburo glared. "Give back the money!"

The older boy hesitated, then he held out his hand. "I'll show you."

Another copper left its string and the boy clambered up the tree like a monkey, jumped to the top of the wall, and disappeared.

A moment later, they could hear angry shouts and a squeal. The other boy ran.

Saburo ducked under the branches of the tree and waited, wondering what had happened to the boy. He heard more shouting, then male voices. Someone seemed to be climbing the wall next to the tree to look over. Saburo stayed under cover until the man climbed down again. After that sounds inside the compound receded into silence.

Saburo waited until night fell and the streets became quiet. Then he climbed the tree, stepped on top of the wall and, taking a careful look around, jumped down into an empty service yard.

11

The Pillow Book

After finding traces of blood in Yukiko's house, Akitada and Arihito made a more earnest effort.

The woman Kimi seemed surprised by the stained *tatami* and denied any knowledge of it. Akitada became suspicious. "I thought you said you cleaned here recently?" he asked, frowning at her.

She twisted her hands. "I dust the floor every day, sir. But I didn't touch my lady's things. How did that happen?"

Arihito studied the stain and some drops leading away from it. "Somebody got hurt." He looked at the woman. "Did my sister injure herself?"

She stared at the spots. "Maybe."

The blood was worrisome. There was not enough to suggest murder, but something violent could have happened. Of course there was no proof that the blood was Yukiko's. Perhaps she had not been alone. Her past life style suggested that this hidden place had been chosen because of a secret affair. Arihito asked the woman more questions, but she just became agitated and claimed to know nothing. It was a futile effort.

Akitada returned to the bookshelf to open each of her books in search of hidden letters. He only found a thin sheaf of notes next to one of the romances. The handwriting was Yukiko's. He hesitated a moment, then told Arihito, who glanced at the pages and said, "It's just some scribblings. And poems."

"I think it's a pillow book. She's been jotting down her thoughts in this. Do you mind if I have a look at it? I'll return it to you."

"No. Keep it for all I care. If we find her, you can give it to her."

They searched the rest of the house and the area around it and then left after a few more questions which the woman could not answer or pretended not to know about. As they rode back down the mountain, Arihito said angrily, "What can she have got herself into this time?"

Akitada said nothing. The alienation between Yukiko and her family accounted for the fact that no one had realized for over a week she might be in trouble. Only Okura had worried, and if Yukiko had been involved in another affair, it was ironic that a rejected lover should have cared more than her family or, for that matter, her former husband. Okura had said as much. He had asked how Akitada could be so heartless toward his former wife.

"That woman," Akitada said after a pause, "either knows something she doesn't want to talk about or else, she is involved in whatever happened to Yukiko."

Arihito protested, "They're servants. They wouldn't have a reason to lie. I think she's just not very bright. Perhaps we should go back and talk to the husband."

"Perhaps later. We need to find out why your sister hid herself away like this. It's not like her. Whatever happened to her must be connected with that decision. Would she have written to either of her parents? Or to a close friend?"

"I don't know, but I doubt it. We all disapproved of her behavior. That didn't encourage confidences. I don't know her close friends, as you call them."

Akitada said mildly, "I was thinking of women friends."

"I doubt she had any."

This struck Akitada as sad. Human relationships tended to be complex. How one felt toward a father was different from one's attitude toward one's mother. Siblings also all were treated differently. Then there was the passionate relationship with a lover, which was unlike any other involvement. And finally there were friends of either gender. Apparently, Yukiko had only enjoyed, if that was the word for it, intrigue and the fleeting moments of lust with men. And this had cost her the closeness to her family and perhaps others.

As it had cost her their marriage.

But he had no right to judge her. If he had not encouraged the young Yukiko in her infatuation with himself, she might have found a younger, more suitable husband and become a happy wife and mother. Yukiko's fate was his responsibility, just as Kobe's was. One gained many obligations in a lifetime. Sadako had been quite right to remind him of them. There was also his daughter Yasuko, and because of her, his obligations at the ministry.

Into these glum thoughts, Arihito asked suddenly, "Do you think she's dead?"

Akitada was startled. "Dead? You mean Yukiko?"

"The blood. Do you think someone killed her? A lover perhaps? Or someone else?"

"It's too soon to speculate. The amount of blood was insignificant. It might have been a cut she or someone else got by accident."

Arihito bit his lip. "What about Okura's story then?"

"I don't know what to think of it, but we need to look more closely into Yukiko's recent relationships. Perhaps there was a new man in her life. If so, could he have taken her away? Perhaps someone else who disapproved may have intervened. The woman Kimi may know more than she's saying."

Arihito stopped his horse. "Then let's go back and make her talk."

"I dislike threatening those who can do nothing about it. There must be others who know something. I'll have a look at her pillow book tonight. Perhaps it will suggest some names or places."

The truth was, he dreaded reading her pillow book. Probing into her private life embarrassed him. Besides, he feared it would bring back bad memories.

Tora and Saburo had not come back yet from their visit to Otsu harbor. This was easily explained by the fact that Tora would surely insist on sampling the local fare before returning to Arihito's house. They would most likely arrive late and seek their beds.

As soon as he was back in his comfortable room in the Fujiwara house, he settled down to the unwelcome effort of reading Yoshiko's journal and found he had been right. The Yoshiko he recalled from the miserable days of their marriage before the complete break-up was back with him.

The small book was no diary. There were no dates. Women called them pillow books, because they were pages on which to write down one's thoughts and impressions in the privacy of one's bedroom. Yukiko's thoughts and impressions ranged widely and seemed to have been written while she served at court. She commented on people's behavior, on their looks, on incidents she found ridiculous, on bad taste, on bad poetry, on silly habits, and on people she found impressive or disgusting.

She had a passion for gossip and court intrigue. She took delight in the frivolous sexual activities of others. She was critical of people's manners, complaining of someone who had nothing to commend him but spoke in an affected tone, trying to use elegant words but looking merely ridiculous. She mocked one high-ranking courtier who had committed the ultimate offense of leaving his shoes on the emperor's dining table, and a lady-in-waiting who had entertained two lovers the same night so that their servants who brought the next-morning letters met each other at her door.

Her attitude came as no surprise to Akitada who had always held that the court would ruin Yukiko. Apparently, though, it had also brought her no pleasure. Eventually she wrote, "Though I had done nothing, people made things difficult for me."

The whole pillow book was a sad record of her doomed career. Only now and then had the old Yukiko surfaced when she reacted with pleasure to a plum in flower, to a new snowfall, to the song of birds, and to the cat that lived in the empress's palace.

He saw nothing useful for finding her. She not only left out dates, she mentioned no names. It was a wise precaution since her pillow book might fall into the hands of some prying person, as indeed it had done now. But it was no help in discovering who had been close to her or who might have wanted to harm her. And the absence of dates meant that he could not learn anything about her recent activities. Still, the final entries might offer some insight into her frame of mind.

These had been written after her departure from court service. Whatever incident had brought it about was not clear, but it seemed significant that Yukiko did not express anger or resentment so much as nostalgia. This suggested that she accepted the responsibility for her exile.

What had caused her flight, or perhaps expulsion?

Toward the end, she quoted an ancient poem from the *Manyoshu*: "Oh, the willow tree on the river in Totomi when the hail came down! Oh, the willow on the river! Though it fell, it will grow again, they say."

Surely this meant that she had found a new hope. But hope for what? What had happened?

There were too many unanswered questions.

Akitada had also begun to wonder about Arihito's relationship with his sister. Even if her behavior had caused a breach with her family, it seemed strange that the siblings could have lived so near each other without Arihito having some notion of what his sister was doing. Had he carried the enmity so far that he no longer cared if she lived or died?

At some point he must press Arihito for answers. And they must both go back to confront the woman at Yukiko's house. Akitada was convinced that she knew more than she had told them and was somehow involved in what had happened to Yukiko.

After he came to this decision, the pillow book slipped from his fingers and he fell asleep.

12

Saburo Finds the Boy

Saburo found himself in a service yard. It was empty and dark. He stood still and listened carefully. In the distance he could hear indistinct voices, then some laughter. It was the right time for the evening rice in a large establishment like this. He had noted that this residence with its stables, storehouses, and servants' quarters was at least twice the size of the Sugawara house in the capital. Land was cheaper in the provinces. Minamoto Norisuke clearly ran his illegal operations from his home and Saburo hoped to find proof of them.

Saburo knew there was danger. They had not turned loose the boy who had climbed over the wall.

And they would have put out watchers even if the boy had not told them about Saburo.

So he remained still in the shadow of the wall and waited, his hand on the grip of a slim, sharp knife that he carried in his quilted jacket. When nothing had moved for quite a long time, except for a cat that crossed the yard without showing any interest in its surrounding, Saburo followed the path the cat had taken.

Cats were night hunters. They were equipped with sharper eyes and ears than humans. He thought the cat would tell him if people were about.

It became clear that the animal was headed for the stables. It passed through an open gate, and when Saburo cautiously peered through it a moment later, he could smell straw and animal waste. He saw the cat as it slipped into the stable by its open main doors. Saburo crept along some walls and made for a small side door. The stable was poorly lit by a single oil lantern hanging from a central column. About a dozen horses dozed in their stalls, but he saw no humans. Apparently the evening rice had taken them away. He could still hear distant chatter and laughter as he moved along. No doubt the kitchen area was close by and with it some building where Lord Norisuke's servants and slaves were fed. His retainers, if they lived in his compound, would have their own houses. But it seemed unlikely that they would not have posted guards.

A moment later, he found one.

A scrawny individual in the dull white clothing of a servant walked into the stable. He belched and raised a pitcher to drink, then belched again. Saburo had shrunk behind some bales of straw and decided the man was drinking wine rather than water. If so, he was not likely to be very alert.

The man traversed the stable, peering at every horse, then sat down on a barrel under the lantern. He raised his pitcher for one more drink and set it down beside him before leaning back against the pillar and closing his eyes. A moment later soft snores announced that he had gone to sleep, and Saburo decided to leave him to his duty. He slipped out of the stable into the darkness through the door the guard had used.

He found himself in another courtyard, this one was apparently used for storage and lumber and broken down carts and equipment. Saburo wondered where the stable guard had found the wine. Perhaps he had a hiding place among the debris. He was about to move on to another locale when he noticed a bundle of stained rags on the ground.

He went closer, saw a human foot, then a hand, and stopped.

The body was small and so still that he had no doubt it was dead. After a moment, he forced himself to look at it. He smelled blood, fresh blood. When he bent to touch the body by its shoulder, he felt the warmth of recent life. He tugged gently and the body rolled on its back. He looked down at the young boy who had shown him the way into the compound. He had been clubbed to death, and his blood was sticky on Saburo's hand. He snatched it back to wipe it on his jacket.

The shock was too great for thought, but now he knew he was in extreme danger. If he was caught, he would meet an equally swift death as this boy. No questions would be asked. His mere presence here would mean death. And, horribly, he had caused a child to be killed.

For a moment longer, Saburo stood as if frozen, listening for the slightest sound of someone approaching. All he heard was the same distant chatter and laughter.

What sort of people were these, to murder a child and then enjoy their evening rice as if such things were common?

He straightened and turned slowly, scanning the yard with its piles and stacks of equipment. He knew he must get out without learning more. But what else was there to learn? The small body was proof enough that Lord Norisuke was guilty.

The problem was how to get out.

He could not go back the way he had come because it was too dangerous. He glanced about at wooden fencing and adjoining buildings but saw no gates or doors. The tallest building was near the stable and probably held straw and food for the horses. Such buildings were open to the roof on the inside and Saburo had once been adept at climbing about in rafters. It was his best option to hide out until he could see a way to escape.

And perhaps he might also learn something more.

He located a small window in the wall of the building. It was above the ground and covered with a wooden grille, its purpose ventilation. He thought he might remove the grille and squeeze through.

There was no time to lose. The sounds from the kitchen yard suggested that the meal was over and the workers were dispersing. The boy's killers would come back to dispose of the body. Saburo climbed a barrel and managed to reach the sill of the window with his hands. To his relief, the grille was loose. A firm pull removed it. Saburo hesitated, then pushed the grille through to the inside. He heard it fall, making little sound. Then he pulled himself up, grunting with the effort. He was still as thin and bony as ever, but he no longer had the muscles and strength of his years as a spy. Fear of a violent death was greater than the pain in his arms and shoulders, and he managed to raise his body until he lay across the opening, gasping for breath. Inside was impenetrable darkness and the smell of straw. He had no idea what was beneath the small window, but took another chance. Pushing himself through the narrow opening, adding another tear to his jacket, he fell.

It was not far, and he landed with minor discomfort on the grille and a bale of straw. He quickly got up and put the grille back into its opening, just in time, because he could hear steps and voices outside and the light of a lantern passed eerily beyond the wooden tracery. His heart beating fast, he sank down on the straw and breathed a sigh of relief.

The cold-hearted murder of the boy had shocked him deeply. Saburo had seen and known cruel violence, but it never been this swift, this violent, and directed against a child. Neither had the motive ever been this slight. What threat could a boy that age be to the mighty and rich Minamoto lord? None. It had merely been a matter of removing a nuisance because the boys had been climbing the wall.

He could well imagine what they would do to an actual spy. He would be questioned and tortured. Saburo touched his scarred face and shuddered.

But here he was, so far undetected, and he had yet to find anything to link Norisuke to a specific crime against the emperor. The murder of the boy would not be discovered. Those men outside were busy getting rid of the evidence and Saburo's word would not be believed.

He considered his next step and decided that staying was too dangerous. They would not go quietly to sleep the night they had killed someone inside their compound. He must get out and report to the master.

It was dark among the bales of straw and he moved forward more by guesswork than any certainty. Eventually he climbed down to what was a clear floor space and crossed it cautiously. A dim rectangle marked a door. It was covered with some sacking. Pushing this aside, he peered out into another yard. This one was deserted. He listened, but heard nothing, so he stepped out and crossed toward a wall he hoped was an outer one. Alas, he saw nothing he could climb, and as he searched he heard a sound and then a light appeared. It was too bright for a lantern and when the man stepped around the corner, Saburo saw he was carrying a torch.

Saburo ran for the darkness, but it was too late. The man shouted, "Over here! There he is!" and all hell broke loose. He ran, and they ran after him, trying to cut him off. He had no idea where he was, but he hoped to stay close to the boundary wall. His flight took him through a number of smaller courtyards, and out into the wide entrance yard, where two gate guards tried to stop him. He veered off toward the main house, up the stairs, and along the broad veranda that turned a corner and led to a covered gallery.

From there he made it into a garden and dove behind a shrub, where he crouched, trying to catch his breath. The main house was now between him and the searchers. The light from the torches gleamed beyond the tiled roof and the shouting continued.

Inside the house, lights came on. A door was flung open and someone stepped out on the veranda. A tall man in a flowing white undergown.

He shouted, "What's going on?"

Someone came around the corner to answer in a low voice. A servant. The tall man cursed. He was joined by a woman wearing nothing but a thin silk gown. With the light inside the room, Saburo could see that she was naked underneath and had a slender and beautiful body.

The tall man told her, "Go inside! The servants will see you. They are looking for an intruder."

She laughed. "How exciting," she said and came forward to lean on the railing and look out into the garden.

He muttered another curse and went to sweep her into his arms and carry her back into the room. The door slammed shut and it was dark again.

Had that been Minamoto Norisuke? Saburo had no idea but guessed that the room the man had occupied with his wife or concubine was at the back of the main house and likely belonged to the master.

But he had no time to ponder this or investigate further. He could now hear voices coming from the corner of the house and then torches flickered. He retreated toward the back of the garden, hoping again to reach a perimeter wall.

The torches spread throughout the garden. Saburo dodged them, but there were too many of them, and he was soon encircled. In desperation, he climbed a tree and clung to its trunk in hopes that they would not look up as they passed.

He was lucky. They did not. But neither did they abandon their search. Men with torches passed below repeatedly. The shouts throughout the garden continued. It was well past the time to meet Tora, and Saburo was trapped. When daylight came, it would be all over.

But he was high enough in the tree to catch sight of the outer wall. He was quite close, though that was not helpful at the moment. His glimpse of the wall had also revealed a small gate in it. He and the boys had checked it earlier and he knew it was locked, but Saburo thought the gate itself might give enough support for him to reach the top of the wall.

He watched the torches carefully. If those between him and the small gate were heading away, he might get enough time to dash through, but he would only have moments, for they would hear him breaking though the shrubbery.

The sky was becoming light in the east when Saburo chanced it. He jumped down and took off. He fell almost immediately, tripping over a root.

They heard him. Shouts alerted the search parties who turned their attention in his direction.

Saburo was up again and running, dodging, jumping, his whole body focused on reaching the small gate.

When he did, he vaulted upward, hoping his hand and feet would find some ledge for support, knowing that they had reached him from the bright torch light and the heat on his back, the hoarse, triumphant shouting in his ears, and then, miraculously, he was on top of the wall. He caught a glimpse of upturned faces before jumping down on the other side and running for his life.

13

The Paulownia Crest

Akitada was woken by a servant. He was so soundly asleep that the man had to shake his shoulder.

Startled he sat upright, blinking against the light in the servant's hands. "What?" he gasped.

"Your retainers have returned, sir. One of them is wounded. Lord Arihito thought you should know right away."

Akitada scrambled out of his bedding and threw on his robe. He followed the servant to the front of the house. "What time is it?" Akitada asked on the way.

"Just past the hour of the tiger, sir."

It would soon be day. What could have happened to make them so late?

He found them with Arihito in the reception room. Tora sat on the dais and Saburo hovered nearby. One of the maids was busy bandaging Tora's head. Akitada winced and hurried to his side. Tora had received many blows to the head and suffered from periodic blinding headaches. He looked white and grimaced with pain.

"What happened, Tora? How bad is it? Who did this? Can you speak?"

Tora tried. "It's nothing, sir." He stopped and swayed a little.

Arihito said, "They were attacked."

Saburo added, "I found him like this at the stables where we left our horses."

Saburo also looked the worse for wear. His clothing was torn and he had bleeding scratches on his forehead, arms, and legs.

"You were not together?"

Both Tora and Saburo tried to answer this. Akitada could only make out that they had separated during the night.

Arihito said impatiently, "Surely this can wait. Tora needs to rest. I've sent for a doctor. Let's help him to his room and make him comfortable."

They did, and Akitada was conscious of how heavily Tora leaned on them. Fear struck him. And guilt. He had sent him out and put him in danger, knowing full well Tora's recklessness when it came to solving crimes. He also knew his age. They had been together since they were both young men and fought many battles together. Tora had mostly got the worst of them and had not been well since some louts had broken one of his legs five years ago. The attack had sapped his physical strength and left him with a limp.

The headaches and dizziness predated that injury and were due do his having been knocked out on several occasions. And here he was yet again with a head injury.

Whatever Akitada's own troubles at the moment might be, he should not have risked Tora. Better he had gone himself, though Tora would probably have been offended. Saburo should have looked after him better. The old resentment against the former spy resurfaced and he had to bite his lip not to blame the man.

But Saburo had his own tale to tell. They listened aghast as he described what had happened to the boy who had dared climb the wall of the Minamoto mansion.

Somewhat reluctantly, Akitada said, "I'm glad you escaped. They would have made short work of you also. What are they hiding, I wonder."

"Well, Tora recognized that their guards at the harbor were wearing fake imperial uniforms. I guessed the compound is full of stolen tribute goods. I was looking for them."

Tora cleared his throat. "Those goods go by wagon train to the capital."

Akitada nodded. "Yes, and I would not be surprised that they are sold in the market where Norisuke's partner, Fujiwara Yoshinari, supervises sales. I expect they split the proceeds. It's a conspiracy."

Tora asked, "Can you stop it?"

"No. They are protected by the new minister. It means I cannot enter any buildings to find proof that they trade in stolen goods belonging to the emperor and the nation."

They fell silent, thinking about the problem.

Saburo broke the silence. "I almost forgot. I think I saw Norisuke. He came out of the main house

103

during the search for me. A tall man, about forty years old, wearing a fine silk night shirt and giving orders."

Akitada nodded. "That sounds like him."

"There was a woman with him. Very beautiful. Young. He was protective of her. She wanted to see the excitement, but he swept her up and carried her back inside. It looked very passionate."

Akitada sighed. "I'm afraid that's not useful. A man like Norisuke must have any number of concubines."

Arihito said, "Norisuke's notorious for the number of women he has pursued. They say he's fathered twenty-six children in his own household."

Saburo grimaced. "Disgusting. I just thought I'd mention it. What shall we do about the murdered boy?"

Akitada looked at him sharply. "You bear some responsibility for his death. Try to find his parents tomorrow. Perhaps we can do something. They should at least know what happened to him."

Saburo protested, "I'm afraid that won't be possible. Such boys have no parents. They live in the street."

"You should feel an obligation. Make an effort anyway. You never know what you might learn in the process."

Saburo said nothing.

Tora had fallen asleep sitting up and was snoring. Akitada regarded him with concern. He hoped the head wound was minor, but he did not like the fact that Tora seemed so sleepy. He asked, "Did Tora seem quite all right to you on the way back?"

"I think so. He's just tired." In a low voice he added, "He's getting old."

104

Akitada felt more resentment at these words. Tora was not old. He was younger than himself. There were many years of life in them yet. How dare Saburo disparage a man who had been with him for most of both their lives and who had served him with courage and devotion? And, of course, if Saburo thought Tora old, what must be his opinion of their master? He thinks I'm in my dotage, no doubt. Not to be trusted to make sense of events. Useless in dangerous situations.

He snapped, "You did a foolish thing today that could have cost both of you your lives. It's only by a miracle that you managed to get home. You should not have gone off by yourself, thinking you could do better without Tora. Never forget again that Tora is my senior retainer. He is a fearless fighter. I owe him my life and cannot do without him. Now go to bed."

Saburo paled, bowed, and walked softly out of the room.

Arihito looked after him. "He's a strange fellow, that one."

"Yes. I'm worried about Tora. Too much has gone wrong lately. Kobe—you recall Kobe?—is ill at my house in the capital. Someone killed his servant and destroyed his property. Then there is Yukiko. And my new superior appears to be involved in this trouble here in Otsu."

"My sister will turn up. It isn't right that you should be burdened with her heedless behavior after all she's done to you."

"She may be in trouble, Arihito. You seem unusually angry at her. Has anything happened between the two of you?"

Arihito bit his lip. "Her life isn't mine. Her friends are not the ones I like to be around. I find I don't like her very much any longer."

105

It was pretty vague but resembled Akitada's own feelings. He nodded and said, "I'm sorry for it. I feel responsible for her and fear that our ill-advised marriage is to blame. It was the closeness of your family that I admired and envied."

"No, Akitada. It was her own doing. She was blinded by the court, and fell for that spoiled boy Okura and all the other useless and immature characters hanging about there."

This made Akitada smile. "You're not much older, Arihito. Were you never tempted by the splendor and the amusements?"

"Father refused to let me go." Arihito blushed a little. "He couldn't stop Yukiko. He never could speak as harshly to her as he did to me."

Ah, yes. There it was. Sibling resentment. Kosehira doted on his oldest daughter the way he had never doted on his sons.

The physician arrived at this point and they woke up Tora so he could examine the head wound. Tora objected, and in the end the doctor said to let him rest. He wrote out a list of foods and herbs the patient was to consume the following day and departed.

And Akitada and Arihito went to bed for another hour's sleep.

A servant woke Akitada. Still half asleep, he struggled up and put on his clothes. The events of his disturbed night upset him anew. He felt tired, confused, and angry. The warm gruel the servant had brought he ignored. Instead he went to check on Tora. He found him still asleep, but he was breathing evenly and his color was better.

Arihito was not up yet and Saburo had already left. Where had he gone? The servants did not know. Akitada dimly recalled having told him to find the boy's parents to tell them what had happened to the child. Saburo had claimed the boy probably had none, but perhaps he had gone anyway. He was still angry with Saburo and now angry again that he had gone off without telling anyone where he was going.

Akitada found himself with nothing to do. He decided it was time to pay the mysterious Norisuke a visit. It was as well to know the enemy, and he could account for it as a courtesy visit he was paying the man on his visit to Otsu and on account of Norisuke's recent promotion. He headed back to his room and changed into his best robe and his court hat. Then he had his horse brought out, left a message for Arihito, and rode into the city.

The Minamoto residence was one of the largest in Otsu as befitted a provincial chief. Norisuke belonged to the Seiwa Genji branch of the Minamoto clan. They were descended from Emperor Seiwa. The Seiwa Genji had risen quickly in the hierarchy and were known for their pride. Akitada was not surprised to see the crest of a stylized paulownia flower above three leaves flying on the banners at the gate. The double gate stood open, and as he rode in he was met by guards in the Minamoto livery. He announced himself and continued to the main house where he dismounted. A senior house servant came, bowed deeply, and guided him up the broad staircase and into the reception room. There he left him.

The large room was decorated with more paulownia crest flags and banners. Its columns were carved and painted, and a large dais held a single cushion covered in the imperial purple silk. Against the wall be-

107

hind it hung a large scroll painting of Bishamonten, one of the gods of good fortune. The warrior god was in full armor, carrying his spear and wearing an ornate, gilded helmet. Bishamonten was believed to be the defender of the nation and the scourge of evil. He also was thought to bestow great wealth. Apparently, Norisuke considered him a representation of his own good fortune.

He was soon to find out. Voices approached. One soft and subservient, the other loud and irritated. It made no attempt to spare the visitor.

"Who is this? I don't know any Sugawara." The soft voice explained. "But at this hour? You should have told him to come back later." The soft voice offered a defense. "Yes, yes. Very well. Let's get it over with."

The door flew open, and in strode Minamoto Norisuke, glowering. He was tall, slender, and very handsome, with a neat beard and mustache. He wore red silk trousers and a fine brocade coat. As he strode forward, it was also clear that he led an active life. This was not one of the pampered, soft-bodied courtiers so common in the capital. Even without spear and helmet, he bore a startling resemblance to the god in the painting.

Akitada bowed and said blandly, "My apologies for arriving so early. My visit was overdue and I was eager to pay it without further delay."

Norisuke stopped and stared at him. "Have we met?"

It was very rude and matched Akitada's original opinion of the man. Smiling with satisfaction, he said, "No, and I'm anxious to correct the oversight. I'm senior secretary in the Ministry of Justice. His Excellency,

Lord Morozane, dispatched me with congratulations on your recent appointment to provincial chief for Omi Province." He made another small bow.

Norisuke's face relaxed into a grudging smile. "That's very good of Morozane. He has also just been appointed to his position, I understand."

"That is so."

Akitada had not yet been greeted, let alone been made welcome and asked to sit down. An uncomfortable silence fell. He did nothing to relieve it.

Norisuke cleared his throat. "Um, I'm obliged for your visit. Even though it is quite early."

Akitada raised his brow. "Surely not all that early for a busy chief. We always start our day at dawn in the capital."

Norisuke flushed. "Well, perhaps not, but we've had a disturbed night. An intruder. I did not get to bed until dawn."

"Ah. That's unfortunate. You dealt with the intruder yourself?"

"Of course not. My servants were careless. But the household was disturbed."

"I see." Akitada waited.

"Er, shall we sit down?" Norisuke gestured toward the dais with its single cushion.

Akitada nodded and went to sit on it, enjoying the momentary outrage on Norisuke's face. Norisuke clapped his hands and had another cushion brought and placed on the dais, then sat down. "So," he said stiffly, "do you have any particular business with me?"

Clearly he wanted to get rid of the unwelcome and offensive guest as soon as possible.

"Well, yes. I regret that a number of complaints have been filed with the government, concerning certain offenses committed by those who deal with goods shipments here. There is some suspicion that even tribute goods designed for His Majesty are being stolen. Thefts and robbery in general appear to be common in Otsu itself and on the roads to the capital. No doubt your appointment signals the seriousness of the situation and the hopes of the central government that you will put a stop to such activities. I am here to consult with you on how best to proceed."

This long, and rather formal explanation caused Norisuke to blink, but if Akitada had hoped for a guilty reaction, he was disappointed. Norisuke smiled. "I see. But you did realize that my appointment is very new? I've hardly had time to familiarize myself with my duties. In any case, it's news to me that such serious complaints have been submitted or that the Ministry of Justice is involved. Who are the persons who made these claims?"

Most of the complaints submitted to the government tended to be made by the victims, and they were usually people without power themselves. Norisuke knew this as well as anyone. Threats and retaliations could put a stop to such irritations. Akitada said vaguely, "I don't have the details in mind at the moment. I wanted to ask what measures you are taking to make the transport system more secure."

Norisuke raised a brow. "At the moment nothing. I have not heard any complaints and you have given me no examples. When I receive instructions from the prime minister's office, I shall know what to do. I control an army if it should be needed." Suddenly his eyes narrowed. "Sugawara? Are you the one who married Fujiwara Kosehira's daughter?"

So his name had finally rung a bell. Akitada winced that it should have been his unfortunate marriage that should have done so. "We are divorced," he said.

Norisuke smirked. "Really? Well, in any case, there was really no need for you to concern yourself."

It was a stand-off and a threat. The man's arrogance was his best defense. He clearly considered Akitada too unimportant to bother with. Akitada smiled a little. "I see. As you told me at the beginning of our conversation, this is not a good time to discuss such matters. What exactly happened here last night?"

"Nothing important. It was just a nuisance, that's all. A thief, one of the street children, climbed the wall. He was chased off, but it woke the entire household."

"Ah. How irritating. Do you have this sort of thing happening often in Otsu?"

Norisuke snapped, "No more so than in the capital."

Akitada allowed himself a small laugh. "You're right. Criminals are busy everywhere these days." He rose. "Thank you for your gracious reception. We will, no doubt, meet again."

If Norisuke had hoped to be rid of the pesky official, he was now on notice that Akitada was keeping an eye on him.

14

Blessings of Adversity

Saburo slept poorly that night. The old ghosts came back to haunt him. He met his other self again, at eighteen, on Mount Koya, being trained in the use of sword, bow and arrow, and unarmed combat.

He had failed miserably at the first two but proved somewhat adept in wrestling his enemy to the ground because of his quick movements. He was clever and well-educated, and so they had decided he would make a good spy. His training had become more intense and had involved certain deadly secrets involving needles and pressure points.

It had puzzled him at first that his present master had not considered the murder of a helpless victim to be another form of warfare, when this type of warfare in the defense of the faith had been approved and praised by his teachers. The monks had made it clear that the price for honor, reward, and salvation was risking his own life while fighting in the service to the Buddha.

His mother had given him to the monks in hopes of a better life for herself in a future world. And the monks had needed soldiers. He had failed both.

It seemed to him now that his entire life had been a series of massive failures. He had failed to be attractive enough to become an older monk's disciple and lover; he had failed to excel in the use of weapons to make a name for himself; he had failed as a spy, because he was caught and cruelly tortured; and he was still failing now when he had found a safe and peaceful occupation and needed to do nothing but please a generous master.

But that was apparently impossible. He had offended again. Was he employed only to watch over Tora who could do no wrong in the master's eyes? What had happened had been Tora's fault. Once again Saburo felt a strong urge to walk away from the Sugawara household. Nothing held him. True he had taken a wife who had brought along a daughter, but the girl was nearly grown now, and there had never been much between him and Sumiko. Sumiko was an *Eta* woman and had been a slave when he had taken her as his wife. She was grateful to him for rescuing her daughter, and he had lost hope of finding any other woman who would want someone as disfigured as he was. Sumiko was grateful, and that was all that was between them and it was more painful even than outright rejection.

Saburo met this new day with the conviction that he must either redeem himself in the master's eyes or die in trying to do so. Death was preferable to going on as he was. And so he dressed in his ordinary clerk's robe and walked into the city. The long walk gave him time to think about Norisuke and the dead boy.

He doubted that the boy had living parents, but he would ask some questions. His first destination was the beggar at the shrine to Ebisu.

The beggar was there, along with a companion, a shriveled, dark-skinned man of uncertain age who appeared to be blind, his eyes a murky, bluish white. Saburo, suspicious of the tricks of beggars watched him carefully before approaching, but the blindness seemed real enough. There were also some children, a few boys and a ragged little girl. The little girl's hair had been cut short with a knife and stood up unevenly in tufts. Nevertheless, she was surprisingly clean compared to the grimy boys.

Saburo thought of the broken child's body in the Minamoto yard and shuddered. He could not rid himself of guilt, even though the boy had seemed to know what he was doing and had given no warning of danger.

The children came running to him as soon as they saw him. He looked over the boys, thinking the dead child's companion might be among them, but he could not remember what he had looked like.

They clamored for coppers, reaching up their grimy hands, while the beggar with the mangled leg cursed them. Saburo handed out coppers, one to each child. Penance, he thought it, for having sent the boy to his death. Then he went to the two beggars.

"You remember me?" he asked the one with the mangled leg.

"Don't be silly. With your face?"

It still hurt, though he looked less repulsive these days than when he was younger. The beard disguised the worst scars. Saburo looked pointedly at the beggar's leg. "I see you make your scars look worse."

The man laughed. "It's good for business. So what do you want today? Did you bring enough silver to pay for it?"

The blind man leaned a little closer and extended a skeletal hand. "A few coppers will do for me," he pleaded. "Please, honored sir. For a poor blind fisherman."

Saburo ignored him. "The boys that were here last time, do you know them?"

The man with the painted leg glanced at the children. "No. But I've seen them here. Not today. What did you want with them?" He suddenly got a crafty look in his face. "Ah. Did you like them? Sweet little boys, weren't they? Is that what you like?"

Saburo almost hit him. "Tell me where they live!"

"On the streets. Here and there. You never know with kids. There are more where those two came from. For a piece of silver I'll get you any boy you like. What age do you like?"

The blind man spat and turned away, disappointed.

Saburo said, "You have a filthy mind, old man," and walked back to the children who greeted him eagerly. He said, "I was here yesterday. There were two boys here, maybe eleven and nine years old. Do you know them?"

They looked at each other.

"Might've been Kai and Masashi," said the little girl. "They come here a lot."

One of the boys nodded. "Masashi's the little one. They're brothers or cousins."

"Do you know where they live?"

They looked puzzled.

"You mean where do they sleep?" the girl asked.

"Yes. If they don't have a family."

The boy said, "They sleep anywhere. Just like us. Sometimes here," he pointed at the shrine behind them, "sometimes at one of the temples. Why do you ask?"

Saburo smiled. "I promised them money for some information. I hoped they'd be back here today."

They looked at each other again. "Which one did you like?" the boy asked, sidling a little closer and smiling up at Saburo.

Saburo thought of the dead boy. "Uh, the smaller one. Masashi."

The boy reached for his hand. "I'll go with you," he wheedled. "For ten coppers."

Saburo jerked back his hand. "No!" he growled. "And don't you go with strange men either. You never know what can happen." He winced at his words.

The boy grinned. "I know what happens, and so do they." He gestured to his companions.

They lived in a terrible world, these children. His stepdaughter at home had once also been the prey of an unscrupulous man. That was why her mother had been grateful to him for saving the child and offering them safety. There was little joy in the knowledge, and Saburo sighed.

The little girl asked, "Why are you sad?"

"Something happened to Kai last night. I wanted to tell his parents if he has any."

117

The three small faces peered up at him intently. "What happened to Kai?" asked the girl.

"He climbed into Lord Norisuke's place. I think they caught him."

They huddled together a little more closely. "Kai shouldn't have done that," said the boy. "He knows better. They beat him, I bet. That's why he isn't here. They hurt him."

And how!

The little girl said, "He went back to see Bishamonten."

Saburo thought he had not heard correctly. "The god Bishamonten? Why?"

"To ask him for gold. Bishamonten keeps his treasure there. He's a big warrior. You can see him in the temple."

One of the boys explained, "He wears armor and a helmet. And he has a spear. And a ferocious face. Kai saw him in that place. He said so."

Bishamonten was one of the gods of good fortune and great wealth. He was worshipped in some temples as a *bodhisattva*. People believed he was a bringer of wealth and defender of the nation. Bishamonten statues were always depicted in full armor and with helmet and spear. Lord Norisuke kept soldiers in his compound. No doubt, the boy had seen one of his warriors on an earlier escapade. In his naïve mind, the child had combined the rumors of Norisuke's wealth with the sight and believed he had seen the god himself.

Saburo told the children, "It was a foolish thing to do. Stay away from the place."

They hung their heads, and he remembered making the boy climb the wall by promising money.

118

True, he had not expected him to jump down on the other side. The boy had done it for a few coppers. So much for winning Bishamonten's treasure.

"Where can I find his friend? Masashi?"

Again it was the girl who had the answer. "They help out in one of the kitchens."

"Which kitchen is that?"

"I don't know." She thought a moment and added helpfully, "They make dumplings and one of the men sells them in the market."

There was no more to be learned here. Saburo thanked her, and then parted with more coppers, giving the girl two of them.

15

The Markets Office

Akitada returned thoughtfully to Arihito's house. He had disliked and distrusted Norisuke instantly. He was a descendent of those who had taken advantage of their imperial lineage to build their fortunes in the provinces and who now wielded such power that the Fujiwara elite were afraid to discipline them even for the most flagrant misdeeds. Instead, they called on them whenever they needed soldiers to suppress an insurrection somewhere in the nation. It was clearly understood on both sides that such services were to be paid for by turning a blind eye to offenses and acceding to requests for additional powers. Norisuke may have felt secure, but his appointment was recent and he could not afford any major scandals yet. Alas,

Akitada's awareness of the man's character fell far short of solving the problems in Otsu.

He was met by Arihito and the news that he was being recalled to the capital. A messenger had arrived from the ministry. Morozane ordered him to report immediately. It probably signaled the new minister's fear that Akitada was interfering in whatever plans were being hatched. Given his decision to keep his position for the sake of his family, Akitada would obey.

Arihito consoled him when he saw Akitada's face. "It may not be much, and you get an opportunity to learn more about Yukiko. You said yourself that something must have happened at court to make her come to Otsu and hide."

Akitada agreed, but he was not at all hopeful.

He went to check on Tora and found him sitting up. Tora still looked pale and was nauseated. The physician had seen him and prescribed bed rest and a diet of gruel. Tora objected to both.

"I want to go back to the harbor, sir," he said. "Something's going on there, and whatever we happened to see or hear yesterday set those thugs on me."

Akitada said firmly, "You're not going anywhere. It's much too dangerous and you're not well yet. I hope Saburo is also careful. In any case, I must return to the capital today. Until I return, I want both of you to stay out of trouble."

Tora looked unhappy. "You'll be back soon?"

"I hope so."

"Don't tell Hanae."

"If you promise to behave."

Tora nodded reluctantly.

122

The journey back was uneventful. Akitada looked carefully at a goods shipment consisting of a line of ten horse-drawn carts laden with assorted merchandise and accompanied by mounted guards. A question to one of them revealed that they were to be delivered to the left market of the capital. There was nothing to suggest that they were stolen goods.

He stopped at his home to change. Sadako greeted him with the news that Kobe had improved rapidly and had insisted on returning home. Akitada thought this rash, but his own problems were more urgent at the moment. He answered Sadako's questions about Yukiko and, in turn, asked about Yasuko. It appeared his daughter was spending time with her cousins at his sister's house. According to Sadako, she seemed to have accepted her father's decision.

Feeling encouraged by this, Akitada changed into his court robe and hat and departed again for the *Daidairi*. His office had once again two clerks in it. They seemed busily at work and Akitada asked what they were doing. It turned out that Morozane had simply transferred them back to Akitada's office to make more room in his own. They were busy with Morozane's correspondence.

He bit his lip in anger, then went to see his superior.

Morozane was reading when Akitada was announced. He looked up and said, "Well, you finally show your face again!"

Clearly they were back to hostilities.

"I returned from Otsu as instructed, sir," Akitada said.

"And what were you doing in Otsu?" Morozane smirked. "Having a nice time, no doubt. Lake Biwa is wonderful place this time of year. Need I remind you that there is work to be done and you need permission to absent yourself from your duties?"

Akitada flushed with anger, but he had spent his time searching for his ex-wife. Still, he was not accustomed to being treated like a clerk. He said stiffly, "You may recall that I was sent to Otsu to look into the irregularities concerning the transport of goods intended for the capital."

"I didn't send you. I expected you to handle the matter from here. Ask a few questions and prepare a response to reassure the central ministry that all is well."

"But all is *not* well, as I found when I started to look around in Otsu."

Morozane stared. "What do you mean?"

The local overlord, Minamoto Norisuke, is making use of his troops to control the loading and unloading in Otsu harbor."

Morozane burst into laughter that made his great belly quiver. "Really, Sugawara, that's too funny for words." He laughed again and the clerks and servants in the room joined.

Akitada froze at the insult.

Morozane eventually stopped laughing. "I shouldn't have to explain to you that Lord Norisuke's appointment authorizes the use of his people to enforce law and order in his area. It has always been considered the wisest arrangement to use local troops to oversee security. They know their people and conditions. And it saves the emperor the cost of keeping an army."

"Thank you for the explanation," Akitada said. "I wasn't quite finished. Norisuke's soldiers masquerade in the uniforms of the imperial guard. I suspect that the tribute goods unloaded under their watchful eyes will not reach His Majesty."

Morozane's jaw fell. He shot Akitada a venomous look. "How dare you make such an accusation against a man like Lord Norisuke? I cannot believe I heard correctly. Are you really implying that he is a thief? A common thief? Do you not know what the punishment is for unfounded accusations?"

Akitada quoted stonily, "Exile or decapitation. The latter if the accusation is directed against someone of significant importance in the government. In that case, an unfounded accusation is considered the same as insurrection."

"Correct. I trust you'll reconsider your hasty words."

Akitada was silent for a moment. Morozane was capable of filing a complaint against him, and he had nothing to prove his accusation but the scene Tora and Saburo had described. He said, "I was under the impression that I was making a report to my superior."

"A report on Lord Norisuke? Did I authorize one? Did I tell you to go to Otsu to spy on him?"

Akitada restrained his anger. He thought of Yasuko and the rest of his family. He bowed deeply. "My sincere apology if I have acted rashly. I must have misunderstood. I believed that you wished to impress the central ministry with the thoroughness of our investigation."

Morozane's face contorted with anger. "You—." He stopped, then said more calmly, "Don't twist my words, Sugawara. I think you understood quite well and decided to do things the way you've always done them. You're a disgrace to your position. You are a lower-ranking official seizing powers he is not entitled to. I shall see to it that in the future your activities follow the guidelines. If they do not, you'll be dismissed. Now go!"

Akitada went. He had handled it badly. His cursed pride had got in the way again. Morozane should have been managed with lies and flattery. But these were repulsive to Akitada and he was probably not convincing with such methods anyway.

He returned to his office and drafted a report asserting that complaints about shipping and transport in Otsu had been unfounded and that the market offices in the capital were operating properly. He indicated that the report had been prepared on orders of Minister Fujiwara Morozane. This he handed to one of the servants for delivery to Morozane. Then he left the building.

He next went to pour out his troubles to his friend Nakatoshi.

Nakatoshi made sure no one was listening when he realized Akitada's anger and misery. Then he waited until Akitada had finished.

"Yes," he said when Akitada fell silent, "I see. I should have known it would come to it. You have at least handled the situation wisely in the end. Morozane will submit the report, thinking he has scored a victory and you obeyed his instructions. Since you did not put your name to it, you can continue your investigation in secret. And he will not notice, being in a hurry to submit the report, because that is how he works." Nakatoshi smiled.

Akitada did not feel like smiling, but he was grateful for the words. "Thank you, but I have achieved nothing. Not only is there the matter of Norisuke and his allies, but I have no idea what has happened to

Yukiko and I'm becoming concerned." He told Nakatoshi what they had found in Yukiko's retreat.

"I'm not close to palace gossip," Nakatoshi said. "From what you have told me, I would think there would be quite a lot about Lady Yukiko."

Akitada grimaced.

"Forgive me," his friend said quickly. "What has happened to you and her grieves me. It is difficult to understand women. I know you think you were too old for her, but surely that doesn't excuse her behavior to you."

"I'm ashamed of myself," Akitada said miserably. "I seduced a child and then expected her to behave like an adult woman."

"No. She was not a child. Women much younger than that become wives of men much older than you were at the time and all goes well."

Akitada shook his head. "Does it always go well? I don't know. Besides, I think sometimes that I've never been young, never was the sort of man who appealed to a young woman brought up to compose poems and receive them from suitors. I've never known how to flatter and how to play the games they enjoy, and I never was the sort of brave hero she expected. Let's face it, I'm hopelessly dull, Nakatoshi."

Nakatoshi laughed. "You? With your history of adventures?"

"She thought I was still that man. I wasn't, and I really never was. What happened was not my doing. I've always been cautious. I was cautious the day she was attacked by a madman, and she thought me a coward."

Nakatoshi said nothing and Akitada was deeply embarrassed. He had never spoken of the incident that finally broke his marriage. She had been ashamed of his

127

lack of action, had not understood that he had been afraid that the madman would kill her, and she had expressed her feelings in the strongest terms. He had known then that it was over. Her betrayal with Okura had come soon after, perhaps in retaliation.

Akitada rose. He avoided looking at his friend. "Well, I'd better be on my way. Please forget what I told you. I'm afraid her disappearance has opened some old wounds I'd forgotten about."

Nakatoshi got up and caught his sleeve. "No, my friend! Don't go yet. Not in this mood. It was her loss that she didn't understand, that she lived in a world of fairy tales instead of reality. Perhaps you cannot blame her, but you must not blame yourself either."

Akitada touched his hand. "Thank you. I shouldn't have burdened you with matters that I should have kept to myself. I'm afraid I sounded like a spoiled child that didn't get a toy. Forgive me."

He left over further protestations by Nakatoshi and walked into the city, having decided to manage his troubles with more resolution.

He headed for the office of the Eastern Market. The city's original plan had created equal halves, the left and the right capitals, each to be managed by separate administrations. Thus there were two markets, as there were two city administrations, and two jails.

Human nature being less orderly, the two halves of the city had developed differently over the centuries. As the western capital declined, the eastern capital grew, and so the two markets had become markedly different. They had been meant to offer alternate services every two weeks, but as the prosperity of the eastern market increased with the population on that side, their character changed. Both markets operated every week. The Eastern Market was larger, busier, and offered more types of merchandise. It had also attracted merchant establishments catering to the elite. The western counterpart served the poor people with the mere necessities of life.

This late morning, the Eastern Market was the usual bustling, shouting, bargaining scene of a cross-section of the capital's inhabitants, men, women, and children, all engaged in their own personal business. Rich smells hung in the air from the many open fire pits, grills, and soup cauldrons. The scent of freshly baked sweet rolls, buns, and fried rice cakes mingled with them as vendors passed through the crowd, their trays held high. Housewives, cooks, and servants shopped for their kitchens, and street children snatched an occasional treat before they could be caught.

Akitada loved the great market because it was utterly alive and mostly happy. Normally he might have lingered and perhaps indulged himself with a fried rice cake, but today he had business with the market master.

He found his office on the top floor of the market gate. The lower floor was cluttered with laborers taking a rest, businessmen engaged in deal-making, a soothsayer, and two beggars. A guard, his uniform tattered and dirty, sat on the steps dozing.

Akitada stepped over his outstretched legs and climbed the wooden stairs. He emerged on the second floor where an empty waiting room greeted him. Light fell through half-closed shutters on a dirty floor. A set of doors faced him, but there was no one there to announce him. He wondered at this, but decided to find out for himself why nobody seemed to work here. He flung open the door and walked into an office where a fat, middle-aged man in a stained black robe rested against a pillar, asleep, while two young males were leaning over the railing looking at the market below.

Akitada cleared his throat. "What is going on here?"

The two at the railing jumped and turned. They were young scribes in brown robes and with ink-stained fingers.

The older man woke, blinked, growled, "Wha—?" and then stared at Akitada as if he were an apparition.

"Who's in charge?" Akitada asked him.

The older man climbed to his feet with some difficulty. "Umm, I'm the senior clerk, Kudara Makoto, sir. Is anything amiss?"

"I'm here to see Lord Yoshinari. Where is everyone?"

"Lord Yoshinari?" The fat clerk laughed. "Here?"

"Yes. He was appointed director of the Markets Office. This is the Markets Office, isn't it?"

"Y-yes, but His Excellency doesn't come here. Only his secretary. And he only comes every other week."

"Then who does the work?"

The fat man bobbed a small bow and chuckled. "That would be me, sir. Those two boys are worthless at calligraphy."

"But you aren't working. You were asleep. And where is your desk? Where are the ledgers, lists, the paperwork that should be kept in a markets office?"

The fat man shuffled over to a small stand. On it lay some pieces of paper beside a dry ink stone and a shriveled brush. A battered ledger rested on a shelf underneath. "Right here!" the fat clerk said proudly. "At hand when needed."

Akitada stepped closer and saw the inky scratches could hardly be called calligraphy. Besides they were minimal. "What do you mean, 'when needed'? I would have thought a busy market like this would mean copious lists of merchants and goods. There should be daily entries in ledgers." His voice had taken on the censorious tone he usually reserved for lazy boys working in the ministry archives.

The fat clerk was becoming defensive. "I've got a fine memory, sir. My memory's wonderful. I can recall the smallest detail and report it to His Lordship's secretary when he comes."

Akitada said nothing for a moment. He was as shocked by the absence of proper bookkeeping, as he was by the lack of an industrious and qualified staff.

The clerk smirked a little. "Besides His Excellency wants all records kept as his house. We just report. His secretary and his clerks take care of the important paperwork."

Well, it might be so because these three people were clearly not competent. Akitada asked, "And what do you and your helpers do?"

"We keep an eye on things and report."

Akitada sighed. "Where does His Excellency reside?"

"He's bought the house of Lord Tadahito. South of Ogimachi and west of Kyogoku. A very fine place."

In the north-eastern corner of the capital, streets and buildings had expanded beyond the original boundaries and into the foothills. Only the great nobles lived in that area. Properties were large. The cost must have been huge. More to the point, it meant a rather long walk back with nothing accomplished. Akitada nodded to the clerk and left.

16

Master Cricket

Tora was frustrated. The master had left for the capital and Saburo had disappeared without a word. No doubt he was busy discovering what was going on in Otsu while Tora was cooped up in his room with strict orders to rest and heal.

As it was, the night had done wonders in easing the pain in his head. He even thought that the thugs might have done him a favor. He felt quite normal and was no longer dizzy. He got up and wandered about the house and the grounds, obedient to his instructions of staying safe, but feeling increasingly restless and dissatisfied with the imposed leisure.

Lord Arihito was gone also, having decided to return to his sister's house. They were all busy, while

Tora was wasting his time watching the servants and eating all the meals they offered. By the time the mid-day rice had been brought and the dishes removed again, he could not stand it any longer. He dressed in his regular clothes and left for the city. His plan was to visit Master Cricket. It should be safe enough, because the hermit was even older than he was and a good deal more decrepit.

The old man had intrigued him and a visit to an ancient wise man could not be considered foolhardy in any way. Besides, Tora would be back home before dark.

The one-eyed woman in the wine shop had said the Master lived behind Miidera.

Miidera, the temple of three wells, lay where the foothills began. It overlooked the city of Otsu and the great lake not far from Arihito's house and in a beautiful location, chosen hundreds of years before. The temple had grown inordinately since then in both size and fame. The Holy Enchin had been its abbot once, and all the emperors had supported it generously ever since. It had also gained an implacable enemy.

Once the great Enryaku-ji on Mount Hiei above it had been its sister temple, but the two had fallen into disputes over which was better or more worthy of imperial generosity. The disputes had developed into outright wars, fought by *sohei*, warrior monks hired and trained for fighting. They had fought and killed their opponents and burned down enemy temples. Miidera had been burned twice, and hostilities were stirring again up on the mountain.

Tora encountered a number of *sohei*, dressed in black and lightly armed, as he made his way past the temple. They made him think of Saburo, who had once been one of them, though his work had been spying on the enemy, a somewhat less martial sport. Tora had been a warrior and had little understanding for the strangeness of such a life. He had never completely warmed up to Saburo the way he had to Genba. He and Genba had a bond that was truly brotherly, while Tora's tongue tended to resist calling Saburo "Brother".

He followed a narrow road along the outer temple walls. The woods closed in at the back of the great complex. Tora almost missed the small house nestled among the trees and protected by a planting of bamboos. A narrow path among the bamboos was all that signified there might be some human habitat among the dense greenery. A small wooden sign was nailed to a tree. It bore the carved image of a cricket.

Tora took the path and found that Master Cricket lived in a small, but very respectable house in a clearing. Its solid appearance surprised Tora who had assumed that a hermit would dwell in a lean-to hut made of twigs, moss, and sticks of bamboo. Another wooden sign at the end of the path read *MASTER CRICKET* in elegant black ink calligraphy. Tora, whose knowledge of writing was spotty, could just make out its meaning.

Since he saw no bell, he clapped his hands twice, much as one does before addressing the god of a shrine, and shouted, "Are you home, Master Cricket?"

A voice answered, "Come!"

Tora noted the cleanliness of the swept path, the scoured steps, the neatly kept dark cedar bark roof, and wondered again. Hermits rarely cared about such things. A black and white kitten lay on the top step in a patch of sun and watched Tora's approach with interest. He stepped carefully over it and went to the door.

The door panel was carved and when Tora opened it, he saw that the back of the house was open and faced the woods behind it. A pleasant green light came in from the outside. The entire house consisted of a single large room with shutters across the back. The shutters were raised, and the sun played through the trees, making moving patterns on the bare wood floor.

Master Cricket himself was almost obscured by this pattern play and Tora did not at first see him sitting near the back of the room, bent over some papers. Tora stood on the threshold, bemused, looking around, seeing many books, perhaps as many as the master had in his study, but few comforts.

"Well, are you just going to stand there gawking?" the deep voice asked. "Come in and close the door."

Tora obeyed and went closer. "Forgive me, Master Cricket. I didn't see you there."

"Even before you see it, a flower is beautiful."

Tora gave an embarrassed laugh. "My eyes aren't what they used to be."

"You have no eyes, Tora."

Tora crept a little closer. The master had not moved or raised his head. How had he known him? How had he guessed his name? Awed, Tora said humbly, "Yes. It's true. I can't see what is happening. That's why I've come. I need your eyes."

Master Cricket finally looked up and gave Tora a penetrating stare. As before, he reminded Tora of ancient wise men he had seen in his master's pictures. His nearly bald head, the long white beard and mustache, and the bristling brows were the same as those of the holy Jurojin who was one of the lucky gods. Tora took the resemblance as a good sign. He could use some good luck.

Master Cricket was old, but the black eyes were bright and sharp. They took in Tora's bruised face. "I warned you to be careful. Your partner is a very unpleasant man, but he has eyes. You, you are as blind as a mole."

Tora hung his head. "It's true," he said again. "I'm only a mangy dog at my master's gate."

Master Cricket snorted. "Well, you try. Your master is a lucky man even with this mangy dog. Sit down and ask what you want to know."

Tora sat. "My master wants us to find out who's behind the crimes that happen here in Otsu. We went to the harbor and saw some things that seemed wrong. I thought I could find out about them by talking to people. I think that was what got me into trouble. Saburo's more impatient. I guess I'm getting too old for this work." He sighed deeply.

Master Cricket nodded. "It happens to all mortal men. A shining face in the morning and white bones by night. Who are you to complain to me about old age?"

Tora said nothing. How could this ancient man know how fiercely he had fought in his youth and how much he wished to serve his master. Master Cricket was a hermit. He owed nothing to any man. He had mastered the desire to impress, to serve, to achieve.

After a long silence, Master Cricket said, "Riches and honors are like floating clouds. Disregard them."

Tora frowned. "I know that. My master is a poor man as such things go, but he's a just man, and he's in trouble. I'd hoped to be of service to him before I die, but I can do nothing."

The wise man smiled. "Ah! That is hard."

Tora tried again. "He must find out if there are thieves stealing from the people. We went to the harbor and there were soldiers pretending to be imperial guards. They were watching the unloading of goods. They threatened us. Were they stealing?"

"Maybe. It is in the nature of armed guards to threaten. A careful man avoids giving offence."

Tora protested, "But how is one to learn what is happening without asking questions?"

Master Cricket stroked his beard and looked at Tora's neat blue robe with the black sash, at his tidy topknot, and at his good boots. "You wore those same clothes then?"

"Well, no. We thought it would be best to seem poor so as not to be told lies."

The master grunted. "You obviously don't know much about poor people."

Tora flushed. "I was poor once."

"But you were young then. Youth and money both buy respect."

Tora thought about this, then nodded. "You mean those guards threatened us because they thought we were poor."

"Poor men steal. And they were guards. It's really very simple, Tora."

Tora rebelled again. "Not all poor people steal. And not all guards are good guards."

Master Cricket moved impatiently. "Of course. But it is what most people believe. Go away! You are wasting my time."

Tora bowed and got to his feet. He said politely, "I'm sorry I troubled you. Forgive me, please."

Master Cricket relented a little. "You will find a way. Remember to be patient and to forgive !"

Tora bowed again and left. Outside he stopped and looked back at the tidy little house in its green setting. Bamboo leaves rustled. Birds chirped. The place was a haven of peace. And yet in the outside world, children were murdered and men robbed and killed each other.

Tora was disgusted with Master Cricket. What sort of advice had that been? How was being patient and forgiving going to help in the present situation? Master Cricket might look like the divine Jurojin himself with his high forehead and white beard, but he had dispensed neither luck nor wisdom.

17

Siblings

It was late by the time Akitada left the Markets Office. He decided to go home and get a good night's sleep before continuing.

As he was eating the evening rice with his wife, he made the mistake of mentioning Tora's injury. She was immediately concerned about his health and did not like keeping the news from Hanae.

She said, "He should be home. You should not have left him."

"I had to report at the ministry."

"Nevertheless." She looked severe. "You must go and bring him back if Saburo doesn't do so."

"I thought he needed to rest." Akitada felt defensive. "And I have work to do if I'm to keep my position."

"At least send a message to Arihito to bring him home."

Akitada dispatched the stable boy with the message.

The next morning Akitada dressed again in his formal court robe and hat to continue his investigation of the Markets Office.

On his way, he decided to visit his sister. He wanted to make sure that Yasuko had accepted his decision and had forgiven him. He also hoped that his sister had managed to learn more about Yukiko's reason for leaving court so abruptly.

He found his sister in their garden, inspecting sprouting and flowering plants and pointing out needed improvements to her gardener. Akitada looked around enviously. His own garden, though older and larger, was untidy at the best of times. He did not have a gardener, and the efforts of his people were reserved for running the household and looking after the horses and repairs to buildings and fences. Akiko's husband was older than she and quite wealthy. She (and their mother) had chosen with care. Akiko had been beautiful and had developed a regal manner to impress her suitors. In the end, she had chosen Toshikage, a man who had both position and property, though no other attractions. Toshikage was not only shorter than his wife, he was pudgy, awkward, and slightly cross-eyed. In the days before their marriage, he had been an object of mockery. Akiko's choice had startled everybody, Akitada most of all. But to his surprise, the marriage was a happy one. Toshikage doted on Akiko and spoiled her with every luxury. In return, she gave him five children before restricting his access to her and turning her interests to her social life at court.

"So you're back," she greeted him. "About time, too. The girls have gone to shop for silk and fans. Let's go inside. I have things to tell you."

Akitada tried to guess from her demeanor whether her news was good or bad. He badly needed some cheering up. Akiko looked grim.

They went to his sister's room. It was hers in the sense that her husband visited rarely and she had had a free hand in surrounding herself with exquisite examples of what a noble lady might take pleasure in. The room held many painted screens depicting flowering cherry trees, flying geese, posing cranes, pairs of ducks, and chrysanthemums. Musical instruments of fine workmanship lay about. A blooming azalea grew in a large stoneware pot, painted lacquer trunks held her clothes, and a large lacquer rack displayed several fine silk robes in the colors of the season.

She gestured to these. "Getting ready for the usual court parties. That's why the girls are off shopping for things. I hope you mean Yasuko to have some spending money also?"

He had forgotten about the need for new spring robes and said quickly, "Yes, of course." He added, "Surely Sadako is seeing to this?"

"Sadako prefers the quiet life. She sent Yasuko to me for advice."

Akitada frowned. "Must she go to court? A few ordinary spring robes should not require much thought."

His sister waved to a cushion. "Sit down and stop fretting about court. She'll be with me."

143

Akitada sat, but he was not reassured. "You know how I feel about the things that go on there. It is totally unsuitable for an unmarried woman."

Akiko laughed. "Don't be silly. That's why parents send their daughters there. How else should they find husbands? Husbands, I mean, who are suitable and can support them and their children."

Akitada said bluntly, "Yasuko finds suitors where her father cannot provide suitable dowries. She needs to look elsewhere."

Akiko stared at him in shock. "Where? Is she to look among the merchants and tradesmen? Just where do you think a young woman finds a husband of her own class?"

Akitada squirmed. "Surely according to custom, they and their family enquire and then a meeting may be arranged in their father's house if both families are interested."

His sister sighed. "Sometimes it may be done that way, but have you made such enquiries? Or have you been contacted by the fathers of suitable young men?"

"There's only been Prince Michiyasu. But she's still very young."

"Oh, Akitada! She's nineteen this year. That's well past her first eligible age, which is fourteen. The poor girl is worried sick she'll have to become a nun."

He was aghast. Time had flown. Was Yasuko really desperate? She was beautiful and any man would be lucky to win her. Was her reaction to losing Michiyasu really just a matter of panic because she was too old to find a man? Should he have made more of an effort to look for a husband for her?"

Reading his mind, Akiko said, "She lost her mother. Tamako, had she lived, would have taken the matter in hand at least two years ago. Your present wife knows little about how such things are done here. That's why I offered to introduce Yasuko at court along with her cousin this year."

Akitada said weakly, "Thank you. Will you keep me informed? I cannot afford a big dowry. And I don't want her falling in love with the wrong man again."

Akiko waved a dismissive hand. "Of course. Leave it to me. Now tell me your news."

Akitada described his visit with Arihito, Arihito's attitude toward his sister, and their visit to Yukiko's empty house with its blood stains. Akiko was a good listener. She interrupted only twice. She asked about Yukiko's relationship with the rest of her family and she asked about Yukiko's servants.

When Akitada explained about the breach between his former wife and her family, she said, "No parent will totally disown a once beloved child. As for her brother, my guess is that she has done something that hurt Arihito himself."

"I know of nothing, except the fact that their father preferred Yukiko to him."

She shook her head. "I've met Arihito. He's not the kind to resent that. Besides, his father has always treated Arihito well."

Akitada nodded. "Yes. He loves all his children, though perhaps not equally. I think Yukiko's behavior hurt him badly. Arihito also."

When Akitada described Yukiko's little house being staffed by only two middle-aged people who claimed to know nothing, his sister's eyes lit up.

145

"They're lying. There's something they are covering up. Go back and question them. You'll find your answer."

Akitada agreed but pointed out that he could not absent himself from the ministry again. "I hoped to learn something about her life at court while I'm here. Something happened that sent her off to the mountain."

"She offended and had to leave," Akiko said bluntly.

"Yes, but how did she offend?"

Akiko threw up her hands. "Oh, Akitada, don't be so dense. Yukiko offended in many different ways. She had hardly any friends. In the end, she offended the wrong person."

"And who was that?"

"I'm guessing it was his majesty's new favorite. Who was newly pregnant."

Akitada let this sink in. The emperor was surrounded by attractive women who hoped to catch his attention. If they did, their future was secure and so was that of their family. And if one conceived, she was likely to be elevated in rank, perhaps even to become empress. He asked, "And who was this lucky favorite?"

Akiko gave him a reproachful look. "I do not gossip about such things."

It was dangerous to spread tales about the imperial bedchamber. Akitada sighed. He said, "I would have thought Yukiko had reached a rank where she was safe."

"No. I told you, nobody liked her. Nobody defended her. She had to leave. I expect even her doting father was shocked, and her brother lost any chance of future promotion. His career is over, and her younger

146

sisters will have to find husbands who are far from court rank."

It all made sense now: Kosehira's silence, Arihito's bitter resentment, the fact that only a minor nobleman like Okura cared about what became of her. Perhaps Okura, the rejected lover, thought Yukiko would be glad to have him now. The story was a sad one.

But it did not explain where she was, the blood in her mountain dwelling, or what had happened to her. He said as much to Akiko.

"Under the circumstances, you should leave well enough alone. Taking up her case can only damage your reputation."

Akitada said, "It cannot be worse than things are already." He told her about his quarrel with his new superior and his suspicion of corruption of the three new officials.

Akiko covered her face with her hands. "Horrible!" she murmured. "Oh! How could you become embroiled in this?"

"Trouble finds me," he said, trying to joke about it.

Akiko lowered her hands to look at him sadly. "Each of those men can ruin you. Did you not wonder how they gained their sudden promotions?"

"I did, but what good is that? Not that I know the ins and outs of it."

"Of course you don't. You never pay attention to the events that might be of interest to your career. Even Toshikage is better at it than you."

Akitada did not point out that Toshikage had no need to worry about advancement. He had enough income to provide for a family much larger than his and for any number of wives as extravagant as Akiko.

Toshikage could devote his time to attending parties. In this manner he had become well-known and liked. Aki-ko had a talent for reminding her brother about the many ways his character was deficient. He said bitterly, "I'm aware of it. I was hoping I might learn something helpful from you."

His sister thought. "Well, Fujiwara Morozane, your new minister, is an unknown. He came back from provincial service only recently. Fujiwara Yoshinaro is sponsored by the crown prince and the Minister of the Left. He's a nonentity, I think, but wealthy. And he has managed to marry a granddaughter of the Minister of the Left and gained a large dowry. He just bought an estate next to one belonging to the crown prince. And Minamoto Norisuke, while not at court any longer, has been the lover of any number of powerful women. He's a soldier and very handsome. Best not tangle with him either. My advice is to stay out of whatever they are do-ing and try to get along with Morozane."

"Even if all three are involved in crimes against the emperor?"

Akiko made a face. "And that, of course, means you must ruin yourself and your family to stop them." She sighed dramatically.

He said stiffly, "I have sworn an oath."

"So did they. It didn't stop them from looking out for their own interests."

"What would you have me do? Ignore what's happening? Oblige Morozane when he wants me to sign my name to a batch of lies? That, too, can lead to disaster."

She stared at him. "Yes," she admitted sadly. "It takes a selfish man to keep his head above the current. You're not that man, Akitada. And you insist on getting into deep water."

She was right, but knowing that was no help. He got up. "I was on my way to pay a visit to the new director of the Markets Office. Thank you for telling me what I'm up against."

Akiko also stood, after extending a hand to be helped up, a sign that she, too, was getting older. She looked at him searchingly. "Be careful, Brother. And leave Yasuko to me. I'll do my best."

He smiled at her. "I know, Akiko. You know, for all your sharp tongue, I've grown very fond of you."

She smiled back and briefly squeezed his hand before letting him go. "Thank you. I always hoped you might find it in your heart to forgive me for being my mother's daughter."

He was speechless that she had known.

She chuckled and gave him a push. "Go on! Do what you must do and come back from time to time to tell me about it."

18

Dumplings

Otsu's market was a modest affair compared to the markets in the capital. Saburo walked its entire length without seeing a dumpling man. Disappointed, he walked back again, looking carefully at the stands and sellers on both sides of the road.

A part of the market was on the street in front of the gates to Miidera where visitors to the temple had to pass by the displays. Business was good here, but it consisted mostly of the sorts of things pilgrims might need or want. First among those were religious objects and charms, both for protection and as reminders of their pilgrimage. Pilgrims, as Saburo knew well, were not necessarily austere and devout. A pilgrimage was a chance to get out of a confining household or away from work. It was intended to be as enjoyable as it was spiritually beneficial. And it was spring again, a good time for travel. Pilgrims also needed to eat, and so food sellers were plentiful. And pilgrims hoped to erase the sins accumulated over the past year, so they gave readily to the many beggars. Old men and women as well as cripples sat near the temple gate, and small, dirty, hungry-looking children in rags darted about among the shoppers.

Saburo tried to recall what the smaller boy, Masashi, had looked like, but boys that age all looked the same to him. Here, too, he was approached and offered sexual favors, in one instance by a girl who could not have been much more than ten years old. What had happened to the parents of all these children? He had told the master that the boy most likely was an orphan. The children of the poor frequently found themselves without parent or home, and many also ran away to the nearest town in hopes of a better life. Some of them, however, were sent out to beg by their own parents.

Finally he found a dumpling seller. He carried his dumplings in two containers suspended from a yoke across his shoulder and called out loudly, "Fine dumplings here! Fresh dumplings! Get them while they're warm!"

Saburo made his way to the man. The smell of the dumplings was tempting, but Saburo told himself that food was free at Lord Arihito's house and asked, "Where are the dumplings made?"

The dumpling man said, "What? They're fresh. I just picked them up."

"Yes, but where did you get them?"

"At our kitchen. How many do you want?"

"None. I just want the name of the man who makes them."

The dumpling seller asked, "What are you? A comedian?"

"No. I'm serious. I need to know."

By now people had paused to look and listen. The dumpling seller saw customers, while the ugly man before him was not interested in buying. He snarled, "Get out of my way if you're not going to buy. Are you mad?" He turned away from Saburo and made some quick sales to the people around them.

Saburo was angry, but it occurred to him that Tora had been right. You had to buy information. He turned away in hopes of finding another dumpling seller when an old woman called out to him. She sat on a reed mat among a collection of amulets and small figures of lucky animals. She said, "He works for Ishimoda. His place is near the shrine of the War God."

Saburo thanked her, hesitated a moment, then pointed to a small, rough image of Ebisu on a wooden disk. Ebisu, god of fishermen, was popular on the shores of Lake Biwa. "How much?" he asked.

"Ten coppers."

Another agonizing moment of indecision, then Saburo relinquished the ten coppers, received the amulet, and consoled himself with the thought that he needed luck very badly, and perhaps the god would be good to him. He tied the amulet around his neck and set off for the shrine of the War God.

This shrine was small when compared with the huge Miidera. Its gate was decorated with thick straw ropes above two warlike statues of fierce warriors and reminded Saburo again of the boys' belief in Bishamonten, also known as Minamoto Norisuke. The

153

shrine was visited by farmers and fishermen, both of whom prayed for luck in their work, but it was also the tutelary shrine of the Minamoto clan. He shuddered at the memory of the small broken body.

Saburo found the dumpling kitchen by following the smell that rose in a cloud of steam from a small, mean building. Inside, a middle-aged man in a greasy smock was kneeling on the floor, busily shaping dumplings from rice dough, while his wife leaned over a boiling vat with bobbing dumplings. A small boy stood beside her, holding a bamboo tray for the dumplings she deemed ready.

The boy looked like Masashi, the companion of the dead child, and he was about the right age.

When he turned his head to look at him, Saburo saw recognition in his eyes. The tray started to wobble and the woman shouted, "Watch out, you stupid brat!"

The man on the floor turned his head also and scrambled to his feet to bow, wiping his flour-covered hands on his shirt. "How can we serve your honor?"

Saburo pointed to the boy. "Is he yours?"

"No, sir. He's useless, but his brother's run away and we're stuck with him."

Saburo took a deep breath. "Masashi?" he asked, looking at the trembling boy.

The child nodded.

"Put down the tray and come here."

The boy started howling. "I didn't do nothing."

Saburo squatted. "Don't be afraid. Nobody 's going to hurt you. It's about your brother."

The child calmed down a little and glanced up at the woman. She laid down her ladle and took the tray, setting it aside. "Go and answer the gentleman," she said.

Masashi crept closer, staring anxiously at Saburo's face. "What's Kai done?"

"Nothing but what you saw. But he was caught."

"Oh." The boy digested this. "Where is he now?"

The woman broke in. "Kai was caught doing what? What has the good-for-nothing done now? Not enough he isn't here, working as he should be, he has to go out and make trouble for us. Just wait until I get my hands on the ungrateful lout."

Saburo stood. He was filled with pity and anger. Glaring at the woman, he snapped, "You won't need to trouble yourself. Beating him would do no good. He's dead."

The child cried out and the man gasped.

Her face hardened. She asked, 'Where? How?"

Saburo squatted again beside the boy. The child had tears in his eyes. "Kai did a dangerous thing," he said. "Don't ever do what he did."

Masashi sobbed and shook his head violently.

The woman demanded, "What did he do?"

Saburo ignored her. "Did Kai ever talk about what he saw in that place?"

Dumbly, Masashi nodded.

"What place?" the woman asked.

Saburo rose and looked at the adults. "Are you related to Masashi and Kai?"

She spat, "No!"

But her husband nodded. "They're my sister's boys."

The woman said, "The slut dumped them on us when she died. They've been eating our earnings.

155

Then they run away and won't work. They've been more trouble than they're worth. Now Kai gets himself killed, and his brother is too stupid to be of any use."

Her husband said, "He's still little. How did Kai die?"

Saburo looked at him a moment, then said, "He was beaten to death."

The man groaned and covered his face.

His wife asked, "Who did it? Do the police have his killer?"

"No. It was someone in the Minamoto compound."

"In that place?" Her eyes lit up. She turned to her husband. "You must report it to a judge. There's blood money owing."

Saburo regarded her with contempt. "I wish you luck demanding justice from Minamoto Norisuke."

Her face fell. "But they harmed us. We lost our best worker. We'll have to work day and night, both of us, to make up for it."

"Life's hard," Saburo said coldly and held out a hand to the boy. "Come, I'll buy you something in the market and you can tell me about Kai."

She protested, but her husband snapped, "Shut up! Let the boy go. Maybe they can figure out what happened and how we can get the body back."

As Saburo and boy walked out, the wife protested shrilly about funeral expenses.

In the market, the boy begged for food rather than a toy. He was skinny like his dead brother. The dumpling maker and his wife were poor people, and the woman was an ogre. Saburo doubted the boys had been given enough to eat. So out of pity and guilt, he fed Masashi with bowls of noodle soup, fried eel, rice cakes, and sweets until he began to look sick.

Then he took the boy to a quiet street where they sat under a large pine to rest and to allow Masashi's stomach to settle. Here, Saburo learned about Kai's excursions inside the wall of Norisuke's compound.

Kai had made three of those before he met his death. On the first one, he watched some of Norisuke's soldiers training with swords and lances and in formations. He was mightily impressed by their colorful uniforms and their armor and decided then and there to become a warrior. At one point, apparently Norisuke himself appeared, resplendent on a horse and wearing a large gilded helmet. Kai had thought him to be Bishamonten himself, especially since all the soldiers fell to their knees before him as he addressed them. It was midmorning and he had crept closer and was seen. Fortunately, armed warriors don't move quickly and so he had escaped easily.

His next excursion had been at night. And on that trip he discovered what he took to be Bishamonten's treasure house. He had found himself in a large garden. The main house was well lit, with its doors wide open to the spring night. In the golden light of candles and oil lamps, Kai saw people in gorgeous silk robes, shimmering paintings, golden tassels hanging from reed shades, golden Buddhas, trunks painted in bright colors and boxes covered with golden lacquer. Even the musical instruments seemed to have gold on them. He had never seen such splendor and was convinced all the beautiful trunks and boxes held more gold. On this occasion, he took a fan someone had left on the veranda railing.

157

He went back the very next night in hopes of helping himself to some small part of Bishamonten's wealth. But on this excursion, he was seen by several servants. He managed to elude them and only picked up a flute that had been left outside one of the rooms. Alas, he dropped it as he scrambled over the wall on his escape.

It all made sense. Kai's excursions had eventually been noted, and when they found proof that the intruder was a thief, the guards were doubled and told to deal with the intruder permanently. That order had come from above, most likely from the master himself. Saburo wished that Kai had found evidence of stored goods, but these were likely wrapped and crated for shipping and the boy would not have paid attention to them. It had been the shining, colorful world he had seen inside the house that he had associated with treasure.

There remained the problem of what to do about Masashi. Saburo hated returning him to the misery that awaited him in his uncle's house. He asked the boy tentatively, "What will you do now that Kai is gone?"

The tears welled again in Masashi's eyes. "I don't know," he whispered. "Kai had a plan for us. He was saving money so we could run away. How much money do you think I'll need?"

"You don't want to stay in your uncle's house?"

"No!" the boy cried. He gave Saburo a pleading look.

Saburo sighed. He owed this child for having taken away his brother and his hope. He could not turn his back on him. But his own home did not belong to him, and the boy's vicious aunt would set the constables on him if he took the child away.

The boy grasped his sleeve. "Can I come with you? I don't eat much and I can sleep anywhere."

Saburo was touched. A bit of food and some kindness had won him the child's trust. He said regretfully, "Your uncle and aunt would not permit it."

"They don't want me."

True enough, but that would change when they smelled money. Saburo sighed again. "You must go back. I'll think about it. Meanwhile, I'll try to check on you from time to time."

The boy's face broke into a big smile. His small hand grasped Saburo's. "Thank you. I'll work for you. I'll do anything."

Saburo snatched his hand away. "You're too young to work. Stay away from men who offer you money if you go with them."

The boy nodded. "I shall wait for you."

What could Saburo say? He reached for the amulet around his neck and put it around the boy's, "I hope Ebisu will look after you," he said and took him back to the dumpling kitchen.

19

A Successful Man

From Akitada's sister's residence, it was not far to the new mansion of Fujiwara Yoshinaro. He headed for Kyogoku Avenue, one of the broad north-south thoroughfares. It was once the outermost road at the eastern side of the capital. Now, however, buildings spilled beyond boundary walls and ditches into the countryside. Ogimachi was an ordinary street that ran east and west. It, too, extended into the foothills, becoming gradually rougher and less straight.

The new markets director had purchased a whole block of land that contained an older residence once belonging to one of the princes. It was easy to find his place, because the sound of hammering and sawing carried for several blocks. When Akitada reached it, he saw that renovations were being carried out, and these were on a large scale. The old gates stood wide open and laborers walked in and out, carrying in timbers and carrying out debris. The street was blocked by wagons drawn by oxen. People were shouting and nobody paid attention to the lone nobleman in court dress who tried to squeeze by to enter the property.

Akitada wished he had worn something less noticeable and subject to damage. But he found the melee of bare-chested workers and shouting overseers of unexpected interest. Such building projects took not only a great deal of money, but they also required influence. Building materials like those enormous tree trunks, intended to support heavy roofs, and that fine, smooth lumber meant for polished floors, were not easy to come by. Mostly such shipments were intended for temples, imperial palaces, and the homes of great nobles.

He slowed his progress to peer at various stacks and piles of materials and to watch the supervisors as they directed the workers. The workers ignored him, too busy to stop and stare, but one of the supervisors finally saw him. He approached, smiling and bowing, a grizzled fellow in a brown cotton robe and striped jacket.

"Welcome, your honor," he cried.

Akitada decided that his costume was useful after all. "A fine sight, seeing such industry in making our great capital more beautiful," he said, gesturing to the work going on around them.

The grizzled man smiled more broadly. "So it is, indeed, though they're lazy and ignorant beasts. But we keep an eye on things. It'll be a magnificent palace when it's done. Is your honor a friend of His Excellency?"

His Excellency? Akitada had not known that markets directors claimed such exalted forms of address. But he nodded and said, "You have some very expensive wood there, I see."

"Indeed. The emperor himself has no finer." The overseer winked, placed a finger on his nose, and invited Akitada to inspect a stack of lumber. Shifting a few boards, he pointed to some marks that had been burned into the end of a board.

Akitada stared at them and shook his head uncomprehendingly.

The man looked over his shoulder, then whispered, "It's the emperor's own mark." And then he held up his hand, hooking his index finger.

This, Akitada knew, suggested thievery. He raised his brows. "Isn't it dangerous to use stolen goods?"

The man placed his fingers to his lips and asked, "Who's to know? The workers certainly don't. I've worked on the crown prince's palace, so I recognized the mark. Please don't mention it. This is a good job. I don't want to lose it."

Akitada nodded and wondered if the shipments had been missed yet. The great distances that such building supplies traveled meant that their arrival in the capital could be delayed. But surely at some point questions would be asked.

He should have expected it. Who is in a better position to abscond with illegal goods than the markets director, especially when his office is kept by three lazy and ignorant clerks. The problem was, what could he do about it?

163

The supervisor had become nervous at the visitor's prolonged silence. He moved a little closer and whispered, "Your Honor wouldn't need some repairs, by chance?"

"Indeed, I do." Akitada's ancestral residence was once again in need of drastic shoring up against the elements. And he had no funds. At the moment, he had pushed such worries to the back of his mind, but they loomed large again when he saw what was happening here. He added, "That's why I stopped to see your work here."

The grizzled man chuckled. "A lucky day, your Honor. I have a small business of my own. If the job isn't too large, I could manage it. And we can always find some good materials. I could make the price very reasonable."

It was tempting. Akitada looked longingly at the fine imperial boards and columns, but he only said, "Thank you. I shall keep it in mind." Theft was clearly rampant in his world. Someone stole goods in Otsu and brought them to the capital where the Markets Master stole them again and thus supplied not only himself but the construction supervisor who ran a business with the stolen goods on the side. Embarrassed by having been tempted, he nodded curtly and made his way to the front of the main house.

And here he encountered the owner of this magnificent project. A finely dressed man with a neat mustache and chin beard stood with a clerkish-looking person, their heads bent over a large piece of paper the clerkish man was holding open. The discussion was not amiable. The well-dressed man was surely Fujiwara Yoshinaro, the new master of the Markets Office. At the moment, he was so caught up in arguing with his designer about overdue payments and unfinished work that he did not notice Akitada's approach until he stood quite close and followed the conversation. Then he suddenly stopped, stared at Akitada, and snapped, "What by all the devils of hell do you want? Can't you see I'm busy? Who let you in?"

Akitada smiled. "Nobody. Your gates are wide open. You really should speak to your people."

Yoshinaro snapped for air and crumpled the drawing in his fists. "I have no time for this. Go away!"

Akitada shook his head. "Sorry. My assignment is to speak to the Master of the Markets Office, and I believe that's you. Or have they seen fit to replace you already?"

The other man paused belatedly to take in Akitada's appearance. "Who are you?"

"My name is Sugawara. I was sent by the Minister of Justice. Central Affairs has received complaints. There are some questions about the way you run your office."

Yoshinaro flushed. He pushed the crumpled paper at the man beside him and snapped, "Fix it. I don't have time for this now." Then he turned back to Akitada. "Let's go inside. It's about some problems left behind by my predecessor, no doubt."

Yoshinaro led the way into a new part of the house. All was in the best taste but lacking the furnishings one would have expected. He seemed to guess what Akitada was thinking and said, "I haven't had time to settle in. The new duties, you know."

Akitada did not comment on this. They went to a room clearly intended to be Yoshinaro's study because it contained a desk cluttered with more paper work for the buildings. At least the noise of hammering and shouting was not as deafening here, but Yoshinaro closed the open shutters, casting the room into twilight. He pointed to a *tatami* next to his desk and said, "Let's sit. Now tell me again what you're here for."

Akitada recited in detail the charges that had been filed against the markets office and concluded with, "I spoke to your clerk there and found him useless."

Yoshinaro had been listening with a frown. Now he said, "Kudara comes highly recommended. You surprise me. But perhaps you should have directed your questions to me and in writing. A certain formality is expected."

Such shuffling of paperwork was common in the administration and designed to let one carry on with whatever one was doing while asserting ones efficiency and glossing over problems. Akitada, who detested it, said, "Sorry. I like to satisfy myself before writing my reports."

Yoshinaro cast a helpless glance around. "But you can see I'm in the middle of construction. I do not have my documents here."

"Where are they then? Your clerk certainly had none."

"Everything will be in good order by the end of the month. You may return then."

"Alas, my own report is due tomorrow."

But Akitada knew that no explanations or numbers would be forthcoming. He had gone as far as he could. And Yoshinaro had found his solution. He stiffened his posture and said firmly, "I shall be in touch with the minister myself."

Akitada rose, bowed, and left in the knowledge that his actions would probably irritate Morozane further. It was not only tempting, but easy to become a successful man. He only had to ignore all the ways in which laws were being broken, and the rewards would come his way also.

He decided to go home and draft his report with one copy for Morozane and the second for the Central Affairs office. It would be a declaration of war.

20

Kobe

Akitada did not return to the ministry. He worked on his reports at home. It gave him considerable pleasure to construct a shocking set of charges against the authorities in Otsu and in the capital. But when he finished, he decided to wait before submitting them. So he drew up a second, shorter report which merely outlined the steps he had taken in his investigation without assigning blame to anyone. It was cowardly, but he hoped to gain a little time to prepare for his dismissal when it came, as it surely must when the original report was turned in.

He decided to deliver the interim version the following morning. Satisfied with his labors, he went to bed, hoping that he had staved off the charge that he had not carried out his duties with sufficient zeal.

But the following morning, Lord Okura arrived before Akitada could leave for the ministry. He looked pale and was apologetic but adamant. "Have you learned anything? It's been more than a week."

Akitada saw no reason to spare the other man. His life was difficult enough without Yukiko's erratic behavior. He had put her firmly from his mind the last two days. He said, "As I promised, I went to Otsu to speak with her brother. I have to inform you that Arihito has lost all patience with her, but he agreed to take me to her house on the mountain. She was not there and the housekeeper had no information, except to say she thought her lady was visiting temples."

Okura cried, "I've been to all, or most of them. She's not there and never was."

Akitada threw up his hands. "Well, what would you have me do? Surely you are in a better position to ask questions than I am. And I am due at the ministry this morning."

Okura actually wrung his hands. "Oh, dear heaven! What can I do? You were my last hope." He sagged and sat down abruptly. "She must be dead by now," he groaned, then covered his face and wept.

Embarrassed by this display, Akitada snapped, "Nonsense. Pull yourself together. If she were, we would have heard. Dead bodies have a way of demanding action."

Okura dropped his sleeve and looked up at Akitada with swimming eyes. "How can you be so cold? Do you hate her so much?"

"I don't hate Yukiko. I find her frustrating, that's all. I do think it's time you realized that she's taken another lover and doesn't want to be found. Especially not by you or by me."

Okura staggered to his feet. He shook his head, muttered something, and left.

Akitada started to leave himself when Genba came in with a young peasant in tow. The peasant fell to his knees and bowed. Genba said, "Bad news, sir."

Akitada looked at the peasant and felt a sudden chill. "What happened?"

Genba sighed. "I'm afraid the superintendent is dead, sir."

For a moment. Akitada stood frozen in shock. Then he asked, "But how is this possible? He was getting better. He left to see to his farm. Was he still very ill, Genba? He shouldn't have been let go."

"He was quite well again. He was eating and his appetite was good. He was quite energetic." Genba paused. "And stubborn. You know how he was, sir, when he 'd made up his mind."

"Yes." Akitada took a deep breath and addressed the peasant, "Please get up. Thank you for coming to tell me about Kobe. He was my friend."

The peasant scrambled to his feet. "He was a good man to his people, the master. There was much weeping when he passed to the other world."

"Tell me what you know."

But the man was nearly tongue-tied. Sadako arrived in the middle of their efforts to understand what had happened and called for some wine. The peasant drank gratefully and managed to speak more coherently.

Kobe had returned four days earlier and immediately set about clearing away the damages and debris of his home with the help of neighbors and his own peasants. On the second day, new materials and furnishings had arrived and the business of fixing the damage started. Kobe was in good spirits and seemed quite

171

well. That day also his son arrived and offered his help. The work progressed with astonishing speed. All was well on the third day also and Kobe moved back into his quarters, but toward evening he suddenly collapsed. He refused offers to send for a doctor and insisted he was just tired. Bedding was spread and he was made comfortable. When the workers returned the next morning, they found him dead.

Akitada shook his head in disbelief. "He must have worked too hard. Oh, we shouldn't have let him leave."

Stung by what she took to be blame, Sadako said, "He insisted. I could hardly tie him up."

Akitada said quickly, "No, no, of course not. I blame myself. I was in Otsu."

Genba said, "You could not have done much, sir. The superintendent had his own mind."

"Yes, I know." Akitada asked the peasant, "Was anyone with him the night he died?"

"No, sir. We all went home, being tired. His son also went back home, seeing that the work was finished."

Akitada frowned. "Strange he should have come to help. I wonder if he was the one who came here that night."

The peasant did not know.

Akitada thanked the man, gave him some money, and sent him to the kitchen for food. He told Sadako, "I'll have to go and arrange the funeral. I don't think there was much money and Kobe probably spent what he had on repairs." He clenched his hands. "I'd like to get my hands on the villain who destroyed his house and killed his servant. He might as well have killed Kobe too."

Sadako put her hand on his arm. "I'm sorry. I know he was your friend and a good man."

Grief suddenly washed over Akitada. He put his arms around her and laid his cheek against her hair. Genba left quietly.

When Akitada reached Kobe's farm, he found it occupied by chanting monks and several strangers. The monks belonged to the Saga temple, and the strangers turned out to be Kobe's sons, one of his wives and a daughter, as well as several of their servants.

The gate was marked with the customary taboo tag made of willow wood. It warned visitors that the house contained a dead body and walking in would mean contamination for anyone ritually clean for a Shinto observance.

Akitada dismounted in the courtyard and was met by a soberly dressed young man who wore a smaller version of the taboo tag. Akitada asked, "Who are you?"

The young man bowed. "Kobe Heishiro. I regret to inform you that a death has occurred."

"Ah, yes. I'm Sugawara. Did you send the peasant?"

Kobe's son looked blank. "No, sir. There was no need to trouble you. Matters are well in hand."

"I want to see my friend's body."

Heishiro bowed again and led the way inside.

Kobe's family was arguing about the funeral. The argument broke off when Akitada walked into the room, but he had already caught some words to the effect that they resented the expense.

Akitada nodded to them. "I just got the news of my friend's death and have come to see to his funeral, so there is no need for you to worry about costs."

There was a moment of relief, then the wife and daughter started wailing. One of the younger sons stepped forward, bowed, and said, "He was our father. It's true, he deserted us, but we've come to make the arrangements because it's proper we do so."

Akitada had not expected this, any more than he had previously expected the other son's arrival at his house to take his father home or the fact that he had returned to the farm to help his father with the repairs. He did not quite know what to say. After all, much as he disliked Kobe's family, they had certain rights that he could not interfere with.

He did not pursue the issue. Instead he sat down, uninvited, and said, "Tell me what happened."

After a moment's hesitation, Heishiro, the older son, also sat down. The women stopped their wailing, and the other two sons moved closer.

Kobe's wife—he guessed she was the senior wife—was no longer young. Her hair was gray and she had become hard-faced, though she must once have been attractive. The daughter had not inherited any beauty from either parent. She was plump, had a round face with small eyes, and a tiny mouth. Her mouth hung open at the moment as she stared at Akitada. The two younger sons were short, corpulent, and had the look of tradesmen. But Akitada's interest was mostly in the son who had spoken to him first. He was almost sure that he had been the one who had come that night to take his father away. He had his father's tall stature and broad shoulders, and would have been handsome if there had not been something watchful in his face and a certain meanness about his narrow lips. Akitada took him to be the eldest and therefore Kobe's heir. No doubt he was also the one who had given his father so much grief over Sachi.

The son bit his lip and gestured to the others. "My mother, Motoko, my sister Takako, my brothers Nakashira and Nakanari. My father's other two wives stayed behind."

Akitada nodded to them. "I'm Sugawara Akitada. Your husband and father was my best friend. As you know, we worked together for many years. His death grieves me greatly."

Motoko began to wail again and her mother put an arm around her, saying, "Hush! Let's hear what his Excellency has to tell us."

The situation was distasteful, but Akitada forced himself to remain courteous. "I'm afraid I know less than you. I hoped you might tell me what happened."

The oldest son answered. "When I heard that my father had returned to the farm, I came to see him. You may recall, sir, that I'd hoped to bring him home when he fell sick at your house."

"I recall you coming one night, but your father had become sick before he came to my house and was getting better while he was with me. He was anxious to repair the damages to this house and look after his property. That's why he left. I was not home at the time, or I would have advised against it."

"I wish you had, sir, because he fell ill again. The work was too much for him, though I helped as much as I could. He was stubborn about getting everything fixed as quickly as possible."

Akitada nodded. "It was good of you to help."

"It was my duty as his son and heir. I only wish he could have enjoyed his life here a little longer."

175

Heishiro had established his claim on his father's property. Akitada said coldly, "I confess I was surprised at your sudden interest. I was told that you had forced your father to relinquish his former home to you and your siblings because you did not approve of the wife he took."

Heishiro's mother snapped, "She was a common bathhouse whore and blind on top of that. We were a laughing stock to our friends and neighbors."

Her son laid a restraining hand on his mother's arm. "That's over and done with, Mother. She died. We wished him to return to us, but he refused."

Akitada said, "He was deeply hurt by your rejection."

The son looked away, but his mother said quickly, "He deserted his family. We didn't deserve to be treated that way. And all the time he kept the income from this farm from his wives and children."

Akitada raised his brows. "I was under the impression that he left you very well off. He gave you everything but this small farm and I see that you did not suffer any deprivation."

She cried, "He left us to starve. He was superintendent of the capital police. He had a fine income until he threw it all away for that whore. And now, what will his sons do? How will his daughter find a husband without a good dowry? How shall his wives live in their lonely old age?"

Akitada winced at the reference to dowries. Before he could answer, Heishiro said, "Never mind, Mother. We shall do what we can. We shall at least have this farm."

Akitada was not at all sure that Kobe had intended the farm to go to his family in the end, but he said nothing.

After a moment, the son said, "You should have let me take him home where he could have been cared for."

Anger and guilt made Akitada rise abruptly. "Show me to my friend's body."

Kobe was still in the room that had served as his study. He had been washed, his hair and beard combed, and he wore clean clothes and lay on a clean quilt, his head resting on a neck rest. An elderly peasant woman sat beside him, her face bowed and a rosary between her fingers. Three or four monks sat in the background, chanting softly.

Akitada knelt on Kobe's other side. His friend's face looked peaceful. He searched for signs of a violent death, but there were none. It was too late in any case. The body had been washed, and if there had been anything more subtle to suggest murder, it was long gone.

They sat like this for a while. Akitada thought back to earlier times, to years when they had both been much younger. The dead Kobe looked smaller, diminished somehow. Akitada grieved the lost past.

After a while, he turned to the peasant woman and said, "I'm Lord Sugawara."

She nodded. "I know. I knew you'd come, sir."

"What is your name?"

"I'm Haruko."

He asked as he had earlier, "How did it happen?"

She paused counting off her rosary. "The master came back and ate two bowls of my soup and then he started working. He was feeling good. He ate rice

177

and some fish that night and went to sleep in his house. The next day was the same." She sighed.

"But something else must have happened."

"That day the master's son came. He ate the evening rice with the master. The master wanted him to go away, but the son begged and so he let him stay." She rolled her eyes.

"And the next day?"

"The master seemed more tired. His son said he must rest and let him do the work." She pursed her lips. "Well, the work got done and all looked good again and the master was pleased. But he only ate a little soup that night and then went to bed."

Akitada asked, "Had he been eating well all day?"

"I don't know. The son wouldn't let me serve the food. He did it all himself."

That seemed strange. Akitada said, "I see. But your master wasn't ill?"

"I don't think so. That night the son told us he had eaten well and then gone to bed. And then he left."

"Did you always cook for your master?"

"No. Hayashi used to do it. I came after Hayashi died."

Hayashi was the servant who had been killed by the robbers. Akitada thanked her, touched his dead friend's hand, then rose and left the house.

21

Suspicions

Outside the farmhouse, he found the peasant who had brought him. He had been joined by a group of other peasants, both men and women. All wore clean but plain clothes to honor their late master. Several wept.

The man who had brought him asked, "What will become of us, sir?"

"I don't know. Your master's family thinks the farm will be theirs."

They all looked at each other. One of the women spoke up, "They never came until now. They didn't care. The master worked hard with us to make this good rice land. Things were getting better. Plenty of rice for him and us and the tax man."

Akitada said, "Thank you for coming. It wasn't your fault."

They hung their heads, grieving and worried.

Akitada had no assurances to give them. Instead, he asked the question that had been bothering him. "My friend seemed quite well when he left my house to come back here. Can you think of anything that might have made him ill?"

They looked at each other and shook their heads. When he pressed them, a few spoke up. They agreed on the events before Kobe's death. He had seemed well and worked hard to make the house livable. His son had come to help him, but only recently.

Along with what the woman inside had told him, this filled Akitada with suspicions of the son. But what of the first time Kobe had become ill? Nothing suggested that Heishiro had seen his father then. Yet the son's visit to the Sugawara home to take his father away could have been an effort to stop his recovery. Akitada wished more than ever that he had realized the danger and prevented Kobe's return, but proving that the son had caused his father's death was another matter.

It took a lot of willpower to be courteous to Heishiro, or indeed the whole family. Akitada wanted them all to be culpable, or at least have knowledge of why Kobe had died. He was angry and miserable because he could not prove that they had somehow caused his friend's death. His anger was made worse because they would inherit Kobe's farm and whatever he had owned at the time of his death. As a motive for murder, the value of the inheritance seemed negligible, which made it even more disgusting. He thought they had acted not just out of greed, but out of revenge which had simmered for many years.

Kobe had known their hatred. It was why he had made no attempt to reconcile with them after Sachi's death.

But what could Akitada do now? Telling them of his suspicions would simply alert them. Much better to let them think he believed them, and perhaps in time he would find a way to prove Kobe had been murdered.

He decided to take care of the most pressing matter and went back into the house. He told Kobe's family firmly that he would make the arrangements for the funeral and pay the expenses. As he had expected, they did not object and he left for the Saga temple.

The Saga temple was where Kobe had worshipped. He had been there the day someone had visited the farm and killed Hayashi. Nothing had come of the police investigation into that murder, and Akitada had put the matter from his mind when Kobe became ill and his own life had filled with problems and duties.

Saga temple, also called *Daikaku-ji*, had started as the country villa of the emperor Saga. In the ninth century he had gathered the learned men of his time there and entertained them. It had become a Buddhist temple after his death but remained under the special oversight of subsequent emperors who endowed it.

He identified himself to one of the monks who met him at the gate and asked to speak to the abbot.

The news of Kobe's death had been received with sadness by the elderly cleric, who said immediately, "He was my friend. I shouldn't grieve his passing into a better world, but I confess his demise has made my own life poorer."

Akitada was surprised. He had known Kobe attended the temple, but little else. The guilt of having neglected him surfaced again. He said, "He was my friend also and I'm glad he found another in you. I blame myself for his loneliness."

The old abbot smiled. "Not so lonely. He came often. We played *go*. He was in good spirits until Hayashi was killed."

Somehow Kobe's death always seemed to go back to Hayashi. The servant's death had started the tragic sequence. Kobe had rallied briefly, but then disaster had struck again. Akitada said, "He must have been very close to Hayashi. I found him very distraught."

The abbot nodded. "He'd been here that day, you know. He always came on the first day of the horse."

Akitada wondered if this was well known. Surely, Kobe's people would have known, as well as the monks at the temple. It had not been a secret. He decided to have another talk with the local police about the outcome of their investigations.

He said, "I came to arrange for the funeral. You will know what Kobe would have wanted."

The abbot nodded. "He would have wanted his friends to do this for him. I think we were both his friends."

"Yes. Though I should have been a better friend."

"From what he said I do not think so." The abbot had a very sweet smile. It brought tears to Akitada's eyes.

"I would be grateful for your advice. His family has arrived at the farm. They have announced their claim to his property. I suppose they would have claimed his body if I had not stepped in."

The smile on the abbot's face faded. "He never lost his anger against his family," he said. "I prayed with him to let it go, but he was a stubborn man."

It seemed to be the final word on Kobe. Everyone was agreed that he had been a stubborn man. Akitada wondered about his own death; what they would say about him? He supposed he had been every bit as stubborn as Kobe and frequently they had frustrated each other. The memory of such past encounters made him smile.

The abbot smiled also. "Yes," he said. "So it was and so it shall be. They don't leave us. Kobe is here with us now and you will find him again and again."

"For forty-nine days." It was the time span allotted to the souls of the dead before they had to leave their homes, families, and friends.

"No. As long as you live."

Akitada nodded. "Yes. I think so."

They turned to the matter of Kobe's funeral. It would be, as custom dictated, at night. Kobe's body would travel in a coffin by carriage to the cremation ground. The abbot himself would lead the rites as the funeral fires consumed Kobe's body. Akitada offered to pay the costs. The abbot smiled. "We shall share them." Akitada nodded. He would also make a sizable donation to the temple.

When he left the temple, he realized his grief was strangely eased. He had forgotten to ask the abbot what to do about Kobe's family. In the end, he decided to let them do as they wished.

At the police station in Kadono, Akitada found the same sergeant he had spoken to on his last visit. The man shot up from behind his desk when he saw Akitada.

183

"My lord. Very bad news about the former superintendent, sir. I was very sorry to hear it."

"Yes. Thank you. Did you go to see the body?"

"No, sir. The superintendent's son came to tell me. The coroner went back with him. He said Kobe-san died from the same illness that he had before. Natural death. Very sad, but he was quite old. Most men don't live as long as that."

Akitada glared at him. "You weren't very troubled by Hayashi's death either. Did you think that natural also?"

The sergeant muttered, "Sorry."

"I've wondered if anyone visited Kobe's farm before or after Hayashi's murder?"

The sergeant shook his head. "I wouldn't know, sir. You should ask his servants."

"He had only Hayashi, and Hayashi's dead. The peasants were busy in the fields."

The sergeant spread his hands and suppressed a smirk. "Well, then we won't know, will we?"

Akitada gritted his teeth. "I'd like to speak to the coroner, if you please."

He had to wait. The coroner was also the local pharmacist and doctor, and he was out on a call to patch up a peasant who had broken a leg. Akitada did not really expect much from him. His training was likely minimal and he had been of little help with Hayashi last time, but he wanted to leave nothing undone.

The coroner arrived in a cheerful mood until he saw who waited. Then his face fell. He hid his dislike for the encounter well enough by expressing his condolences on Kobe's death.

He clearly also expected little from the meeting. He was as nervous as before and immediately on the defensive when Akitada asked him if he had had any more insights into Hayashi's murder. He said again, echoing the sergeant's philosophy, that Hayashi had been old and it would not have taken much to kill him. Akitada had seen the condition of Kobe's house and knew that whoever had delivered the fatal blow must have been a strong man. He asked, "About how tall do you think the murderer had to have been?"

This gave the man pause. He frowned. "Well, Hayashi was short. The person hit him on top of the head. Toward the back." He pointed to a place on his own skull.

Akitada nodded. "It would almost seem then that he came upon Hayashi while the servant's back was turned?"

The pharmacist considered this and said, "It might have been that way. Or Hayashi was bowing to him." Then he shook his head and laughed. "But that couldn't be. Hayashi would not bow to a robber."

Akitada smiled a little. "No. I doubt it. Thank you. You've been very helpful."

He left the pharmacist and the sergeant looking puzzled.

22

Family Council

Tora had already made up his mind to return home when Saburo walked into his room.

"What's ruined your disposition this time?" Tora asked, seeing the deep frown on Saburo's face. "I thought you were busy proving what a master spy you are."

Saburo flushed. "Don't blame me. It's not my fault you were careless."

"At least I didn't let a small boy get killed," Tora snapped back.

Saburo sat down abruptly and hung his head. "I'm not likely to forget it," he said bitterly.

Tora regretted his remark. "I shouldn't have said that. It wasn't your fault. Kids get in trouble all the time."

Saburo gave him a dark look. "I found his brother."

"Good for you. Did you find the parents?"

Saburo sighed. "No parents. They lived with an uncle and aunt."

Tora went to sit beside Saburo. "It must've been hard, telling them. I'm sorry."

"That's not the problem."

"What do you mean?"

"They were only upset because they lost their best worker. The woman beats the boys."

"Well, they're poor people. What sort of work?"

"The father makes and sells dumplings."

"Ah. Well, it's done. Maybe we can give them something toward having some prayers said. I don't imagine the body will be found."

Saburo shuddered. "The boy who died was called Kai. His little brother is Masashi. Masashi will run away if I don't do something. He wants to come with me and be my servant."

Tora chuckled. "I'd like you to explain to the master why you need a personal servant."

"I know. I can't take him." Saburo paused. "And I can't leave him."

Tora's face softened. "I'm going home. I can ask the master what he wants you to do."

Saburo gave him a long look. "Are you feeling better?"

"Yes. And there's nothing for me to do here." Tora smiled a little sadly. "Master Cricket says I have no eyes."

"That old fake. Why do you bother with him?"

"He also said you are unpleasant."

Saburo nodded. "He got that right anyway."

"He did say you have eyes. So what have you learned?"

"That Norisuke keeps a great treasure at his place and that his men guard it."

"I could've told you that. Men like Norisuke who have their own soldiers have the gold to pay for them."

Saburo said, "Maybe, but to the poor he's like a god. The boys called him Bishamonten. Kai climbed over that wall because he believed the god would help him and his brother escape their misery."

"Poor boys. They're better off begging. I hear Norisuke's a devil."

"Gods and devils. I learned early there's no difference."

Tora frowned. "No, Saburo. You're wrong. The difference is in how we see things. Gods are good. Devils lie to us."

Saburo laughed bitterly. "Well, Master Cricket said you have no eyes. He thinks I can see, but I see only devils."

Tora sighed. "Well, I'm going home. I'm no use here."

"I haven't exactly impressed anyone myself. After the boy's death, I'd be surprised if the master keeps me."

"That's ridiculous. You've been with us for years now and your family too. Where would you go?"

Saburo stared into space. "No idea. Heaven help me. They'll be homeless because of me. Sumiko and young Tokiwa. Thank the gods my mother didn't live to see it. I'm cursed. The master's never trusted me."

"No, Saburo. He'd never turn you out. How can you think so little of him?"

"I think so little of myself."

They looked at each other. Then Tora put an arm around Saburo's shoulder. "Well, it looks like we're both failures. Let's go home and lick our wounds."

Saburo said meekly, "Yes, Brother."

They met the stable boy on the road and arrived home a short while before Akitada. Genba shouted a welcome, and Hanae came running. She exclaimed over Tora's black eye and bruised back, but was reassured to see him walking and in good spirits.

Sadako also came to greet them. She wisely refrained from making a fuss over Tora, and their return was unremarkable until Sadako told them about Kobe's death.

Tora stood shocked into silence. Saburo immediately asked, "Who killed him?"

They had no answer. Genba mentioned the night-time visit from Kobe's son and how he had demanded the return of his father.

Saburo cried, "There! You see? Didn't you think it was very strange for that son to be so anxious about his father when the whole family rejected Kobe after he married the blind bath house girl? That son was up to no good. How could the master let him leave?"

"Oh, the master refused. The superintendent made up his own mind to leave later while the master was gone. We didn't think any more about the son. Maybe he was just worried about losing the farm if his father died."

Saburo nodded. "That sounds like him."

Barely an hour later, Akitada himself arrived home. They all gathered in his study. He was glad that Tora was back and apparently in reasonably good health. He had not expected Saburo but said nothing. They all settled down among Akitada's books in that pleasant room overlooking the garden. Sadako came with wine and bowls of nuts and fruit.

Saburo and Tora were full of questions about Kobe's death, and Akitada tried to answer them. There was little he could tell them that satisfied them.

Saburo's report about finding Kai's little brother and the conditions of that household caused Akitada to grimace and Sadako to cry out, "Oh, the poor child!"

Encouraged by this mild reaction, Saburo said, "I wanted to bring him home with me. I feel responsible for him since it's my fault his brother died."

Akitada frowned. "You exaggerate. The blame falls entirely on Minamoto Norisuke and his thugs."

Sadako said quickly, "That doesn't change the boy's need, Akitada."

Akitada looked at her and felt helpless. "Sadako, we cannot simply take the child from his lawful guardians."

Saburo had known this, but his master's use of the word "we" encouraged him to feel more hopeful.

Sadako said, "You could buy him."

Akitada stared at her. "What? Make him our slave, you mean?"

His wife made an apologetic gesture. "Well, not quite like a slave. We could raise him here. He could do small chores and get an education."

Akitada said icily, "That may be customary up north, but here we do not keep domestic slaves any longer. If you want to make another family's child a part of your family, you must adopt him."

They all looked aghast that a street urchin might become a Sugawara heir.

Sadako cried, "Oh, no, Akitada! I wasn't thinking. You cannot adopt a child you've never even seen. It was very thoughtless of me."

Saburo muttered, "It's unthinkable. I was thinking of adopting him myself, but I don't have the right." He paused. "Or the money. They're greedy people."

Genba was practical. "We could use another stable boy. Ours is getting too old for the job. He plans to look for better work."

"Surely Masashi is too little to do much work," Sadako objected.

Akitada sighed. "Let me think about it. I'm too preoccupied with Kobe's death at the moment. I think he ate something that poisoned him. We managed to save him the first time, but he went back, and this time he died. I blame myself."

Saburo muttered, "I bet his son murdered him."

Tora said, "You couldn't have known, sir. We were in Otsu, and he wouldn't stay."

Sadako said nothing, but she hung her head and twisted her hands. Akitada touched her arm. "Don't fret. Nobody could stop Kobe once he made up his mind."

Saburo said, "I'm sorry for all the bad news, sir. And we didn't bring better news from Otsu."

"Not your fault. Once I've dealt with Kobe's death, we'll put our heads together and see what we have learned about Norisuke and the new Market Master."

"And Yukiko?" Sadako asked.

Akitada shook his head. "Let Arihito and Lord Okura worry about her. I simply don't have the time. And that reminds me. My sister has offered to present Yasuko at court with her own daughter."

Sadako looked worried. "You don't mind?"

"No. She knows my wishes."

"Then I'm glad. I didn't know what to do."

Akitada smiled. "Let's all go and eat. I'm hungry after all that riding."

Peace and tranquility with his family was short-lived for Akitada. Soon after their meal, a clerk arrived from the ministry. The new minister expected Akitada to report immediately. The clerk's face promised trouble.

Akitada changed into his good robe and hat and took his report with him. The clerk had waited to make sure Akitada obeyed the command and remained silent on the way, offering only curt answers to the casual comments Akitada made about the weather and the signs of spring. Akitada abandoned the effort quickly. He had always been treated with friendly respect by the clerks in the ministry, but clearly this had changed. People learned quickly to disassociate themselves from those who had fallen into disfavor.

Prepared for the worst, Akitada entered Morozane's office. His Excellency was seated near the open doors, leaning on an arm rest and reading a letter. A timid clerk knelt before him holding a tablet and making notes. Other clerks sat at their small desks, busy copying materials.

Akitada cleared his throat and made eye contact with the minister, then bowed.

"So!" Morozane said with a scowl.

"You sent for me, sir?"

"You have been absent for days. Why have you not been working?"

"I've been working, as you instructed, on the investigation of the markets office. But I'm afraid I received news of the death of a close friend in Kadono and went to arrange his funeral. I had just returned from there when your messenger arrived."

"What friend?"

The question was rude and none of Morozane's business, but Akitada answered. "Superintendent Kobe, sir."

Morozane frowned. "Who?"

"The former superintendent of the Capital Police, sir. We've frequently worked together over the years."

"That man has been retired for a long time. Some scandal, I think. You should pick your friends more wisely, Sugawara."

Akitada bit his lip and stared up at the ceiling. A brief silence fell.

Morozane said, "I trust you haven't come in contact with the corpse and been contaminated. I attend on His Majesty later today."

Akitada almost smiled. "I'm afraid I sat with my dead friend last night. Will this cause you some inconvenience, sir?"

Morozane struggled up, red with anger. "Inconvenience? I shall be unable to attend. How dare you come here unclean?"

Akitada looked surprised. "I'm very sorry, sir, but your clerk was adamant that I come. He would not leave until I obeyed your command and would not hear of any excuses."

Morozane waved his hands. "Leave! This very moment! Go home and remove the contamination before you return to work. And be more considerate in the future. Now that I have the honor to attend upon the emperor, I shall do so frequently. I would have expected you to know that no one who is unclean is admitted into the palace. Thanks to you, I shall now have to waste precious time to go through all the required rituals to remove the contamination."

Akitada bowed, handed the report to a clerk, and went home.

23

Mourning a Friend

Akitada chuckled to himself on his way home from the ministry—having caused the hated Morozane an inconvenience he could not be punished for was highly satisfying—but the fact of Kobe's death fell ever more heavily on him now that some time had passed and normal activities had resumed.

He would miss Kobe's good sense and support. Perhaps he had not availed himself as often of them as he should have, but now the finality of the loss was very painful. Even their recent encounters, though they had mostly concerned the events in Kobe's own situation, had given him strength when his world appeared to have taken an ominous turn.

On an impulse, he turned his steps to the *Shinsenden*, the imperial garden where they had first

197

met over the case of a murdered girl. The garden was no longer as well kept as he recalled it. Weeds sprouted on the walks, and the little lake was choked with reeds. But the cherry trees, many old and crippled, still bloomed, and the air was delicious with their scent.

They had both been much younger then. But Kobe was the older, of course, and he had already made a name for himself in the senior ranks of the capital police. He had been affronted by the young nobleman poking his nose into police business. With that case had started several years of contention during which they had both been angry with each other. Akitada's behavior had been shocking on several levels. Descendants of the aristocratic families did not dabble in murder. Akitada's interest could not be excused because he served in an unimportant position in the ministry of justice. The ministry of justice dealt with legal matters of the dry and learned variety. Kobe worked with actual messy crimes, the sorts of crime scenes the aristocracy shunned in horror. And perhaps it had been that incongruity which had ultimately gained Akitada some grudging respect from Kobe.

That, and the fact that he had solved a number of Kobe's cases.

They had become friends slowly but strongly nevertheless. Akitada had reason to be grateful to Kobe who had frequently helped him when matters had become dangerous. And now? Who could take Kobe's place? Who would listen sympathetically to Akitada's frustrations with his duties and send him away with renewed strength and patience?

As men grow old, they not only face the challenges of declining health and infirm bodies, they become lonelier and suffer greater disappointments. Akitada longed for his youth and for Kobe.

The sight of pink blossoms against the deep blue sky provided little solace. Already the path was covered with fallen petals. Nothing lasted. Eventually, Akitada left the gardens behind and walked home. He still had his family, had children to provide for, and he had Sadako. There was still a life to be lived.

When he explained his early return from the ministry to his wife, she laughed and clapped her hands. Her joy was infectious and he took her into his arms gratefully. They spent the afternoon together, sharing the midday rice, and then, after inspecting the over-grown garden, they worked in the warm sunshine, trimming and clearing, pausing to admire new growth, discussing changes and additions. Pleasantly tired and quite dirty, they returned for a hot bath before eating their evening meal. And after that, they sat together on the veranda under a full moon, and Akitada played his flute for his wife.

It was to be the last time of true contentment for Akitada.

The next day, he returned with his three retain-ers to Kadono for Kobe's funeral. The temple had been generous. A large number of monks had come to pray and chant at his house. Toward evening, many mourners both from the area and from the capital, gathered. The procession formed in front of Kobe's farm. Six torchbearers were followed by ten monks. The front monk carried a yellow silk banner with a Buddhist prayer inscribed on it. Then came the litter with the coffin. It was carried by ten of Kobe's peasants and preceded by another peasant who carried a burning lamp. The mourners followed in loose groups.

Akitada took his place behind Kobe's family, followed by Tora, Genba, and Saburo. Arguing precedence with Kobe's family would have been unseemly. Behind them followed a large number of Kobe's former staff and friends from his days in the capital. Local officials, including the sergeant of the Kadono police and the coroner-pharmacist walked among them.

The funeral procession wound for two miles through the rice paddies and woods to the cremation site, a large space covered with white sand. Here, too, the temple was in charge, and the abbot awaited them with his senior monks. The litter with the coffin was placed in the center of the white sand. At this point, Kobe's sons and Akitada opened the coffin and filled it with prepared firewood. Then they surrounded the coffin with more wood. They lit the fires, while monks chanted invocations.

During the cremation, Akitada struggled with his thoughts and memories and a bitter anger at his friend's death when he should have been mourning and praying for a better life in the other world for him.

He could not bring himself to speak to Kobe's family afterward, but he thanked the abbot and talked with some of Kobe's peasants, a small group of bareheaded men in hempen shirts. They mourned Kobe's death, but they also worried about their future. To a man, they disliked Kobe's oldest son.

It was while Akitada was talking to them, that a curious fact emerged. Kobe's eldest was no stranger in the area. It appeared that he had visited before and asked questions about the crops, the taxes, and what rents they paid.

Heishiro had clearly taken an interest in the small property, but Akitada did not think that the value of the farm was great enough to cause a man to kill his father, the worst crime that could be committed. At best, the farm would serve as a dowry for one of the daughters, and Kobe had left his family well provided for when he had chosen to live apart from them.

As Akitada thought about this, one of the old men suddenly said, "That Hayashi. He hated the master's son. Hayashi said he was like an evil spirit. May the Buddha help us if we have to work for that one!"

Akitada asked quickly, "When did Hayashi say that?"

The old man shook his head. "Can't remember. Long time ago."

With a sigh, Akitada thanked them and turned away. But the old man followed him.

"That Hayashi. He loved his master," he said.

Akitada stopped. "Yes, and Master Kobe loved him, too. He was very upset when Hayashi died. They must have been close."

It still seemed a strange relationship, quite improper between a man of rank and a lowly servant, but Akitada saw no reason to deny it. Loyalty was a great virtue and it went both ways. Such was his bond with Tora. He would grieve at his loss much as Kobe had grieved for Hayashi, and Kobe had had even more reason. He had been very much alone in his final years.

The old one nodded. "Hayashi was my cousin. He told me he would die for the master." He paused to shake his head. "I think he did."

Surprised, Akitada asked, "You think the robber who killed Hayashi was there to attack his master?"

The old peasant nodded. "Not much to steal there. I think an evil spirit killed them both. May the Buddha protect us!" He bowed and walked away.

Peasants were a superstitious lot. Their lives were filled with all sorts of beliefs in spirits, demons and changelings, like *tengu, kappa,* and *oni,* creatures that had human characteristics, but came in odd shapes and with supernatural powers. Many of them were evil. The rice culture had always fostered such beliefs. Peasant lives depended on successful harvests, and failures were often only to be explained by supernatural evil.

But Akitada was struck by the man's insistence that both Kobe and his servant could have been killed by the same agent, and that he had associated such evil with Kobe's son. It was too close to his own suspicions. There was no proof for such things, but even in the current enlightened age, a judge might hear such testimony and order an exorcist to look into the truth of the matter. Was the son possessed by an evil spirit? If it was so, then surely Kobe's entire family shared this possession. They had all acted abominably toward him.

Akitada's refusal to accept the court's belief in spirit possession, exorcism, and other practices involving the unseen had caused him problems in the past, not the least of which had concerned one of the imperial princesses who had practiced as a medium and decided to seduce him in order to get away with murder. What filled most people with fear, Akitada considered at best as a form of madness, and he resisted the temptation to accuse Kobe's son of being possessed. No doubt, an exorcist would claim to have removed the evil agency and cured Heishiro, who would then go free.

Akitada decided to look for witnesses and proof that Kobe had been poisoned.

24

Pharmacist and Physician

They rode to Kadono together. Tora, Genba, and Saburo were silent and sober after the cremation. Dawn shimmered on the horizon when they reached the Kadono River. Here they paused for the customary ablutions. Then they continued into the town and stopped at a small food shop for a bowl of gruel and a cup of wine.

They sat outside on rough benches, still in their mourning clothes. The young woman who brought their food, asked, "Did he have a fine funeral, our Master Kobe?"

Tora said, "The best! Everybody was there. Both the good people and the peasants."

She smiled. "I'm glad. He was a good man."

It pleased them all and broke the heavy silence that had fallen between them.

Genba said, "He shouldn't have died. It was wrong."

Saburo looked at his master. "It was that son of his, that sniveling, worthless bastard. I know it. What are we going to do?"

Akitada finished his gruel. He had not really tasted it, but he had been hungry, having skipped the evening rice the night before. He said, "We have no proof. We may think the son guilty and we may want him to be, but that is not proof. You have to have proof to make an accusation."

Tora said, "Can't we find the proof?"

Akitada drank his wine and put down his cup. "Perhaps. We can try." It cheered him that all three of his retainers wanted to join him in proving Kobe had been murdered.

They had several options: they could speak to Kobe's neighbors and his peasants or the medical men, in this case Akitada's physician, who had seen Kobe at his house, and the pharmacist who had dealt with both Hayashi's and Kobe's bodies. He told the others they would talk to the pharmacist first since they were already in Kadono.

It was still early in the day, but they found the small man already busy in his shop. The place was no more than the front room of the pharmacist's house, and his house was very modest. Into this small space, he had inserted a large number of shelves, drawers, a counter, a few barrels, and many clay containers of assorted sizes. The clay containers stood mostly on the shelves and were marked with brush and ink as to contents. The drawers were below the shelves and also bore the names of what they held. The barrels stood on the floor and left barely enough room for the pharmacist and his customers. A pleasant herbal scent greeted them.

The pharmacist had his back to them when they arrived at the door. He was stirring something at the counter.

Akitada cleared his throat, and the small pharmacist said irritably, "A moment, a moment. I'll be with you as soon as . . ." He finished what he was doing and turned around. When he recognized Akitada and saw that he had come with three other men, he gasped, his eyes wide with shock. "What . . .?"

Akitada stepped inside and smiled reassuringly. "Ah, I see you recognize me. Sorry, I never asked your name."

The pharmacist gulped. For a moment, Akitada thought he would refuse to answer, but then he stuttered, "I-I'm N-nagaie, s-sir. What's wrong?"

"Nothing as far as you're concerned. We've come from Kobe's funeral."

The pharmacist bowed. "I also went. I regret it deeply, sir. He was a fine man."

"Thank you. You may recall that he was quite ill the last time you saw him."

The pharmacist nodded and finally relaxed a little. "I wanted to offer my services, but he was angry with me at the time."

"Yes. You cannot be blamed. I wondered though if you might have guessed at what was wrong with him."

The pharmacist thought, then said, "He looked very uncomfortable and held his belly at one point. Perhaps he took a purge of some sort? I sell a number of those and prescribe them."

Akitada asked, "So you thought it was something he ate?"

"He looked quite ill. Did something not agree with him? Is that what caused his death? If so, I'm afraid he must have continued eating it."

"He didn't. While he was at my house, he got better. It was only after he returned to his own place that the illness came back and killed him."

The pharmacist frowned. "But then whatever killed him must have been at his house. I think it would be well to look for it. Someone else may also become ill."

Tora grunted. "Poison! I thought so."

Saburo and Genba said quickly, "Yes, poison."

The pharmacist looked at them, but he said nothing.

Akitada thought there was little chance of anyone getting poisoned by accident. If Heishiro had poisoned his father, then he would hardly do the same to himself or his family. He asked, "Can you identify the substance that killed my friend?"

Nagaie shook his head regretfully. "There was no autopsy. If you find what he ate, I can possibly guess at the poison."

Akitada sighed. "Where would I look? A lot of time has passed."

"I sell some herbs and powders that can make you ill if taken in excess, but I would have known if someone had bought them recently. That leaves only certain plants gathered in the woods and added to his food."

Akitada did not see how this was possible. Hayashi had prepared Kobe's food. Still, could that old man have become senile and cooked up the wrong vegetables? It was possible, but he did not like that explanation, for Hayashi was already dead when Kobe succumbed to his final illness. After Hayashi's death, Kobe had presumably prepared his own meals or they had been cooked by the old woman Haruko who had mourned her master. It was worth checking into it, though. Akitada thanked the pharmacist and they left.

Outside, Tora asked, "What will you do now?"

Akitada swung himself into the saddle. "We'll all go home now. I must report at the ministry, and you need to put your heads together. Tora, are you up to doing some light work?"

Tora said eagerly, "Of course. I meant to find out what killed the superintendent. We can't let that rest."

Akitada nodded. "I agree. You and Saburo will go home to rest and to change your clothes. Then I think you should both return to Kadono and ask questions. We need to find out how Kobe got poisoned both before and after he came to my place. Saburo, you'll make sure that Tora doesn't overexert himself."

Saburo nodded, not very eagerly and with a worried glance at Tora.

Genba cleared his throat.

Akitada smiled at him. "I need you at home, old friend. Someone has to look after my family while we're stirring up trouble here and there."

The three retainers chuckled as they turned their horses homeward.

After getting home, Akitada donned his usual court robe and hat and walked to the ministry. He had not slept the previous night and exhaustion was beginning to set in. It could not be helped. He was in enough trouble already and had taken off more time for Kobe's funeral.

He expected another lecture laced with threats of dismissal, but Morozane was positively affable.

"Ah," he greeted Akitada, smiling like a happy Buddha *Hotei*, "you're early. Wasn't the funeral last night?"

"Yes, sir. We were careful to purify ourselves before returning."

"Yes, of course. Was it well attended?"

"It was. Many of his former friends and colleagues from the capital were there."

"Good, good. I've read your report. Excellent work. You see, this is exactly what is expected of you. And I can see that you were very thorough. I have passed on your findings to the controlling boards and to the administration of the capital. I trust we can now work together for the betterment of our nation."

Akitada swallowed his pride and bowed. "Thank you, sir. I hope so also."

He returned to his office where he found that his two clerks had been returned to him and awaited him expectantly. He was momentarily at a loss about what to do with them and it took all of his concentration to think back to the projects they had been working on before Morozane made his rude entry into their lives. Eventually, he sent them back to their own rooms with assignments, and he sat down behind his desk to go through the messages and new requests that had accumulated on his desk during his absences.

In the back of his mind were two unresolved matters. The first concerned Kobe's mysterious death; the second was his conscience. The report he had delivered to Morozane had given him back his position but it had been a lie. On his desk at home lay a second report, a detailed and honest investigation of flagrant abuses involving the transport of government goods and their theft by high-ranking courtiers. That report would end his career and worse, it would expose him and his whole family to the vengeance of men far more powerful than he was. In the meantime, he was no better than they, someone who lied and cheated to protect his career. It sickened him.

The day passed uneventfully in the ministry. After leaving the *daidairi*, Akitada sought out the physician who had treated Kobe.

He did not have far to go. Doctor Ishimodo, retired court physician and former university lecturer, tended his garden in his family home just outside the government enclosure. It was one of the older properties, though Ishimodo had rebuilt the main house after a fire. The garden was enviable since it contained many rare and venerable trees in addition to the meticulously maintained shrubberies and gravel walks.

A servant led the way around the house. The physician was at work carefully raking the sand outside his veranda into patterns of swirls around islands of rugged rocks and outcroppings of mossy hillocks.

"Ah, Lord Sugawara," he said when he saw Akitada. He was embarrassingly formal at all times though they did not differ very much in rank and he was twenty years older than Akitada. "How may I be of assistance? You're not ill yourself, I think? Your lady perhaps, or one of the young people?"

"No. Nobody is ill, though I'd be glad to hear your opinion on Tora's headaches some time. No, I came today because my friend, Superintendent Kobe has died."

Ishimodo instantly looked alert. "But he is the one I saw not too long ago. His condition worsened?"

209

"No. He improved, but then the illness returned and he died."

Ishimodo looked astonished. "But you did not send for me."

"He had gone home by then. Also, from what I was told, the second sickness must have been much quicker and more violent. He went to bed and died soon after the evening meal." Akitada wondered again about that evening meal. But it had been prepared by the old woman. Soup, she had said.

The physician pursed his lips. "Very careless," he muttered. "He should have stayed under my care. A major derangement of his wind perhaps. He was suffering from severe melancholia, you recall."

Akitada frowned. "He was mourning the death of his servant. What do you mean by 'wind'?"

"There had been both nausea and vomiting. When I saw him, his belly was distended by wind."

Akitada nodded. "Ah, I see. Yes. But the nausea had stopped and he was eating without vomiting."

"Even so. Disease is brought about by cold *chi* when the *ying-yang* balance is upset. Sometimes hot food may temporarily dissipate the cold *chi.* That could explain why he got better but later died."

Akitada sighed. "I wish I had been there. He left my home without my knowledge."

The physician said, "It is regrettable."

"You don't think it could have been something he ate?"

Ishimodo pursed his lips again. "Of course, but why would he eat the same thing again?"

More confused than ever, Akitada took his leave from the learned physician.

25

The Old Robe

The next day, Tora and Saburo set out again for Kadono, while Akitada returned to his duties at the ministry. The paperwork had accumulated in his absence and he was kept busy until late. At least, Minister Morozane had decided to treat him a little better, though he made sure that Akitada understood what was expected of him. Fortunately, the work was routine and tedious rather than more cover-ups of illegal activities. Only the knowledge of the report waiting at home made up for the lies Akitada had been forced to tell.

When he finally reached his home, it was already fully dark. The night sky was clear and there was a moon, so he managed to see enough not to stumble over wheel ruts in the streets. But his own street was dark because large trees hung over the walls of the adjoining houses and gardens. He aimed for the familiar small lantern at his gate. It was not until he stood practically in front of the gate that he noticed the small figure huddled in the corner between gate and wall.

A child.

A small boy in rags, perfectly filthy with mud not only on his bare feet and legs, but also on his face and plastered into his hair. The boy peered up at him hopefully.

Akitada reached for his money. "What are you doing here? The nights are still cold. You need to find a warm place to sleep."

The boy said, "Saburo. I want to find Saburo."

Akitada's jaw dropped and a memory returned. "What's your name?"

"Masashi."

"Masashi? From Otsu?"

The child nodded.

"But how did you get here?"

"I walked." He slowly got to his feet, and Akitada saw that he carried a bundle.

"You walked all the way? Did someone bring you?"

The boy shook his head. "Does Saburo live here?"

"Yes, but he isn't home right now."

The boy's face crumpled and his body sagged a little. "Where is he?"

"In Kadono."

"Is it far?" Tears spilled over and made tracks in the dirt on his cheeks.

"Too far for you to walk. But I live here and you can stay until Saburo returns. I'm Lord Sugawara."

The boy sniffled and nodded, and Akitada un-latched the small side gate, inviting him to walk through.

The gate rang a bell, and Genba appeared with a lantern, saw the dirty child and shouted, "Hey!"

The boy froze just inside the compound. Akitada followed him in and closed the gate behind them.

Genba said, "Oh, it's you, sir. But who or what is this?"

"This is Masashi. Masashi, say hello to Genba."

The boy blinked at the light and peered up at the large man who towered over him. A dirty hand reached for Akitada's and clung on. He murmured something.

Genba bent down a little and smiled at the boy. "Masashi? You mean this is Saburo's little friend?"

Akitada squeezed the small hand reassuringly. "Yes, it is. He says he walked here. All the way. I suppose it accounts for the mud."

Genba shook his head in wonder. "Bet those little feet are bloody under all that mud. Shall I take him and give him a bath?"

"No, thank you, Genba. I'll take him myself."

Akitada took the boy directly to the bath. The water was hot. Sadako saw to it that her husband always found it ready when he returned from a day's labors. Masashi looked at the steaming water in astonishment and panic. He shook his head. "No," he whimpered, clutching his bundle to his chest. "No, I don't want to."

Akitada said firmly, "We must wash the dirt off. You cannot eat your evening rice in that condition."

The promise of a meal overcame the child's aversion to water. He allowed himself to be undressed, though he clutched his bundle throughout the process and would have taken it with him into the tub, if

Akitada had not firmly removed it, saying, "You can have it back as soon as you're clean."

Masashi cringed and whimpered through the first scrubbing. He was all skin and bones. Akitada shuddered at the stripes on his back, left by beatings he had received not long ago. His feet were not as bloody as Genba had thought, but they were calloused. Masashi's barefoot life had prepared him for the rigors of walking the long road to the capital.

Once the boy was in the warm tub, he relaxed and smiled at Akitada. "Thank you," he said. Akitada's heart twisted. He was so little and so alone in a hostile world. Suddenly he felt like a father again, a young father to a small boy. His first son, Yori, had been about this age when he had died. He had been well-nourished and white-skinned, while Masashi was skinny and muscular and quite brown, but there was a strong similarity, and when the boy took his hand, Akitada felt tears in his eyes. Oh, to be given again the lost pleasure of a small son!

The door opened behind them, and Sadako appeared through the steam of the bathroom. "Genba says . . . oh, he's so little!" She came to lean against the tub and smile down at the child. "Poor baby," she crooned. "Did you really walk from Otsu?"

Masashi had clutched Akitada's hand again when Sadako appeared beside him, but when she spoke, he relaxed and the smile came back. He was a pretty child for all his miserable upbringing. "I'm Masashi," he said, by way of introduction.

"I'm Sadako," she returned. "I'm Akitada's wife."

The boy frowned in confusion.

214

Akitada chuckled. "My personal name is Akitada. Sadako is my wife."

The boy nodded. "I can work," he said, uncertainty returning. "I'll be very good."

Sadako laughed. "I'm sure you will do very well, but perhaps it's time to get out of the bath and have a nice bowl of rice."

Masashi instantly scrambled out of the tub and allowed himself to be dried off. Both Sadako and Akitada got wet in the process. Their eyes met over the boy's tousled head, and a look of deep emotion passed from one to the other.

Masashi was returned to Akitada's study, wrapped in one of Akitada's underrobes and a quilt. He still clutched his dirty bundle, but he ate ravenously as husband and wife watched like a pair of doting parents.

Sadako murmured, "He's starved."

"Yes. I doubt he found much food on the road."

"Someone beat him."

"Yes."

"Can we keep him?"

Here it was—the question that had been in Akitada's mind since the moment the boy had reached for his hand in the bath. "He asked for Saburo."

"Oh!" There was disappointment in her voice. He touched her hand. She was childless and now past childbearing and he felt her pain and longing. In truth, he had felt it also when the small boy had held his hand the way Yori had so many grief-filled years ago. He sighed and said, "He can certainly stay with Saburo if he chooses."

"What if Saburo and Sumiko don't want him?"

"We'll find a way."

215

And so the Sugawara household added another member, another mouth to feed, another child to raise, another dependent to be responsible for.

The next afternoon, Akitada received visitors from Kadono.

The two peasants came first. Akitada recognized one of them as a man he had spoken to after Kobe's death. They stood there, in their ordinary field-working clothes, but they had been at some pains to wash their hands and faces before knocking at the gate. They knelt and bowed when Akitada came out to see what they wanted.

The one Akitada had spoken to after Kobe's death said, "Your Honor, please help us. The master's sons are taking our rice and they are beating our women. They have taken away Sueji's daughter."

The other man murmured, "She's promised to my wife's cousin. She's only fifteen."

It was unspeakable and Akitada should have foreseen it. Kobe's sons had taken over the farm and they were not kind masters. Akitada felt utterly helpless. The law was very clear on the rights of children. The fact that the whole family had rejected Kobe did not weigh against their taking the small farm, the only thing he had kept for himself, now that he was dead. Any peasants living on and working the land were at the mercy of his heirs. They could not even leave legally, though many peasant families did just that, preferring to become vagrants rather than suffer under a cruel master.

Even if Akitada could prove that Heishiro had, with the knowledge of his family, murdered his father, the land would still have to pass to one of Kobe's de-

216

scendants. All Akitada could do for them was to speak to Heishiro again and perhaps gain better treatment and the return of the girl.

He told them so, and they hung their heads. Even a good meal before their return to Kadono could not lift their spirits.

Akitada went to tell Sadako about the visit and his promise. He found her busy sewing clothes for Masashi who sat beside her looking at one of her picture books. The peaceful domestic scene gave Akitada another pang. He regretted now that they could not have a child together.

Sadako said happily, "Masashi will look very fine. I managed to cut up this old gown of yours to make him trousers and a jacket."

Akitada looked at the fabric and recognized it. "I liked that gown. It was very comfortable."

"Oh, Akitada. It was badly stained at the hem and there was a large tear."

"But I liked wearing it to work in the garden." Akitada saw the boy looking at him nervously. Ashamed, he smiled at the child. "But you're quite right. I don't really need it. I have other clothes."

Akitada gave the old robe another regretful glance and said, "I must return to Kadono. Kobe's peasants have come to ask for help with Kobe's son."

She nodded. "Tell Saburo about Masashi, but there's no hurry. We're quite content, aren't we, Masashi?" They smiled at each other.

217

26

The Inheritance

Kobe's farm was an unhappy place. The peasants
should have been in the fields planting rice, but
most of the fields were empty.

They had arrived near midday from the capital.
Tora was the first to notice things amiss. Having been
raised in a peasant family, he saw the half-planted fields
and missed the bent backs in them. It was rice planting
time. He said, "Something's happened."

Saburo raised his brows. "What? You've got in-
tuitions of disasters now?"

Tora gave him a pitying look. "No. I thought
you had eyes. Nobody's working."

Saburo looked around. It was a pleasant spring
day; the air was still cool and birds twittered in the trees.
"What do you care when they start working?"

219

Tora only grunted and made for a nearby peasant hut. Saburo followed reluctantly. They dismounted and Tora called out a greeting. The door opened and a woman glared at them. "What do you want?"

Tora approached. "Is anything wrong, Sister?"

"I'm not your sister," she snapped, but her face cleared a little.

"We serve Lord Sugawara and came to see how things are going for the superintendent's people. My master is concerned."

She looked surprised, then her face crumpled. She came out. "Things are bad, very bad. Tell your master. We'll have to leave the land."

"Leave the land? But why? You and your family have been here for ages."

She wiped her eyes. "There's a new master now and he took all our rice. We'll starve before the new harvest. He doesn't care. My husband went to talk to him, to tell him if he takes our rice we'll leave. That's when the new master had him beaten. The others," she swept an arm toward neighboring dwellings, "are afraid. Some of them will leave, too. If they don't, they'll starve or have to sell their daughters."

Saburo came up. "But can he take their rice? Is it legal to do such a thing?"

She looked at Saburo. "He's not very bright," she said to Tora.

Tora grinned. "No, not this early. I thought Kobe-san's heir would have more respect for his father's people. His father is barely gone and he drives his peasants from the land already."

She nodded. "He says the land is his and so's the rice."

Tora shook his head at this. "He's from the city. He doesn't understand about farming. If the peasants don't plant rice, nobody eats. But he seemed so worried when his father was ill. Can this be the same man?"

"Pah! It was all show. We went to see the master after Hayashi died. The master grieved for old Hayashi as if he'd been his brother." She smiled a little. "Older brother. Hayashi was getting past it. The master had to help Hayashi instead of Hayashi helping the master. The son said it was high time Hayashi died. May the Buddha reward the master for his kindness. How can such a man make such a son?"

They fell silent, contemplating the strangeness of it.

After a moment, Saburo said, "The family resented his marriage to a bathhouse woman. They're still angry."

The woman nodded. "She was so beautiful even though she was blind. The master doted on her. They were happy and she was a good woman. His own family, they never showed their faces. Not once in all those years. Not until now. And then the son wanted the master to get rid of Hayashi. It's like he didn't want his father to have anyone to love." She paused. "Maybe they were jealous."

Tora growled, "Shame on them! He had little enough. He gave them everything else."

This comment puzzled her. She looked uncertain, then said again, "He was very kind. May the Buddha help us now!"

They left after this, feeling depressed and angry. Tora especially muttered imprecations against Kobe's son.

221

On their way to Kobe's house, they came across on old woman who was searching among the ferns and grasses under the trees.

Tora reined in. "Have you lost something, grandmother?"

She straightened to peer at them, then came over. Slung across one shoulder she wore a large square of cloth that made a bag. She grinned up at them tooth-lessly. "No, sirs. I find things."

Saburo muttered, "Let's go! You're wasting time."

Tora smiled at the old woman. "You must be lucky. I never find anything good among the weeds."

She cackled and reached into her bag to show him a handful of mushrooms and leaves. "For my sup-per," she said. "The woods are full of good things to eat."

"My own grandmother used to go out, looking for mushrooms," Tora said. "She was a fine cook."

The old woman nodded. "Those young ones, they know nothing. All the time they say, 'No time to gather berries or mushrooms. There's fields to tend and babies to raise. We need to work.' And then they have nothing to put in the soup pot."

Saburo said impatiently, "We've got work to do ourselves. Let's go, Tora!"

But Tora still lingered. "You've got to know your berries, and herbs, or mushrooms, though. If you don't, you can get very sick."

She opened her bag again. "Look! Every bit is wholesome. I know my stuff."

Saburo lost his temper, muttered a curse, and kicked his horse into a trot that made the old woman jump aside. She lost her footing and fell, spilling her

gatherings across the dirty road. Tora climbed down
and helped her up, apologizing.

The old one thanked him. Tora tied up his
horse. Together they gathered what they could. As they
worked, she named the herbs and leaves and explained
where he might find certain mushrooms and how to
avoid others. When they were done, Tora thanked her
and got back on his horse to follow Saburo.

He found him talking to some peasants who
were working in their field. Tora said, "Sometimes I
think you have no heart."

"Why?"

"You made that poor old woman fall down."

"You were wasting time. Look!"

"Why are they working?"

The government supported the rice culture
even where peasants were mistreated. The loss of a
crop could spell disaster. The men and women wading
through the mud as they planted young rice plants had
paused only briefly to explain that Heishiro had threatened them with the law.

Saburo said, "Heishiro has moved into Kobe's
house. He has an overseer who goes around with two
hired thugs to make sure the work is done. It's clear the
peasants will run the moment they relax their vigilance."

Tora cursed. "They'll walk away and starve in
the streets of the capital or work at some harbor like
Otsu, and Kobe's farm will fail unless those lazy sons
work the land themselves. Then what will he do with his
fine inheritance?"

As they sat there on their horses, looking glum-
ly at the bent backs of the peasants, five monks came
walking down the road. A senior monk led them. They
paused to look at the working peasants and then greeted
Tora and Saburo.

"May the Buddha be with you," the senior monk said politely. "It's a lovely day, isn't it? How good to see people working. We heard reports that some of the fields were being neglected and came to see what the problem is."

Saburo said sourly, "They don't like their new master, but it seems he has threatened them with the law."

They withdrew and put their heads together to discuss this information. When they returned, the senior monk said, "We think this land belongs to the Saga temple. Who is this new master you spoke of?"

Tora said, "Kobe Heishiro, the son of superintendent Kobe who died recently. His funeral was at your temple."

They looked at each other and nodded. The senior monk said, "Perhaps there has been some mistake. We must go back and report."

The monks departed. The peasants continued their labors.

"What did he mean, the land belongs to the temple?" Tora asked.

Saburo looked after the monks. Beyond the line of trees they could see the pagoda of the Saga temple. "I wonder," he said, frowning. "Maybe Kobe knew his son well enough to prepare against him."

"What! You think he gave his land away to the temple?"

"I think it's about the only thing that would keep Heishiro from inheriting."

Tora shouted with glee and clapped his hands. His horse nearly shied. "Why the wily old fox!" he cried. "I bet that's what he did! Good for him! Let's tell the peasants to stay. The temple will treat them well."

Saburo was still frowning. He said, "No, wait. Let's go home and tell the master. He can make sure. Then we can drive that bastard off Kobe's land."

27

Men and Their Women

They arrived home before the evening rice and Genba greeted them with the news that Masashi had arrived.

Saburo's face broke into a broad smile. "Is he all right? How did he get here? What did the master say? Where is he? I want to see him."

Genba laughed. "Slow down. He's well and in the main house. He's been asking for you."

"Has he?" Saburo slid out of the saddle and ran toward the house.

Tora looked after him. "I never thought I'd see Saburo look happy. He's crazy about that child. I guess the kid has found a home with him and Sumiko."

Genba chuckled. "If her ladyship's willing to share him."

"Really? That should be interesting. What did the master say?"

"He found him on the street outside the gate. That boy was covered with dirt, but the master took him himself to bathe him. That's the last we saw of Masashi. He's been in the main house ever since."

Tora dismounted more slowly than Saburo and stretched his sore body. "It's good to be back," he remarked. "Maybe we'll have some smiles in this house for a change. We bring some news also." He told Genba what they had learned from the monks. Genba turned the horses over to the stable boy and said, "I'll come with you. I want to hear what the master thinks of this."

Inside, they found Saburo and Masashi reunited in the master's study. Masashi sat beside Saburo. He was telling him excitedly about his journey and his new life. Saburo smiled but he looked slightly stunned. His eyes kept going to Masashi's new silk trousers and jacket.

Akitada and his wife also smiled as they watched this scene. Eventually Sadako took Masashi away so Tora and Saburo could report and the men could talk.

Akitada received their news with great satisfaction. The likelihood of Kobe having had the foresight to give his land to the temple suddenly seemed completely in character. Kobe had worshipped there and had found a friend in the abbot. And then, when Hayashi had been killed, he had surely thought of his own death and how it would affect his peasants. Yes, it made sense.

The next morning, at the ministry, Akitada went directly to the archives. The usual group of youngsters had their heads together, chatting and laughing. When they saw Akitada, they jumped to their desks or dove into the warren of shelved manuscripts. Only one, the smallest and slowest, remained. Akitada suppressed a chuckle. Not much had changed here since the days of his own servitude among the dusty archives.

With a straight face, he asked for the records of Kobe's farm. The boy looked blank, and Akitada sighed. "Well, get me what you have about title transfers on land in Kadono." The young man, he was surely not older than sixteen, bowed and dashed away.

After some excited whispering and shuffling of papers, he returned with two companions, each carrying boxes of papers.

Akitada said, "Good. Put them down and find the list of owners."

They searched their boxes and eventually came up with the list. Akitada scanned it and pointed. "There. That must be Kobe's farm. Now find the papers that go with it."

Kobe's property was a very small piece of land and this search took a while. Akitada noted with approval that several older youngsters joined the three, rather frightened, boys to help them.

In due time, a number of manuscripts appeared and Akitada sat down to peruse them. An unnatural quiet fell on the archives. The boys stood around him, waiting. Going back in time, Akitada found that the farm had been in Kobe's family for several generations as part of the Kobe family property, which was once significant but had recently shrunk in size. This suggested poor management after Kobe left most of it to his oldest son. The property transfer from father to eldest son was duly noted. Only the little farm that the father retained for himself had gained in size and value because he had added new land and cleared it for rice farming. He had been rewarded with tax relief for the new fields. However, the lands left to his oldest son had undergone quite a number of sales recently. Mismanagement indeed.

Akitada had wondered and worried after Kobe had given away most of his property to his family He saw now that by hard work and good management, Kobe had made a success of his little farm.

The farm should by law also pass to his oldest son at his death. But now there was a chance that it had been donated to the Saga temple. In cases where land is given to a temple or shrine, the law recognized passing over one's own family.

The trouble was, Akitada did not find any document of such a transfer.

His disappointment was heavy until he remembered that the gift would have been made recently and therefore nothing would have been filed in the archives yet. What he was looking for was probably lying somewhere in someone's office, and he could not go and demand to see it.

He thanked the boys, returned to his own duties, and that evening he walked away from the ministry in a state of dejection. His thoughts were preoccupied with his own inadequacies, and he was startled when someone suddenly stepped into his path.

"Sir?"

He looked up and found Lord Okura blocking his way.

"I'm glad I ran into you," the man said, looking anxious. "I was afraid to call on you in your office or at home, having made a nuisance of myself in the past."

Akitada snapped, "What do you want?"

Okura took a step back and gulped. "O. . .only to ask if there might be news. I . . . forgive me, but it's been such a long time with no word, and nobody seems to care. How can a young woman disappear so completely unless she's dead? How can her family forget her existence? I . . . it breaks my heart." He choked and started to weep.

Irritation and frustration gave way to embarrassment and shame. Akitada said, "Come away from here. Let's walk in the Imperial Garden. It's more private there. I'm very sorry that you've had no news."

Akitada's concern made matters worse. Okura now sobbed openly. Akitada took his arm and walked him quickly through the main gate of the *Daidairi* and across broad Nijo Avenue to the *Shinsenyen*.

The "Divine Spring Garden" had been intended for an imperial pleasure ground. It occupied thirty-three acres. Entertainments of all sorts were held there, and it was used not only by the emperor, but also by the members of his court and administration. Banquet and poetry contests were held here, and eventually also more common entertainments like wrestling matches. The common people gained access to fish in the lake and to worship at the imperial shrine. The gardens contained several imperial villas for use on special occasions.

On this spring evening, nothing special had been planned and the garden lay quiet. They walked along graveled paths under flowering and budding trees, and Okura poured out his heart.

Akitada made soothing noises and wondered that a woman capable of the cruel and cutting remarks she used to make to her husband could have inspired such love and devotion in this young man. As irritating as Okura had been, he pitied him and disliked Yukiko even more.

She had been quite outspoken about Akitada's unfeeling neglect of her, and yet she had also left this man who was clearly besotted with her. What could have brought that about?

He asked cautiously, "What made her leave you in the first place? She seemed clearly in love with you."

Okura wiped his eyes. "She went to visit her parents . . . and the child . . . and just did not come back."

"The child" was the result of Yukiko's affair with Okura. She had still been married to Akitada at the time, and her father had adopted the little girl to spare her reputation. And yes, Akitada could imagine that Yukiko had tired of Okura and used the excuse of wanting to see her child to leave him.

Akitada decided to be a little blunter. "Was there another man? Did you hear any rumors of a friendship with someone?"

Okura had calmed down. He said quite steadily, "I've racked my brain to think of someone. She had so many friends. I suppose it could be anyone. But it all seemed very casual." He paused, then said sadly, "I never suspected . . . but I have to accept she may have found someone else, someone more to her taste. She used to complain that I bored her."

Yes, that sounded like Yukiko. She tired quickly of the men in her life. But unless Okura could be more specific, it did not help much. "Have you asked her friends?"

"Oh, I could not speak of such things to others." He gave Akitada an uncertain look. "In your case, well, you knew her." He flushed. "I mean you were intimate."

Akitada flushed in turn. The conversation was becoming embarrassing. Would all of Yukiko's lovers become so unbearably familiar in the future? He snapped, "I was not suggesting you speak to all her lovers. I meant women and men she knew socially."

Okura's color changed. He clenched his fists. "You speak of her as a loose woman, one who behaves like a whore. I was right. You hate her. Your words dishonor both of us and I resent them."

Well, so Okura did have some spirit. Akitada said, "I'm sorry. I didn't mean that."

Okura said nothing.

"Can you not stop worrying? I told you, we should have heard if something serious had happened to her. She is after all free to live where she wishes and go wherever her mood takes her. I suppose it would have been better if she had told someone of her plans, but Yukiko tends to be somewhat abrupt."

Okura nodded. "You must be right. And I can do no more." He bowed and walked away quickly.

Akitada looked after him as he disappeared among the flowering cherry trees, a tall figure walking briskly but with a bowed head.

Did women know they could have such a profound effect on men? They complained about their restricted lives and how men treated them like helpless children. Was the custom of confining one's wives and daughters to the safety of the inner pavilions of the home due to women behaving like Yukiko and causing such pain to their husbands or lovers? He did not know, but he wondered if there were others like Okura and himself, men who had been unwilling to force the woman they loved to submit to their wishes.

Okura was right. Akitada did feel something close to hatred for his ex-wife.

When he got home, Saburo was waiting for him.

Akitada noted the worried look on his face and the way he kept wringing his hands and wondered what new unpleasantness awaited him. "What's the matter?" he asked.

His tone caused Saburo to retreat. "Sorry, sir. It's not important."

Akitada said sharply, "You stood here waiting for me. I assume it is important. Speak! I'm tired and troubled by too many things already."

Saburo almost cowered. "It's nothing, sir. I'm sorry to have bothered you."

Akitada sighed. "Now I'm curious. Tell me!"

"It's about the boy, sir."

"Yes. Well, he seems to have found a home. Why are you concerned?"

"Thank you, sir. You and your lady have been very generous. And he seems to be happy."

"So? What's the matter?"

"What will become of him, sir?"

There it was. The problem he had pushed away because he had too many other things to worry about. What were they to do with this street urchin who had crept into their family and was even now making room for himself in their affections?

He said, "Surely that isn't something that must be decided today? This very moment?"

Saburo looked at his feet. "No, sir. Of course not. Only I feel responsible."

Akitada stared at him. "What do you mean?"

Saburo shuffled his feet. "I thought I might adopt him, sir."

"Oh!"

It was a solution, but what about Sadako? He recalled vividly her mothering of the child. Sadako, who had wished for children. A child. And was denied. Sadako, who had blossomed and softened in a glow of happiness when she tended to Masashi. He knew she hoped the boy would stay with them, to be raised as theirs. He had seen it in her eyes. And he himself had also warmed to the idea. No, he had loved feeling that small hand in his and longed to raise another small boy.

Saburo finally looked up. "Sir? Would you allow it?"

"What about your wife? Sumiko. Have you discussed it with her?"

"No, sir. I saw no point in it. It's *my* wish."

"That seems hardly fair. He will be part of your household. Your heir."

"Sumiko has her daughter. I have nothing."

It was a strange marriage if that was the way he felt. But then, Saburo was a strange man. Akitada shook his head in wonder. "You surprise me. That isn't the way it usually is in a marriage, Saburo. Surely one's wife's feelings must be respected."

"Sumiko was a slave and she and her daughter were abused. I married her to take her away from that. And because I needed someone to cook and keep house for me."

Akitada's jaw dropped. "You mean . . . there's nothing between you, no intimacy?"

Saburo shuffled again. "Oh, I also sleep with her now and then. She seems to expect it."

Well, he had the grace to blush. At least what Akitada could see under the beard and the scars had turned a deeper color. "I don't know, Saburo. The child needs a family, and yours is not quite what I had in mind."

"I see, sir." Saburo raised his head to give him a look filled with resentment and disappointment. He bowed and walked away.

28

Of Mushrooms and Fans

Akitada watched Saburo leave and knew he had handled this badly. After all, Saburo had found the child, and clearly the boy was attached to him. He had no right to decide the life of either. But there was Sadako. How to resolve this tangle? Besides, while he felt that he owed Saburo an apology, his antipathy for the man had just grown immeasurably because of his heartless behavior to the woman he had taken to wife. Could he even be trusted with the life of a child?

Before he could escape back into his house and tell Sadako of the conversation, Tora joined him.

"I've been thinking about the superintendent," he said. "His illness, I mean."

Kobe. Akitada had momentarily forgotten about Kobe. What would Kobe have done about the child? He would never know now. With an effort, he turned his attention to Tora. "Yes? What's on your mind, Tora?"

"He must've eaten something, right? Some poison."

"Yes. I think so. We've suspected his son."

"Well, but he got sick before the son found out. What did he eat then?"

"I don't know Tora. It may have been something else."

"Well, what if it was the same thing and it wasn't the son at all?"

Akitada did not like the notion, but he nodded. "Go on!"

"You said a woman had been cooking for him after Hayashi died. What if she gave him something that made him sick?"

Akitada thought back to old Haruko mourning beside Kobe's body. She had loved Kobe. He told Tora about it and added, "I cannot believe it of her."

"It may have been a mistake. I ran into some other old woman in the woods near Kadono. She'd been gathering herbs and mushrooms. Some mushrooms are pure poison. The old woman said it was easy to make a mistake."

"But surely . . . surely such old women know the difference."

"Well, but if they get old and their eyesight isn't so good, they might not."

"Maybe not. But if you're right, then we can do nothing. In that case, she did not mean him any harm but just made a tragic mistake. And proving it will be more difficult than proving it was murder."

"I can go back and talk to her, sir."

238

"Tora, she'll be upset. She loved her master and grieved. And if it was an accident, terrible though it was, there is no point in hurting her."

Tora thought about it. "Yes. I see that. But can we just forget it?"

Akitada said bleakly, "No, we cannot forget. But this doesn't help."

Tora nodded and they parted.

Akitada went inside to share what he had learned from Tora.

As it turned out, Sadako knew quite a bit about mushrooms. "Of course," she said quickly. "Tora is right. That must be it. There are several kinds that cause the nausea. The *benitengu-take*, *tamago-take*, and *tsukiyo-take* all do that. And they look like harmless mushrooms. It takes an expert to know the difference."

Akitada was surprised. "You didn't mention the possibility. Is it possible to die from eating these mushrooms?"

"People can get very sick, but then they stop eating them and get better."

"Kobe got better when he was here."

"Yes. He did. He must have eaten what made him sick when he was in Kadono. Who cooked for him?"

"Hayashi before he was killed. After that, it was one of the old peasant women."

"Would either have made the mistake to gather the wrong mushrooms?"

"I don't know, but both were old."

Sadako sighed. "That's difficult."

"Yes."

They considered the problem and Akitada said, "At least it may be possible to keep Heishiro from

239

benefiting from his father's death. The monks at the temple seem to think the land is theirs."

"But how can that be? I thought it was Kobe's from the beginning."

"It was, but I think he made it a gift to the temple before his death. Apparently nobody knew."

"Oh, how wonderful for his people!"

Akitada said, "Well, it was done out of anger. He knew his family well enough."

Sadako's face fell. "Yes. I see."

"We have another problem. Saburo wants to adopt Masashi."

He saw the shock in her face. "But why? He has a family of his own."

Akitada knew what she meant. He had a daughter, while she had no child at all. In fact, their situations were not so different. Saburo's daughter Tokiwa belonged to his wife, and Sadako was stepmother to Akitada's two children. He said nothing and saw her flush with embarrassment. She said in a small voice, "Yes. I see. He found the boy. And Masashi is very fond of him and grateful. But he cannot do for him what you can do."

"I have no right to interfere. And Saburo seems to feel strongly about it. I think he's always wanted a son."

She hung her head. "Well, then . . . we should let Masashi decide."

Akitada sighed. "I'm not at all sure Saburo will make a good father. He hasn't shown much love for his wife and daughter."

She looked up. "Oh, have they complained to you? They haven't told me of any problems. But maybe they don't trust me. Sumiko comes from the same province as I, only her people were slaves. I blame myself for not looking after them better."

"Don't. They have not complained and seem quite content. It was a comment by Saburo that I didn't like. He doesn't seem to care about Sumiko's feelings in this matter. He wants the boy and that's all that matters. He struck me as far too selfish to raise any child."

"Perhaps it's just his disappointment that Masashi seemed to have preferred living with us."

"Perhaps. How is he? Did he talk much about Saburo?"

Sadako nodded. "He looks up to him as his hero. The amulet he wears he got from Saburo. He wouldn't let me touch it when I dressed him. But he showed me his treasures."

Akitada chuckled. "He trusts you more than he does me. What was he carrying in that bundle?"

"Some polished stones he thinks are jewels, three silver coins and four coppers—his entire wealth—a colored bead, and a fan."

Akitada laughed. "A fan? What does he have a fan for?"

"I think it used to belong to his brother. It's broken. Someone threw it away, I think. A pity. It was quite a fine one once. An unusual one with snow made of gold dust."

"I wonder if the brother found that in the Minamoto place. If it was an expensive item, it would make sense. Let's have a talk with Masashi tomorrow."

They found the boy with the women in the kitchen. He was explaining his uncle's dumplings to them. Both Hanae, Tora's wife, and Sumiko, Saburo's spouse, had taken on some kitchen and house duties after Saburo's mother had died. They were smiling as they listened to the boy.

Akitada greeted them and then said, "Will you come and show me your treasures, Masashi?"

Masashi hesitated. Perhaps he only shared such confidences with a few. But he relented and went willingly to where he had hidden his bundle behind one of the trunks in the small room where he slept. He undid the knot, spread out the tattered cloth neatly, and revealed his collection.

Akitada admired his wealth first. "How have you managed to save so much money," he said. "Didn't you need it on the long walk here?"

"No. I begged for food. Kai said you must always save your coppers for when you really need them." He pointed to the two silver pieces. "They're silver. They're worth many coppers each."

The boy was bright for his age, and streetwise. "Do you miss Kai?"

"Yes. He was my brother. We slept together. He told me many things."

Akitada touched the broken fan. "Where did you find this?"

"It's a fan. It belonged to Kai. So did the silver. The coppers are mine, and the precious stones."

"But where did Kai get such a fan? It's a very fine one."

Masashi watched anxiously as Akitada reached for it and opened it. "Be careful. It's broken," he said.

The fan was delicately painted on pale silk. It showed a wintry landscape of snow-covered hills, a deep blue winding river, and snow-covered pines. The snow was made of gold dust and misty golden clouds drifted across the scene shedding their shimmer over it. It was exquisite, but the lacquered bamboo sticks were broken in several places, and the silk had been ripped. It was also quite dirty.

Masashi said, "Kai found it in Bishamonten's treasure house. He almost dropped it when the guardians chased him. Then he broke it climbing over the wall."

Bishamonten again. The poor boys dreamed of wealth, because that was what poor boys did. And the wealth Kai had found had been in Minamoto Norisuke's palace in Otsu. Provincial chiefs tended to control large properties and were well-to-do, but their expenses were also great if they guarded their lands with armed retainers and hired soldiers. Norisuke seemed considerably better off than even some of the Fujiwaras. Most likely his martial bearing and good looks contributed to his godlike image in Otsu. All of this made him a dangerous adversary and possibly a threat to the current government.

Akitada was about to lay the fan back down, when he noticed that the scene on it seemed familiar. Dirt and damage made it difficult to see clearly. He brought the fan closer to his eyes. Yes, the shape of one of the hills was unmistakable and he saw parts of the famous bridge. The scene was of the Uji River crossing. He had given just such a fan to his former wife after their marriage. It had been to commemorate their journey together as newly-weds on their way to the capital and his home. He had asked the artist to paint a winter scene, because Yukiko's name meant "child of snow".

He turned the fan over. There was a poem there, or rather part of it.

Beneath the piling snow . . . the path to love among the nodding bamboos . . .

He had forgotten and it did not matter any longer. Whatever he had felt when he bought the fan for his new wife was long gone, a mere dim memory of a consuming passion. Alas, it had not melted Yukiko's cold heart in the end.

But why was this fan in the ragged bundle of a street child?

Masashi eyed him anxiously. He was afraid for his treasure. "That's gold on there, isn't it?" he asked.

"Yes." The fan had been expensive. Akitada, normally sparing with money, had felt extravagant in his effort to please the beautiful girl who had made love so passionately in his arms at night. No wonder other men adored her. Lord Okura among them. "How did Kai get the fan?" Akitada asked.

"Kai stole it." Masashi looked at him anxiously. "Do you think the god was angry and killed Kai?"

It was likely, but Akitada did not say so. He returned the fan to Masashi.

Had his gift ended up in the boy's hands to return as tattered and spoiled as their marriage? It was surely most unlikely. Years had passed since then, and the artist must have sold other fans with that famous scene and poem.

29

Kobe's Legacy

Akitada did not tell Sadako about his reaction to the fan. He knew it would pain her to be reminded of her husband's former passion for the faithless Yukiko. He merely said that the picture was of a famous scene, and Sadako commented that it was very beautiful still and must have belonged to a very highly-placed lady.

They went to bed with the matter of Masashi unresolved. Both avoided the subject.

The following day was not a work day and Akitada did not have to go to the ministry. He decided to use the time for a return to Kadono to resolve the problem of Kobe's property. Tora and Saburo came with him, having expected the summons.

"When we're in Kadono," Akitada said, "I shall speak to the abbot at the Saga Temple and perhaps talk with old Haruko again. You will urge the peasants on Kobe's land to have patience for a few more days."

Saburo looked stubborn. "What about Masashi, sir?"

Akitada nodded. "If the boy agrees, I shall not oppose your adopting him." He wanted to warn Saburo about his lack of consideration for Sumiko and her daughter but bit his lip. It was none of his business.

Saburo brightened instantly. "Thank you, sir. I made a promise to Masashi and he's eager." He paused then added with a smile, "The boy is grateful. Perhaps it's wrong of me to take advantage of that."

"He needs a father and a stable life. I think you'll give him that."

Saburo smiled more broadly. "And I can teach him. He's very bright."

True. Saburo, unlike Tora or Genba, had received a good education from the monks. Akitada felt more content that he had done the right thing and hoped Sadako would also come to accept his decision.

This time the mood was lighter as they rode together to Kadono. Tora was eager to deal with Kobe's son, and Saburo was cheerfully agreeable. They stopped at the farm first and found that Kobe's family had left to return to their own home in the capital. The place looked deserted except for two snarling, barking dogs tied to a tree.

But Heishiro had left an overseer in possession. This man, a big fellow with a mean face, came out of the house and glowered at them. Akitada wore a simple hunting coat and was bare-headed, and his companions were similarly dressed.

Akitada introduced himself by name but without title. The big man responded rudely, "Kojima, manager. What do you want?"

"I was the late superintendent's friend and have come to speak to Haruko, the old woman who used to cook for him."

The man growled, "She's busy. This place belongs to Master Heishiro now and I'm in charge. And we don't like strangers here."

Akitada raised his brows. "I think you must be mistaken. The farm belongs to the Saga Temple. Heishiro and you are breaking the law by staying here without permission."

This surprised the overseer. For a moment he stared, then he raised a fist and threatened, "Get out or I'll set the dogs on you."

Tora and Saburo urged their horses forward and Tora put his hand on his sword. "Watch your tongue when you speak to his lordship, you lout," he warned, "or you and your dogs'll be sorry."

Kojima retreated a step. "You can't threaten me. I work for the rightful heir. If you don't go, I'll report you to the police. In fact, I'll report you even if you do leave."

Akitada saw no point in facing off with the man and said, "We shall be back."

At this point, they separated. Tora and Saburo went off to speak to the peasants, while Akitada rode to the temple to consult with the abbot.

Akitada found the elderly cleric in council with his senior monks. News of events on the farm had been reported, as had the fact that some of the peasants were rebelling and talking about leaving the land.

247

The abbot said, "After Master Kobe's generosity I don't like to expel his family, but we've been told that his son has been sending his people to whip any peasants who aren't out in the fields planting rice."

Akitada told him about finding only the supervisor at the farm. He added, "I've checked the archives but couldn't find the gift listed. It may be too early. Do you have any paperwork on it?"

"I do." The abbot sent one of the monks to get the documents, then said with a sigh, "Kobe made the gift to the temple a short time before Hayashi died. He was in very low spirits and did not think he would live much longer and he did not want to risk having his oldest son claim the land. He also hoped to provide for Hayashi. We agreed that, if Hayashi outlived his master, he would stay on the farm for the rest of his life. We would not claim the house until after Hayashi's death and we would look after him. I have the deed, but there was no time to file it properly. We shall do so now."

Akitada inspected the signed bequest, read it, and nodded. "Good. It looks very much as though Heishiro, Kobe's son, will fight for his inheritance, even though he doesn't deserve it and his father did not want him to have it."

The abbot pursed his lips. "We'll send that overseer on his way and put someone from here in his place. The peasants will be reassured. I should have kept an eye on things, but it seemed unkind to drive the family out so soon after the funeral."

"Did Kobe speak to you about Hayashi's murder?"

"Yes, of course. He grieved and was in great need of consolation."

"Did he have any suspicions?"

The abbot looked puzzled. "What kind?"

Akitada hesitated, then asked bluntly, "About his family being involved?"

The old cleric looked shocked. "No. Of course not. You mean you think they killed Hayashi? But that's surely unbelievable. His family never came to see Kobe at all until his death. It was his loneliness that made him cling to old Hayashi the way he did."

Akitada felt the old pang of guilt again. He should have been a better, more attentive friend. He said, "His eldest son visited twice before Kobe's death. Maybe even more often."

"But why would the son want to kill Hayashi?"

"I wondered if he was looking for the will and Hayashi surprised him."

"Well, the robbery happened shortly after Kobe gave us his gift." The abbot shook his head. "There wouldn't have been any point to it. I cannot believe that the son could be so evil."

Akitada sighed. "I have no proof, but Kobe's illness made me suspicious. He may have been poisoned. We shall speak to some of his people again, but we may never prove anything against Heishiro."

"It would be a terrible story if it's true."

Saburo was whistling. Tora looked at him from time to time. Finally he asked, "Why are you so happy? Aren't you at all bothered by Kobe's death and by what's been happening here?"

Saburo stopped whistling. "Sorry. I was thinking of Masashi. What a boy! Can you believe he walked all that way from Otsu? Alone. With no money. And he's just six years old. Have you ever heard of such a thing?"

Tora relaxed and smiled. "Never. He'll grow up to be somebody!"

"I think so too. And I'm going to teach him. What a boy!"

"Yes, but do it later. We have a job to do."

They began a systematic series of visits to Kobe's peasants. One family had already left, but most were still in their houses, frightened and desperate, or out in the paddies, planting. Two of the able-bodied men had been beaten by Heishiro's overseer when they refused to turn over the rice that was supposed to feed their families until the next harvest. They lost their rice anyway. One of the young women had been taken away. The rest had simply submitted. They planned to subsist on a few vegetables, grains, and beans. They all talked about leaving the land. Tora and Saburo reassured them that the land now belonged to the temple and there was no need to leave. The monks would see to it that they had enough.

They were coming from the last house when they found the irate overseer and three large, mean-looking males waiting for them. The three men carried cudgels.

"There they are!" the overseer shouted. "They're spreading lies about my master."

The three louts surrounded Tora and Saburo before they could reach their horses.

Tora said calmly, "Kojima lies. The peasants are leaving because you steal their rice and their women, and you beat them."

"More lies! Go on, get them!" Kojima urged.

The leader of the three thugs was long-haired and bearded with an ugly scar on his cheek. He growled, "If you touch that sword, you're dead!" He swung his cudgel.

Only Tora was armed with a short sword, and his gray hair and beard must have made him appear a negligible opponent to the younger and more muscular thugs. They pressed closer, grinning in anticipation.

Tora glanced at Saburo. "It's a stand-off. I could lop off the big fellow's head, but the rest would gang up on you."

Saburo grinned. "Go ahead!" He tucked the hem of his short robe in his belt and flexed his arms.

The thugs hesitated. Their leader said, "We can kill you both. Nobody would blame us."

Tora put his hand on his sword. "If you attack us, you attack Lord Sugawara. We're his retainers. And we're here on behalf of the monks of the Saga temple who own this land."

Kojima shouted, "Don't listen to him! He's lying. The land belongs to my master, Kobe Heishiro. Go ahead! Hit them. The police will be on our side."

The thugs moved in again and raised their cudgels.

Tora sighed. He looked at Saburo. "I told you, it's a stand-off." He drew his sword.

The thugs, on their part, roared and attacked.

Cudgels make excellent weapons. They can disarm a man with a sword quickly, and they can kill. But Tora did not scare easily. When the big thug lashed out at his head, Tora pivoted and arched away, then swung around and slashed with his sword. He deflected the cudgel but did not stop his attacker. He merely roared louder and came again. This time Tora dodged forward and aimed at his shoulder. There was a jarring impact and a satisfying scream. The big man's knees buckled. He dropped his cudgel and sat down, still screaming.

Tora ignored him. He turned to assist Saburo. Saburo had ducked under the cudgel of the first man to attack him while drawing a thin chain from his sleeve. Gripping this firmly, he had whirled it in the air. It made a high whistling sound, then caught his attacker around the neck. He dropped his cudgel when Saburo jerked the chain hard, making him fall to his knees, choking and scrabbling at the chain around his neck.

But the remaining thug now brought his cudgel down on Saburo's back with a fierce blow. Saburo gasped and fell forward as Tora arrived, sword raised to decapitate his opponent. The thug squealed and jumped away. Then he ran.

Tora lowered his sword and looked around. The leader of the three sat on the ground moaning, cradling an arm, and bleeding profusely. The thug with the chain around his neck was also down and gasping for air. And the third and final thug was gone. That left Kojima, who had turned quite pale and was backing away from the scene.

Tora shoved the sword back and put a hand on Saburo's shoulder. "How are you, Brother?" Saburo was on his hands and knees and groaned in answer. Tora helped him up and felt his ribs and shoulders. "Can you ride?"

Saburo winced but nodded. "Sure," he croaked.

Tora helped him into the saddle, then got on his horse. "Bastards!" he said with feeling. "I should've killed them all."

"It would've caused trouble." Saburo's voice sounded stronger. "Let's go back to the farm and see what they've been up to. I expect that Kojima and his thugs will keep their distance now."

They saw that the overseer had made himself at home. His bedding still lay tumbled on the floor of the main room, and dirty bowls and cups littered the area around it. The kitchen smelled more like a stable. Food remnants rotted in bowls and dishes. A small keg of sake was half empty. But the ugliest surprise awaited them in one of the small storage rooms under the eaves. This one had walls and a door that was bolted from the outside. Inside was a young girl, naked, weeping, and clutching some torn clothing to her body. She stared with large, frightened eyes at Tora and Saburo. Her hands and feet were tied with rope and what showed of her pale skin was bruised and scratched.

Tora cursed loud and long. The girl whimpered.

Saburo said nothing. He left and returned from the kitchen with a knife to cut her bonds. Tora was trying to talk to her, to reassure her, but she backed away as far as she could into a corner.

Tora said fiercely, "She looks about ten years old. A child. I should've killed him. I should've killed them all."

Saburo shook his head. "She's older. They said he'd taken one of the peasants' daughters. That's the girl, I guess. Young, but marriageable."

"He raped her!" Tora said, outraged. "How can you be so calm?"

Saburo glanced at the naked girl. "She's small for her age, but she's not a child."

Tora muttered another curse, then went to get one of the quilts from the bedding in the main room.

Saburo cast another glance at the weeping girl, shook his head, and walked outside.

30

Haruko

When Akitada returned to the farm, he heard their story. He asked Saburo how he felt and, when reassured, said, "Ride into town and get the constables. It's high time they arrest that overseer and his thugs."

Then he went with Tora and had a look at the girl, who cowered in the main room, wrapped in her quilt. She was no longer crying but shivered from time to time.

"She's just a baby," Tora said.

"She's very young, yes." Akitada knelt beside the girl, saw her flinch away, and got up again. "We'll get your mother. Tell Tora where you live."

She looked from him to the big, gray-haired man with the kind face and finally murmured a few words.

Tora smiled at her and said, "It's not far, sir. I can take her. Shall I go now?"

"Yes, of course."

"You'll be alone. That overseer and those thugs are still about."

Akitada's lips quirked. "Clearly you think me unable to defend myself even after all of our practice. I have a sword. Go!"

Tora told the girl. "Come, I'll take you home." She nodded and scrambled to her feet, clutching the quilt to her. Akitada followed and helped her get on Tora's horse. Then he went to look around Kobe's place. He, too, saw how the overseer had abused Kobe's tidy home and shook his head at it.

When he heard a noise outside, he stepped to the door to look. To his surprise, he saw Heishiro ride up and dismount. When Heishiro saw him in the doorway, he stopped, flushing angrily, and demanded, "What do you want now?"

Akitada said calmly, "I came to check on things."

"You've no business here." Heishiro came to the steps. "This is my place now. You're not needed or wanted any longer."

"There've been complaints. I take it you appointed that overseer who's been living here?"

"Of course. I can't be bothered running a farm. What complaints and why are they any of your business?"

Heishiro started up the stairs. Akitada stepped aside and let him walk into the house.

Heishiro glanced around and made a face. "Where's Kojima?"

"He set some thugs on my retainers. They defended themselves, and he took to his heels. It seems he's better at beating peasants and raping children than fighting."

Heishiro glared. "I repeat, you have no business here. And you've no right to interfere with my servant."

Akitada caught a movement from the corner of his eye and glanced past him. He saw an old woman limping across the courtyard.

"Haruko!" Pushing Heishiro aside, he ran out of the house and after her. His pursuit frightened her. She fell to her knees and cried, "Sorry, Master. Sorry. Don't hurt me." She looked terrible. Her face was bloodied and there was dried blood in her white hair.

He stopped. "What happened to you?"

She cowered away from him. "Nothing. Nothing. Don't hurt me."

"Don't you remember me? You and I sat together that night to mourn your master."

She blinked and looked at him uncertainly. It had been dark that night, and her old eyes were getting dim. She asked, "Was that you, sir?"

"Yes. I'm Lord Sugawara. Kobe's friend from the capital."

"Oh, sir!" She struggled to her feet and he helped her. "Oh, sir," she gasped again, "they tried to kill me. The young master made me go with them. He said, 'Get out, you old hag!' And I'd served Master Kobe all my life, from before he put on trousers." The tears came again.

Akitada put an arm about her shoulders. "Don't cry. I know you're a faithful servant."

257

She sobbed. "I don't know where to go. Nobody wants an old woman like me. I should have gone up the mountain to die, but I'm hungry."

Heishiro's version of housecleaning.

Akitada wondered why Heishiro had been so cruel. More immediately, she needed food. The town was too far for her to walk to and he hated to leave Heishiro in possession of the farm. But Heishiro had no business there and she did. He led her back to the house. She resisted at first, but he held her firmly.

Heishiro blocked the door. "What's she doing back?"

Akitada stopped at the bottom of the steps. "Get out of the way. She's hurt and she needs food."

"I'm not feeding the old crone. She's useless."

"She served your family all her life."

"Well, now she's senile and can't work. She's a liar and she shows me no respect."

Akitada snapped, "You don't deserve it. And you're trespassing. This place does not belong to you."

Heishiro stood his ground. "I'm my father's eldest son. What was his has become mine."

"It wasn't his when he died. He gave the farm to the temple."

Heishiro gaped. "He couldn't have. Why would he? No, I know that's a lie. I know because he was already ill, and then after he came back from your house, he didn't have time. I was here. I know he didn't." Having convinced himself, Heishiro regained some of his color and defiance.

Akitada thought his words revealing. Heishiro had tried to make sure Kobe could not give his property away before he died. Perhaps he had also made sure that he would in fact die quickly.

258

He said, "Do you want me to come up there and remove you myself or will you let us inside?"

Heishiro moved aside reluctantly. "I don't want her here. She's mad."

Akitada did not reply. He helped the old woman up the steps and into the kitchen area. There he sat her down on one of the barrels and then looked around for food.

Rice was simmering away in the cooker in the corner, and someone had chopped some radish. Akitada found, with some difficulty, a clean bowl, ladled out rice and put some radish on top. This he took to the old woman, who had fallen into a hunger-weakened doze.

Heishiro had followed them.

The old one woke a little and seized the bowl. She raised it shakily to her mouth and shoveled the food in with a finger. Akitada had not found chop sticks, but it did not matter. When the bowl was empty, she lowered it and looked up. "Thank you, master. You must be a god." She smiled. "Like *Daikokuten* himself, come to feed the hungry. Your hat, that's what Daikokuten wears in the pictures."

Akitada felt faintly flattered. *Daikokuten*, another god of good fortune, was usually depicted in scholarly garb. He was one of the Chinese gods and popular with the common people. He chuckled and said, "Thank you, but I'm only Sugawara, the same one who kept watch with you over Master Kobe's body."

She looked a little stronger, but there was the blood on her face and her right arm was bruised and scratched. He saw a clean rag, dipped it in the water container, and dabbed the blood from her face and arm. "Who did this to you?"

She flinched away and tried to take the rag. "They were going to kill me, so I ran. I fell down in the woods, but I found a place to hide and there I stayed until they were gone."

"Who tried to kill you?"

"Those men. The young master said to go with them."

Akitada stared at her. "But why did they want to kill you?"

"Nobody wants me. I'm useless."

"Master Kobe wanted you. You were a faithful servant to him."

"Oh, Master Kobe! May he be reborn! Always kind, always good. He suffered so much." She wiped away a fresh tear.

"Was he in pain before he died? Do you remember the day?"

"His children were not filial," she said, shaking her head. She sighed.

Akitada said, "Well, his son seems to have cared. Didn't he stay with his father?"

"In the end. But then the master died, and he changed."

"Do you mean Heishiro? How did he change?"

She leaned forward to peer past Akitada. "He sent me away. When it was me that held him on my lap and me that wiped his bottom when he was small. He came here and the master talked to him. They quarreled and then he went away again."

Akitada was becoming confused. The woman was old and rambled. He asked again, "But Heishiro only came once, after the master returned from the capital?"

260

"No. He came after Hayashi died. He said the master needed better food, more good rice and vegetables. I said there weren't any vegetables in the garden yet. He showed me where to find fresh herbs in the woods."

A helpful Heishiro was very suspicious. Akitada thought about it and a memory stirred. "Did he also find mushrooms?"

She nodded. "Yes. Such fine mushrooms. He knew where they were growing."

Akitada suddenly felt weak. He sank down on another barrel and looked at her. "And you cooked the mushrooms and went back for more."

She smiled and nodded again. "I went every day and the master praised my soup."

She had labored faithfully and lovingly and had slowly but surely poisoned him.

She fell into a doze after this. Little wonder after the day she had had and the food she had finally eaten.

Heishiro was gone. Akitada had not heard him leave and wondered how much he had overheard.

He sat with her, hoping Tora and Saburo would return soon. Saburo would bring the constables, but he could not give them old Haruko. He had no doubt that Heishiro had given her the poisonous mushrooms. In the beginning, they had merely made Kobe ill, but repeated doses had weakened him and he would surely have died eventually, except that Akitada had come and taken him away from Haruko's soups and Heishiro's plans. Heishiro had tried to take his father back to the farm, but had failed. It had been Kobe himself who had returned to his deadly diet.

Could it be proved that Heishiro had provided the poisoned mushrooms? Perhaps, if Haruko told her

261

story clearly. But she was nearly senile, and Akitada still hoped she would never learn that she had caused her master's death. It now made perfect sense that Heishiro should have ordered his thugs to kill the old woman. It would have been easy: take her up the mountain and push her off a cliff. It would have looked like an accident: a feeble old creature who did not see well was likely to take a misstep.

That left the murder of Hayashi, another faithful servant. Kobe had inspired such loyalty in his people. Akitada was now convinced that Hayashi had been murdered because he surprised Heishiro in Kobe's house. The son must have come to check on his inheritance and when Kobe had told him what he intended to do, there had been the quarrel Haruko had witnessed.. The shock must have been considerable. Heishiro had returned to search for documents of the gift to the temple and Hayashi had surprised him and objected. Then Heishiro must have killed him. Haruko's rambling account suggested that Heishiro had visited his father several times during those weeks.

But why the sudden interest? Heishiro had not bothered with visits for years. What had brought him now? Why had the farm become so important? Akitada remembered how Heishiro's mother had claimed they were left to starve. If Heishiro had so mismanaged his property that things had become dire, the farm might well have become very important to him.

The sound of his horse whinnying outside startled him out of his thoughts. He rose, wondering if it was Tora who had returned or Saburo had arrived with the constables.

Alas, it was neither. Heishiro was back. With reinforcements.

31

A Cornered Rat

They were armed. Heishiro and his overseer carried short swords and their two companions had cudgels. The two thugs with cudgels, no doubt, had been the men who had attacked Tora and Saburo. Heishiro looked murderous. If he had overheard Haruko earlier, he knew the trouble he was in and had nothing to lose.

Trying to defuse the tension, Akitada said, "What do you want, Heishiro? Whatever it is, we can settle it later. I've sent for the constables. Your overseer is in trouble."

Heishiro sneered, "We'll be done before the constables show up. They're lazy bastards." He turned to the others, "Let's teach him a lesson!"

Akitada cursed his negligence. He had left his sword with his horse when he had arrived earlier and joined Tora and Saburo. In any case, it had not occurred to him that Heishiro would dare attack him. He said, "You'll never get away with it."

Heishiro laughed. "I own this land. You attacked me. We defended ourselves." He waved his arm. "Get him!"

They started toward him, running up the stairs, Heishiro and the overseer in front. The veranda and house were too cramped for evasive movement, and Akitada swung himself over the veranda railing and dropped down into the forecourt. The landing sent a jarring pain through one leg. He sank to his knee.

On the stairs, a brief tangle ensued as his four attackers turned back. The respite was too short. Akitada jumped up and flung himself toward his horse and the sword tied to the backpack. He ignored the agony when his left foot touched the ground and supported his weight for a moment. His arm was reaching for his saddle when a well-aimed blow from a cudgel caught his shoulder. He stumbled, then felt a blinding pain at the back of his head and fell.

Heishiro shouted, "Kill him!"

After that, things became a blur. The crushing blows fell hard. He tried to cover his head with his arms and roll himself into a ball, but it did little good against the onslaught by the two thugs standing over him and delivering mind-numbing strikes to every part of his body.

Expecting Heishiro's sword any moment, he wished for unconsciousness as he waited for them finish.

An ignominious death in some small farm yard and at the hands of thugs. Nothing in his life had prepared him for this in spite of all the disappointments.

The beating stopped suddenly, and he thought here it comes. Let them make it quick and not carve me up slowly like an animal.

He dimly heard some confused shouting and running footsteps. A horse whinnied and there was the sound of metal striking metal. His mind was numb, but somehow he knew. A swordfight!

Someone had come to his aid.

Akitada lay where he was and blinked against the sun. He wondered why he had not fainted from the pain, but pain has a way of blocking that escape. Akitada's whole body throbbed with it, his arms and legs, and, dear gods, his back. He closed his eyes again, but the darkness did not bring blessed relief. Instead, his mind woke up. He thought: a single horseman has arrived. Only one. Not Saburo with the constables. It must be Tora who had returned before Saburo.

Tora alone, facing four much younger men, two of them with swords.

Tora, who had only recently suffered another attack and was still not very well. They would kill him.

Fear seized him, along with a furious anger. He opened his eyes again and moved his head a little to see. The pain of that movement made everything turn dark for a moment. But he had seen enough to know they had indeed ganged up on Tora, who was fighting desperately from the back of a rearing horse.

When the pain eased, his thoughts came back: it would not be long before Tora would be unseated, and once he was down, he was at their mercy. They would kill him before turning their attention back to their first victim.

He tried to move and almost passed out from pain. He lay spent until the horse screamed. Then, he made a desperate effort. Ignoring the agony in his back and shoulders and the blinding dizziness that seized him, Akitada got to his knees, then staggered to his feet, and hopped the few feet to his horse. He fell against it, clutching the saddle, and tried to grab his sword but found that he could not raise his right arm. It hung limp and useless, and blood trickled from his sleeve and into his palm.

With another desperate lunge, he got hold of his sword with his left hand and pulled the blade from the scabbard. Then he forced himself to turn around.

Tora was no longer on his horse. The animal had galloped away, and Tora half lay and half crouched on the ground, sword in hand, clearly stunned, but clumsily fighting off the overseer and one of the men with a cudgel. Heishiro hovered behind them, ready to lend assistance.

Akitada started toward them and promptly fell. With a groan, he got back up, putting his weight on the good foot, and took several hopping steps. This attracted Heishiro's attention. He shouted a warning and ran toward him.

Under normal circumstances, Heishiro would not have been much of an adversary. It was unlikely that he had much use of a sword as a minor official in the city administration. But he was much younger and for some reason desperate. Akitada could only use his left arm and right leg and he had no fighting skills with his left hand, even if he could have moved on two healthy legs. But if he could remain upright, he might parry a blow or two and give Tora a better chance.

266

He got in position, sword held firmly in his left, eyes on Heishiro's sword. Perhaps Heishiro saw his determination, because he suddenly slowed and hesitated. He came to a stop a few feet away. Akitada saw fear in his eyes. "You poisoned your own father, Heishiro," he said through clenched teeth. "And you killed Hayashi and tried to kill Haruko. But Haruko talked. You're a dead man."

Heishiro started shaking. "My father hated me. He deserved to die. They all deserved to die. And you'll die, too." He glanced over his shoulder for his thugs.

Gasping with fury and pain, Akitada attacked.

Too late Heishiro tried to step aside, stumbled, and fell. Akitada practically fell on top of him, driving his sword into the man's belly. Heishiro screamed and convulsed under him.

Akitada lay on the twitching body for a moment, then rolled aside. He missed the blow to his head that a thug tried to deliver. He could not have escaped another, but by then there were shouts, and suddenly red-coated constables seemed to be everywhere. The thug was gone, and Tora was bending over him.

"Sir?"

Akitada muttered, "Y-yes. A-are you all right?"

"Yes, but you?"

"I'll get up in a moment."

But not yet. Just then lying still without moving was bliss.

Saburo came. "How badly are you hurt, sir?"

Tora snapped, "Can't you see? They nearly beat him to death before I got here. Then they attacked my horse and were on me. I couldn't get to him. We'll need a cart. And a stretcher."

Akitada muttered, "N-no." He should get up. If he did not, he would face the embarrassment of being transported home like a slaughtered animal. Sadako would faint with the shock. Just a little more time. He said, "Go away!"

They did not obey, though the constables seemed to demand their attention. Heishiro had stopped screaming. That, too, was a blessed relief. Someone was touching him, feeling his head, his shoulders, his arms. They were trying to be gentle, but they hurt him, and he groaned.

Tora said, "He's hurt badly. There's a lot of blood."

Akitada decided they would not leave him be. Resentfully, he pulled his remaining wits together and made an effort to raise himself by propping himself on his left arm. He immediately got dizzy and felt sick. The pain returned to all the damaged places on his body, returned more violently now that his mind was not distracted by his attackers, and he gasped, then vomited.

Tora cried, "Lie still!"

That was what he had tried to do when they would not let him. He lay on his side and glared at Tora. "No!"

Then he saw that Tora was also bleeding. "You're wounded."

"It's nothing. That bastard overseer nicked me, that's all. He paid for it." Tora sounded proud.

"He's dead?"

"Yes. Good riddance! And so's that bastard Heishiro. You left your sword in his belly. One of the others is wounded."

Akitada made a move to get to his feet, but Tora stopped him. "No, you mustn't get up yet."

Gritting his teeth, Akitada snapped, "Shut up! I could use some help."

Finally Tora understood and helped him stand. The nausea did not return, but his body would not obey. He leaned on Tora's arm, swaying and dizzy. "We must make a fine pair," he said, and managed to raise a chuckle.

Akitada looked around. Saburo was bent over a body with the sergeant of the constables. The other constables were tying up the surviving thug. It was over. Little thanks to them. He said, "Help me to the stairs. I'll rest there for a bit."

"You need to lie down. They've sent for the doctor."

That would be the pharmacist. Kadono did not have a physician. Akitada did not bother to explain. The pharmacist was also the coroner and would be needed to look at the dead. He took a step toward the house and Tora helped him.

It was harder than Akitada had thought. Tora's arm was around his waist, and together they staggered drunkenly across the rough dirt to the steps. There Akitada sank down with a grunt of relief and said, "Sit down yourself. We've done our part." And after a while, he told Tora about Haruko and what she had said.

Together they watched the activity. Saburo came back and asked, "How are you, sir?" Akitada assured him that he had only suffered a small scratch, and Saburo held out a boot. It was missing a piece of its sole. "Heishiro's?" Akitada asked and Saburo nodded.

They did not talk much. Tora adjusted a blood-soaked rag he had tied around his leg and Akitada was preoccupied with flexing the muscles in his shoulders, back, and arms and in stretching his legs. His right ankle was hot and painful and he still could not put any weight on that foot. But he was determined to get on his horse after a rest.

In time, the pharmacist arrived with his box of implements and plasters. He looked at the bodies, spoke briefly to the sergeant and Saburo, and then came over.

Akitada nodded to him. "Have a look at Tora first, Nagaie. He's still bleeding."

Tora objected, but the pharmacist overruled him, unwrapped and checked his wound, covered it with some paste and then rewrapped it more tightly. "It's not deep," he said. "Leave it alone and let it heal."

Akitada wiped sweat from his face and wished for a breeze. Intense pain tended to make one hot. It also sapped one's strength. Perhaps he could sit a little longer. He leaned back and closed his eyes.

"Where are you hurt, sir?" The pharmacist broke rudely into a slight doze that had calmed the various aches and felt blissful.

Akitada said drowsily, "It's nothing. Just let me sleep a little." He closed his eyes again but the pharmacist's inquisitive fingers started crawling all over his head. When they reached the back of his head, Akitada started and opened his eyes. "That hurt," he protested.

"Yes." The pharmacist showed him bloody fingers. "You have a wound on the back of your head."

"It's all right. It only hurts when you touch it. And there's some blood on my arm, but very little. It must be from a scratch. And I hurt my leg when I jumped from the veranda. I just need a short rest."

The pharmacist glanced up at the veranda above and shook his head. He next looked at Akitada's arm. "The blood is from a small wound on your head,"

270

he said. "They bleed a lot and it ran down your arm."
Then he investigated the ankle, which was swollen so
badly that he had difficulty removing the boot. "You
need to lie down. Any head wound may be serious.
Time will tell. I'll bandage it, and then your people can
make a bed for you inside."

Akitada sat up. "No. I'm riding home as soon
as I've talked to the sergeant over there."

The pharmacist gave him a look. "As you wish,
sir." He busied himself with a small bandage for
Akitada's head. Since the patient would not allow him
to cut off his topknot, it was of necessity small. "It may
bleed again," he warned.

"Never mind."

Tora, who had stood by, said, "You should stay
at least until morning."

"No."

The pharmacist eventually finished with his patient and departed. The sergeant had been waiting.
Akitada waved him over. "What is the situation?" he
asked.

The sergeant bowed. "A valiant battle, sir. Four
against two, and they were all young."

Akitada frowned at him and Tora snorted.
"Experience is twice as good as youth," he said.

The sergeant smiled and bowed again. "Why
did they attack you?"

"We threatened to put them in jail," Akitada
said. "They were trying to take over the farm, which
belongs to the Saga Temple now. They've been beating
the peasants and stealing their rice, and they raped one
of the girls."

The sergeant required a few more explanations,
but then declared himself satisfied. The constables

271

gathered the bodies and the prisoner and they all departed.

Akitada stood up, clutching the stair rail. "Get my horse, Saburo, and help me in the saddle."

32

Life's Disgraces

That ride home was among the most painful experiences in Akitada's memory. At least by then it was getting dark, and the others did not see his face as he slumped in the saddle. Neither did they hear his groans over the sound of hooves on the rocky roadway. If he had hoped to reach his home and dismount without disgracing himself, he soon found out that his entire body had stiffened to a point where he could not move at all.

Genba with his lantern, of course, saw the way he barely clung to his saddle and how white and sweat-covered his face was.

"What happened, sir?" he cried.

Nobody answered. The horses moved forward, the gate clanged shut, and then arms reached up for Akitada and peeled him out of the saddle. He tried not to moan with the pain and failed. Muttering under their breaths, they half walked, half carried him inside, where Sadako came and cried out in alarm.

She did not faint, however, being made of the stern stuff of a northern upbringing among warriors and bloodshed. Instead, she got Akitada settled on his bedding. They removed some of his bulkier clothes even though he cursed and begged them to leave him alone. And they brought warm wine and food. He drank but turned down the food. Finally, while listening to Saburo and Tora explain what had happened, he fell asleep.

He woke to a dark room and his wife's warm body curled up next to him. Her breathing was steady and deep. Akitada tried to move his limbs and found he could, a little, but that anything beyond that was absolutely forbidden. So he lay still, enjoying the absence of pain and the sound of Sadako's breathing, and thought. He found he had an amazing clarity of mind after his ordeal.

Kobe's death had been avenged and justice served. That matter was closed.

The same was true for poor, brave Hayashi. Their killer Heishiro had reaped a terrible reward.

But many other problems remained unsolved. They had already begun to be dim memories after the events of the past week. As he lay there, he found that he could concentrate on them and recall details.

Most of all, he faced again his shame for submitting to Morozane's pressure. He had been made to lie about the gross corruption in the transport system. After a long career of the utmost rectitude, trying to live up to the example of his ancestors, all the way back to the great Michizane, he had sold out his honor. He had done so to protect his family, or more accurately, in order to keep his position so that they would not suffer hardship and penury, so that his son might make a good career in government and his daughter marry well. So that his children and Sadako would not suffer the miseries of a punitive banishment to some far distant and unhealthy province. And of course he had also been too cowardly to face such a fate.

Realizing the extent of his failure was more painful than his battered body.

In those silent hours, with only the soft sound of his wife's breathing to support him, Akitada came to a difficult decision.

But there were also other results of this strange mental acuity. He thought of Okura and his dilemma and as he did, a vague idea formed in his mind. It was strange and far-fetched, but utterly possible. He did not yet know what to do about it, but he would do something.

Somewhere in the darkness outside his room, beyond the trees and walls of his home, a night watchman called out the hour. It was close to dawn. Another day lay ahead.

He thought of his daughter who had fallen in love with a man far above her station and who was even now in the care of his sister Akiko. Akiko was trying to find another, more suitable husband for her. Yasuko's disappointment grieved him. Had he made the right decision? Could Akiko be trusted to handle this matter delicately? Probably not, but he trusted his sister enough to know that she would do nothing to hurt his child. He would speak with her when she came, as she surely would when she heard about his injuries.

He sighed. They were in for a difficult time, even if he managed things well.

Morning came and with it the need to move. Sadako helped him to the privy. Sadako brought him tea and gruel and later hot water so he could shave. Sadako combed his hair with gentle hands and tied his topknot. When she was done, he took her hands in his and said, "I love you. Whatever happens, remember I shall always love you."

And Sadako brushed away tears and whispered, "I'm sorry I hurt you."

"It doesn't matter. During the night, I made a decision that may bring us discomfort. I beg your forgiveness for that."

She looked anxious. "What will you do?"

He told her, watching her face. When he was finished, she smiled. "I'm glad," she said.

He next wrote a note to Morozane, excusing himself from his duties for the time being because of his injuries. This he asked Saburo to deliver.

His physician arrived, having been sent for by Sadako. Told about the pain and stiffness, he insisted on inspecting Akitada's back. Both he and Sadako cried out when the undershirt came off. Sadako said, "You're terribly bruised. Your entire back is marked. What happened to you?"

Akitada said nothing.

The physician peered more closely and answered, "It looks like someone gave him a beating. Either that or he fell off his horse and the animal trampled on him."

Akitada snapped, "I don't fall off horses and my horse would never trample on me. Now see what you can give me for the pain so I can get dressed. I have some work to do. I need to be able to sit up and write."

The physician shook his head. "You're mad!"

Akitada decided to plead. "Please humor the madman!"

"You need to lie still. Movement will be very painful."

Akitada muttered with frustration and Sadako said, "Please do as he wishes, doctor. He knows what is best."

The physician humphed and departed after rubbing ointment on Akitada's back and leaving him some pills intended to take the edge off the pain. With some difficulty, Akitada got up, put on his old house robe, and then sat down at his desk to start work.

Shortly before the midday rice, a clerk arrived from Morozane. Akitada took to his bed again, where the clerk verified that the patient was indeed bedridden. He asked some nosy questions about the injury, was shown the plaster on Akitada's head and his black and blue arms. He left satisfied and Akitada returned to his desk. He was pleased to find that it was a little easier to move and that he was no longer as dizzy as he had been in the morning. He spent the rest of this day polishing his report and making a new copy.

But there were interruptions.

Akiko arrived, eager to learn about her brother's latest accident. When she heard what had happened, she became concerned. Typically she rebuked him. "You will kill yourself some day with your determination to right every wrong single-handedly," she said. "Really, Akitada, you're no longer a youngster. You have grown children and soon you'll be a grandfather. It's time to take things easy."

Akitada laughed. "Stop before you have me in my grave and buried."

"The way you go on, that will be next." Akiko sat down and smirked. "Speaking of grandchildren, I also have some news."

Akitada clapped his hands. "One of yours? My congratulations!"

"No. Yours. You have a daughter, or had you forgotten."

She meant Yasuko. Akitada's heart plunged; then he got angry. "So this is what happens when you send a young woman to court. I thought I could trust you. What have you done?"

"Is that the thanks I get? After working a miracle? After plotting and planning for weeks to get your daughter a husband? You might be a little bit grateful when you have done absolutely nothing in that respect."

He made an effort to control his fury. "Tell me!"

"I've managed to negotiate on your behalf, and Yasuko is now betrothed."

Akitada gritted his teeth. "And who is the lucky man you pawned her off on? Against her will, no doubt?"

"Against her will? You must be joking. The girl's been absolutely besotted from the start. And yes, fortunately it all worked out, because I'm sure they met quite frequently over the last few weeks. I wouldn't be surprised to see you holding your first grandchild by this winter."

Akitada took a deep breath. "Who is the man?"

Akiko's face broke into a triumphant smile. "Michiyasu, of course. What were you thinking?"

There was some relief in that, but Akitada shook his head. "Akiko, I told you I cannot pay that dowry."

"The dowry is paid. It was quite modest. Michiyasu is completely taken with Yasuko, and when his father saw how popular she is at court, he allowed his son to make the arrangements." Akiko giggled. "Michiyasu made a very generous settlement on Yasuko and her future children. Toshikage almost lost his voice, he was so startled. Yasuko's a very lucky young woman."

Akitada shook his head, stunned. "I don't know what to say. I suppose if Toshikage negotiated for me, it's all done. What am I to pay?"

"Oh, only what I knew you'd set aside for her."

"Only the small farm and the land in Mikasa Province?"

Akitada had neglected to enrich himself during his governorships, but he had bought some land in Mikasa, his last appointment. He had intended it from the start as Yasuko's dowry, but the income in rice was modest, and her proposed marriage to the son of a high-ranking nobleman, a grandson of an emperor, again shamed him.

Akiko saw his face. "Don't worry. Toshikage gave her a present also."

"But why? You have children of your own."

"Because we love Yasuko like our own. And we love you."

This unexpected answer brought tears to Akitada's eyes. "Thank you both," he said. "I'm in your debt. I'm always in your debt and I'm beginning to think I shall never repay it."

Akiko looked smug. "Not at all. Now tell me what else you've been up to."

279

Akitada repaid her generosity by informing her in detail about the Kobe case as well as the other problems that had been burdening him lately.

She passed over the details of Kobe's murder with a nod and asked, "What about Yukiko? What will you do about her?"

He hesitated. As yet, his suspicion about his former wife's whereabouts was vague and unsupported and confirming it would be extremely difficult. He said, "Okura will have to contact all of her admirers. I'm convinced she's living with one of them."

Akiko said, "Not around here. I have asked everybody and I would've found out."

"Okura will find her. And I have decided to file a new report on the problems in the transport system with the Council of State."

She sat up straight. "What? Akitada, what are you going to do?"

"The report contains evidence of gross malfeasance by the authorities in Otsu and in the capital."

"No! I take it some very important men are involved. You can't. You'll be dismissed. Maybe worse. Akitada, think of your daughter, of her marriage. What if this ruins everything?"

Akitada sighed. "I don't think it will. In any case, I cannot live any longer with the lies Morozane forced me to submit earlier."

"You accuse him also? Does Sadako know about this?"

"Yes."

"You're a fool! I don't know why I try to help you." Akiko rose, her face bitter, and walked out.

33

Moonlight and Boiled Rice

There followed days of intermittent pain. The physician's pills eased it somewhat, but whenever Akitada moved he felt vicious stabs in his back and side that turned into agonizing muscle cramps. He was afraid that the cudgels had broken a rib and fretted at the delay. Now that he had come to his decision, he wanted to see it done and face the outcome. Instead he was housebound and barely able to leave his room to relieve himself.

Sadako was a blessing, but her constant care and worry got on his nerves and he ended up snapping at her to leave him alone. He felt guilty about Akiko. He should have known that she would do her utmost to promote such an advantageous marriage. She had spent most of her adult years lecturing him about his lack of ambition. His marriage to Yukiko had pleased her because it had brought him property and recognition. He had returned Yukiko's dowry when he divorced her, and the misery of that marriage plagued him to this day. He suspected that she had got herself into a particularly unpleasant liaison.

Tora and Saburo came to see him. Both were healing far more quickly than he was. Both were proud of their battles. Saburo showed off a bad bruise across his shoulders with a grin and said that Akitada would soon be back on his feet, too. Akitada doubted it and felt resentful in his pain.

Masashi came with Saburo. He looked happy enough and clung to Saburo's hand the way he had clung to Akitada's not long ago.

Akitada saw it and the longing for a child was there again. And with it a certain amount of self-pity. Not for him the small successes in life. Not for him the consolation that he had saved a child. What lay ahead was more pain and the humiliation of dismissal.

They left and he cursed himself for his weakness.

In the afternoon Yasuko came to see him. She put her head in the door shyly and asked, "Father?"

With an effort he put aside the upsetting matter of dowries and busy-body sisters for a cheerful greeting. "Yasuko, come in! I've been wanting to see you. Are you alone?"

"Yes." She ran in and he saw what a beauty his daughter had become and wondered that he had not noticed. She was also beautifully dressed—trust Akiko to see to that—in iridescent rose colored silk and a white embroidered jacket; she looked like a garden in bloom.

She knelt before him with a rustle of silks and bowed. Then, raising her head, she asked anxiously, "How are you? Aunt Akiko says you've been beaten with sticks until you were near death."

Cudgels, actually.

But he smiled, touched by her concern. "It was nothing and I'm mending. There's just a little stiffness, that's all."

One lies like that, he thought, and maybe it is even true when it is to someone one loves and who looks as happy as a spring morning.

She studied his face. "Are you sure? I've been so afraid."

He felt a sudden warmth and happiness. She did not hate him as the ogre who had forbidden her the man she loved. It was worth everything, even the shame of being too poor and insignificant to give his daughter to an emperor's grandson and of being indebted to Akiko and her husband.

And what did it matter? They loved him. Yasuko and Sadako, and even Akiko. And he knew Tora and Genba cared deeply for him. That was a wealth greater than mere gold.

He said, "Your aunt has told me of your betrothal. You will leave me soon."

"No. Never. I shall be close and I shall come to see you all the time. Oh, Father, isn't it wonderful? Everyone has helped, and Michiyasu has found a house for us. It's in the foothills. He's taken me to see it, and it's really quite large. There are the most beautiful views of the mountains and it's not very far. You and Sadako can come to see us every week."

283

She was bubbling with excitement and happiness. Tears came to his eyes. Ignoring his pain he reached out to pull her close and held her. "I've missed you," he said. "I'm sorry I've hurt you."

She hugged him back. "Never mind. I know why you did it. You'll see, you'll love Michimasu as much as I love him! And perhaps soon you'll come to play with your grandchildren."

There it was again. He released her to look her over. "You are not by chance already . . .?"

His daughter blushed and hid her face. "No, Father. Not yet."

It told him that Michiyasu had lain with her and he suspected that his sister had aided and abetted the affair in hopes of bringing about the marriage. She had taken a chance. Young noblemen did not, as a rule, acknowledge their affairs with proposals of marriage. He felt another stab of anger, but then he realized that his daughter was grown and it had been her decision also. He had no right to be angry with those who loved him.

"Did your aunt come with you?"

"Yes, but she's gone to see Sadako."

So Akiko held a grudge.

"Aren't you happy for me? Is it Michiyasu? Father, he truly is the kindest man. He's so much like you. I know you'll come to love him."

The comparison startled Akitada. He had always felt that nobody was like him; that he was in every way different and odd and that this accounted for the fact that he shied away from social occasions. He said, "I'm happy for both of you and I like Michiyasu. I've always liked him. It was just that I didn't think . . . I worried that he might not hold you in regard when he learned . . . my circumstances."

His daughter laughed. "You're wrong. He admires you. And so does his father."

He did not believe it, but Yasuko did and she was happy, and so he nodded and smiled and said, "I'm very glad."

Yasuko left eventually with Akiko, who did not come in to see him. He ate his evening rice with Sadako who was excited about the upcoming marriage and told him that his sister was certain that the connection would result in advancements and promotions in rank for Akitada.

He knew better.

He was about to spoil whatever benefits might have accrued to him by his declaration of war against some of the most powerful men in government. And perhaps that would end his daughter's happiness.

The night was not comfortable. There was not a single place on his back that did not protest under the pressure of lying on it. He lay awake, occasionally shifting slightly to ease the pain, counting the passing hours by the watchman's cries, and worrying about the future.

He also spent some time thinking how to solve the problem of Yukiko. Since her situation might become entangled with the crimes within the transport system and who knew what other dangerous schemes, he was at a loss how to proceed.

He reminded himself that Yukiko was not his problem any longer. Let her brother search for her, or Okura, or any others of her past lovers. And had her parents been informed? Kosehira and his wife were getting older also and neither was in good health. Yukiko's brother had refused to write to them, afraid that they would set out on the long journey home from their distant province. Such journeys were dangerous, even if a governor like Kosehira could command an entourage. And since Akitada suspected that all was not well with Yukiko's latest adventure, he was also afraid what the knowledge would do to his friend.

But perhaps it was unavoidable. He would have to return to Otsu eventually.

Morning came at long last. He found he had become so stiff that he could not move. Sadako was anxious and wanted to send for the physician again. He forbade it and instead asked her to help him to the bath. Somewhat to his surprise, his ankle was less swollen, though it was still very painful. The trip down the corridor and along the gallery in the back was slow and agonizing, but immersing his beaten and bruised body in the deep tub filled with steaming water proved a perfect curative.

He stayed for a time, luxuriating in the heat of the water and the gradual loosening of the muscles in his back. If he expected to emerge a new man, he was disappointed. His foot still hurt and so did a couple of ribs in his back whenever he moved. But he managed to dress himself. His hair had been matted with blood, but he had removed the bandage and steam and water had dissolved most of the blood and he had rinsed out the rest. Sadako tied his topknot and when he peered into his mirror to shave, he was pleased to see himself looking almost normal again.

He was apologetic about dirtying the bathwater, but Sadako was so pleased to see him on his own two feet and dressed that she laughed and said, "I can skip my bath until tonight."

Again he thought how much his family loved him. They would not stop loving him if he lost everything. And why should he worry about his poverty, or his position at the ministry, or even about his reputation. As the saying went, there would always be moonlight and boiled rice. A man needed nothing else as long as he had his family and his friends.

34

The Audience

The day had begun a great deal better than the previous one, and Akitada, perhaps rashly, decided he was well enough to deliver his report.

In this he was encouraged by the fact that his wife, who, seeing him so much improved, announced that she would go out to shop for Yasuko's wedding clothes and the rolls of silks and brocades that a young bride brought into the marriage. It had been decided—by Akitada's sister and the groom—that Yasuko would enter her new husband's home rather than receiving Michiyasu in her father's house as was customary for the first years of their marriage. Michiyasu's circumstances were much better than Akitada's, and apparently Akiko had felt that adding a new son-in-law with numerous attendants would put too great a strain on

Akitada's household. This was another matter which embarrassed Akitada, but he had decided to suppress such feelings for the sake of his daughter's happiness.

In any case, Sadako was safely out of the house, and Akitada took his carefully written report, wrapped the pages in a piece of figured silk, and tied the package with silk tape.

Then he got his court robe and the small black lacquered silk hat with the two long ribbons from their trunk. The process of getting dressed would be slow and painful. There were many awkward layers to the formal outfit he considered proper for this visit.

Limping out onto the veranda, he called the stable boy and sent him for a sedan chair. He rarely used one, but today's errand and the fact that he could barely move justified the luxury.

Back in his room, he took off his every-day robe and undershirt and began putting on formal court wear. Normally Sadako helped dress him on such occasions, but he had been afraid to tell her of his errand because she would have stopped him.

He began with the silk undershirt, then put over this the *hitoe,* a silk robe. Next came the trousers, very full and of thin silk worn over a starched divided skirt to give them body and width. The trousers and skirt had to be tied with ribbons around his waist and the ankles.

At this point, Akitada was bathed in perspiration and had to lean against a wall to rest.

Eventually, he continued with a thin jacket that had a short train in the back, and followed this with several single layers of silk shirts. Over these, he put a sleeveless vest.

Shoes were next. They were soft, lacquered court shoes worn over white silk socks. His injured foot was only slightly swollen, but the voluminous white silk trousers hampered his movements and bending was extremely painful to his back and ribs. This state of affairs made him doubt he would be able to perform the required obeisance when he was admitted. He rested again, wishing he could simply collapse into the layers of his costume.

Finally, a loose black silk mantle went over all the rest. It was a garment that was quite long and had very wide sleeves that covered his hands. A fine, decorated leather belt held everything in place around his waist. The last touch was the lacquered hat, tied with a black silk cord under his chin.

Akitada was leaning against the wall again when the boy returned to tell him the sedan chair waited outside.

Taking up up his baton and the carefully wrapped documents, he made his way supported by the boy down the steps to the sedan chair and sank into it with a grunt of relief.

"To the *Daidairl* The *Dajokanjo,*" he told the bearers.

The *Dajokanjo* was the building that housed the great Council of State. The prime minister's office was there.

A sedan chair voyage was by no means as comfortable as Akitada had thought. The chair swung and bounced as the bearers ran, turned corners, dodged traffic, or came to sudden stops. Akitada felt shaken and pummeled and climbed out of the conveyance dizzy with pain and misery. He stared up at the gate and the stone steps leading to it. The gate was guarded by uniformed imperial guards. This explained why the chair bearers had decanted him here and were about to depart.

"Wait!" he told them. They set down the chair again and made themselves comfortable on the steps. And Akitada began to climb.

His formal costume with the wide stiff trousers and the dragging train was a problem at the best of times. He was bathed in perspiration again when he reached the top and stood swaying between the stiffly posed guards in their full ochre-colored uniforms and with their bristling array of weapons.

"I'm here to see the prime minister," he informed them when he could catch a breath. They nodded, and he passed through the gate and into the courtyard. It was paved, making progress easier and being kinder to his train. He hated the costume so much that he steadfastly refused to attend nearly all official meetings and observances. This time he had no choice. His report, his honest report, must get into the prime minister's own hands.

The prime minister was Fujiwara Yorimichi, father-in-law of the emperor and grandfather to the crown prince. Akitada knew him from the case of a massacre involving his noble relatives. He had been fair and efficient then, but he had acted out of family interest. Now the situation was very different, almost the exact opposite. Akitada was charging highly placed officials, most likely tied to his Excellency by marriage or past obligations, with gross improprieties. The outcome could very well mean a swift end to his career and the sort of enmity from which his family would not recover.

Never mind!

He looked at the building that contained the great man's office and saw a servant detach himself from the entrance and come swiftly toward him. Akitada limped forward and told him that he wished to see the prime minister.

The servant, wearing sober black and therefore most likely a clerk of some sort, eyed his robes approvingly, then looked at his face. "Are you quite well, my lord?"

"Yes." Akitada brushed away moisture. "A warm day."

The clerk said dubiously, "And who are you, sir?"

Akitada came so rarely to these chambers that he could not expect recognition. "Sugawara Akitada. I last spoke with His Excellency a year ago. In the matter of the massacre at Shirakawa."

"Oh!" The clerk looked at him with more attention. "His Excellency is busy and does not expect you, but I shall tell him you're here." He led the way inside and to a waiting room where already some thirty people of all ranks and professions sat or stood in hopes of being heard. Akitada's heart sank. His report was hardly of sufficient significance to get him a hearing. He was tempted to leave it and make his escape, but there was the danger that it would fall into the wrong hands.

He had mentioned last year's troubles in hopes of gaining access to the prime minister, but now he worried that he had presumed too much. To be sure, their last encounter had ended very well. The prime minister had been affable and expressed gratitude for his service. But he had also attached a reprimand to his praise. And certainly no other acknowledgments had followed since. Akitada had once again been passed over for either promotion or a governorship. As he waited, he became convinced that he had acted rashly and that demanding

293

an audience had been quite wrong. He was sorely tempted to flee.

Just then, however, the clerk returned and gestured to him. Akitada, his heart beating faster, straightened his train and lifted his long trousers so he would not stumble, and followed the clerk. He was conscious of his limp as the other waiting dignitaries watched him curiously and with envy.

The prime minister was pacing in his office, engaged in a discussion with a tall man whose rank colors and robe marked him as a *sangi,* one of the handful of men who directly advised the emperor. Akitada knelt—or rather, he intended to kneel and bow deeply, but his leg and his back simultaneously protested with a blinding pain and he fell headlong with a cry.

The prime minister and his visitor were, not surprisingly, startled by this strange way of approaching them. As Akitada attempted to scrape himself off the floor to apologize, he heard the visitor ask, "Who, for Buddha's sake, is that?"

The prime minister sighed. "It's Sugawara, I think."

Akitada managed to raise himself to his knees, but the pain returned and he became speechless. He tried to bow but gave up when he felt a sudden bout of nausea coming on. He could not, must not, add to this disastrous moment by vomiting at the prime minister's feet. He should not have come.

He swallowed, then croaked, "Forgive me! A recent injury."

The prime minister said, "Oh. Well, don't kneel then. Ono, help him up."

The imperial counselor approached to pull on Akitada's arm and Akitada regained his feet with a gasp.

He thanked him, then made a small bow from the waist toward the prime minister and a second toward the counselor. In an unsteady voice he said, "I should have followed my doctor's advice, but I found it hard to delay this any further."

The prime minister frowned. "What has happened? Why the urgency? Not another massacre, I hope?"

"No, your Excellency. My report—my corrected report—concerns malfeasance."

"What do you mean, 'your corrected report'?"

"I was asked to submit another earlier. I have now corrected several . . . mistakes in it."

The prime minister stared at him for a moment, then snapped, "Surely there was no need for dramatics, Sugawara. Leave the report and go home to tend to your injury."

Akitada felt he had not explained himself well, but the expressions on the two men's faces suggested that he had better obey instantly. He looked around for someone to hand his report to, saw nobody, and bent to place it on the floor at the prime minister's feet. His back protested again and dizziness seized him. He more or less dropped the papers and turned away. The room seemed to move and the floor was rising to meet his feet. He lurched drunkenly to the door and through it into the corridor.

He did not know later how he got back to the sedan chair. Somehow, it deposited him at home where Genba unloaded him and walked him up the stairs to his room.

There Genba removed most of his formal costume before Akitada collapsed on his bedding and fell fast asleep.

35

The Laws of Men

For two days, nothing happened. Akitada spent the first day resting, if it could be called that. He turned the scene in the prime minister's office over and over again in his memory and cringed anew. He expected momentarily to receive the punishment for having dared to make such accusations against officials favored by all, and if not that, then punishment for having submitted a false report.

Sadako had returned from shopping, chattering excitedly about the fabrics she had seen. Akitada had listened with half a mind. There might never be a wedding, and that would be his fault. What price a clean conscience?

The day following his visit to the prime minister, he felt better physically and occupied himself with tidying his books and papers and wondering if he should report for work. He decided against it. If the prime minister had read his report, the news of what it contained might already have reached Morozane. No, he could not face a furious Morozane until he knew what, if any, effect his accusations had had.

Masashi came to keep him company and cheered him a little. He still chattered about the magnificence of Bishamonten and how he thought the fan had brought him luck because he was now living here with Saburo and Master Akitada. Akitada did not remind him of his brother's death. He took out his flute and played a little for the boy.

In the afternoon, Nakatoshi stopped by. He walked into Akitada's study, frowning heavily, and Akitada's heart sank.

"I heard you were attacked," Nakatoshi said. "Why didn't you send for me?"

Akitada's welcoming smile faded. "I'm sorry. A lot has happened."

"How are you?"

"Anxious. I'm waiting to hear my fate."

"Waiting to hear? Why?"

"About my report. I took my report about the transportation business and delivered it into the prime minister's own hands. I couldn't trust it to regular channels. Now I await my fate."

Nakatoshi sat down, shaking his head. "I'm confused. I heard you'd been wounded in an attack."

Akitada blinked. The dangerous report had wiped Kobe's murder and the dreadful drubbing from his mind. "I'm much better. It was just a few thugs with cudgels and my own carelessness."

"They said you were at death's door. And you look pale. And why are you sitting so stiffly? And grimacing every time you move? And why didn't you let me know?"

"I'm sorry, Nakatoshi. It's very kind of you to come. Please forgive me. I've had so much on my mind."

Nakatoshi relaxed a little. "I had not seen you for such a long time. You missed all of our usual meetings and without a word."

More apologies were needed. Eventually, Nakatoshi recalled the report. They were alone, the doors were closed, and Akitada's household seemed occupied elsewhere, so he explained the problem of the two reports, one full of lies, and the other, much longer, full of serious charges. When he was done, Nakatoshi gaped at him.

"And you didn't think to discuss this with me? Clearly I have lost your trust."

"No, Nakatoshi. Kobe's murder happened and my mind was occupied with that. Then the cursed Heishiro attacked me. It was during the night after that attack that I saw what I must do or be lost completely. It did not matter any longer who would be offended and what the outcome would be. I couldn't live with those lies. I had to write a new report, do you see?"

Nakatoshi said nothing for a long time, then he sighed. "Yes. I see. And in any case, it's too late now."

Akitada felt a stab of panic and disappointment. "You disapprove?"

Nakatoshi looked at him sadly. "No. I understand why you did it. It was a question of honor. But I doubt many people would understand, and that's the problem. You'll make some powerful enemies. Again! And your circumstances are due to just that dilemma. If

299

you were a wealthy or powerful man, you wouldn't have to fear for the future. I feel great sadness for my country and my people."

"Come, it isn't so bad. We have the laws. All it requires is for someone to restrain greed. That's all I've been doing."

Nakatoshi sighed again. "What exactly did you say in this report?"

"That I was correcting the mistakes in an earlier report. And this time I cited the reasons for my concern."

Nakatoshi said, "Making a false report means demotion for the reporting official. That's in the Taiho code."

"Yes, I know. 'A false report shall mean demotion for the reporting officer.' But I was ordered to do so by my superior."

"Who will deny it."

"The Taiho code also says 'always correct evil that comes to your attention'."

"Oh, Akitada! They will say you're accusing your superior because you wanted the position yourself. The punishment for false accusations is severe."

Akitada knew it. Feeling suddenly hopeless, he muttered, "I had no choice, Nakatoshi. I couldn't live with myself."

"Well, Morozane cannot be expected to forgive you, but you may have a friend in the prime minister still."

"I was counting on it, but he didn't seem very friendly. Of course, I made a fool of myself while he was talking to one of the imperial advisers. I arrived in full court costume and then fell on my face trying to kneel."

"You did?" Nakatoshi's long face broke into a smile. Then he laughed out loud.

"It wasn't funny!"

"No, I'm sure it wasn't for you, but I think it may have helped you."

Akitada was becoming irritated. "That's ridiculous!"

"Yes, I'm sure it was." Nakatoshi laughed again, then stopped. "Oh, forgive me! That was thoughtless. Come, don't be angry. I'll do anything to help. And I brought some news that may be useful."

Akitada relaxed a little. "I was deeply embarrassed. I shouldn't have tried to deliver the report when I couldn't even walk properly. You may be right. He may have forgiven me my foolish appearance and make allowances for the report. What news?"

"Well, the men you asked about. I talked to more people and checked a few more documents. Since my ministry works on ranks and promotions, I have access to some things others don't see." Nakatoshi smiled.

"You mean things like demerits?"

"Those and even rumors. We have to be very careful that appointments and honors don't become an embarrassment later."

Akitada nodded. "Go on! What did you find? Anything on Morozane?"

"Not Morozane I'm afraid. He's an inept official but a cousin of the prime minister."

Akitada grimaced.

"But the others. Now that was interesting. Fujiwara Yoshinaro, the director of the markets office and Minamoto Norisuke, the new provincial chief of Omi Province." Nakatoshi paused, still smiling.

"Yes. What? One is a thief and the other a murderer. Do you have anything better?"

Nakatoshi sighed. "I doubt you can prove either of your charges. But Yoshinaro left his last post under a cloud. He was serving as temporary governor of Sagami Province. The entire contents of a tribute warehouse were sold there, and Yoshinaro's signature was on the bill of sales. He denied being involved and claimed someone faked his signature and seal."

"The seal too? That was careless of him."

"Yes. My point is that any charges you made against him are likely to be taken seriously."

Akitada nodded. "Yes, that's good. What about Minamoto?"

"Ah! Nothing about malfeasance, I'm afraid, but some very unpleasant tales about his sexual tastes."

"That won't impress the court much," Akitada said with a snort.

"Well, it might if it turns murderous."

"He kills women?"

"Accidents will happen." Nakatoshi grimaced. "Mind you, nothing was proved, but a woman died at his family home in Izu Province. Apparently, he had invited a number of entertainers to a party and one of them ended up dead."

Akitada frowned. "Clearly that was some time ago and a long way from the capital, and no doubt the case was never associated with him personally."

"Well, it wasn't proved, but a number of other women have since complained that Minamoto Norisuke enjoys inflicting pain on his partners. Whips have been mentioned, and one or two women have ended up scarred. He tied them up and marked them with his sword. Apparently he likes to see them bleed."

Akitada stared at his friend. "Dear gods! Why is such a man free to practice his repulsive perversions?"

"Norisuke commands only a small army in Otsu, but he has large military resources in eastern and northern Japan. The government expects to go to war with the northern barbarians again shortly. He requested an appointment in the capital, and his appointment to Otsu was the response. He's being groomed to lead the government forces, but they did not want him too close to the court."

Akitada thought of his visit and the image of the warrior Bishamonten in Norisuke's reception room. He said bitterly, "I see. Well, it's always good to know one's enemy."

"Yes. But consider, the gossip about him will be known at court."

"Yes, thank you. I expect to hear soon. Wish me luck!"

It was an unfortunate remark. Akitada remembered Masashi's unlucky brother who had believed in Bishamonten, and all the other divinities of good fortune and had reaped death instead.

But Nakatoshi's information had given him some hope that his report would at least not be used against him.

The following day brought the summons.

36

The Summons

Akitada had barely bathed, shaved, and put on his ordinary robe, when the first visitor arrived. It was one of Morozane's clerks who wanted to know when he expected to return to work. Akitada, who was well enough, promised to report to the minister later that day. The clerk left without giving any hint about Morozane's mood.

The second visitor was from the prime minister's office. He was polite but businesslike when he asked if Akitada was well enough to see the prime minister. The question was accompanied by a sharp inspection of Akitada's appearance. Akitada assured him that he was better and asked when he should be there.

"At the hour of the ox. His Excellency asks that you not trouble with formal court robes and that you dispense with kneeling."

Akitada flushed. By now everyone would know about his embarrassing fall at the prime minister's feet. It would make an excellent joke in all the ministries and bureaus. He thanked the official and walked him out.

The time chosen was right after the midday rice, but Akitada had no appetite for this meal. He changed into a robe of brown silk and a coat of brown and black brocade. Instead of calling a sedan chair, he walked. His foot was nearly back to normal, and he hoped the exercise in the fresh air would calm his agitation.

This time he was expected and, for better or worse, given no time to collect his thoughts or add to his panic. He was shown into the prime minister's private study. The prime minister was alone. The room was small and under the eaves. The doors were closed and a number of candles burned on tall stands. Document boxes were stacked everywhere, but the *tatami* mats were thick and of a shiny newness.

Akitada automatically attempted to kneel, but the great man called out, "Don't!" and then added, "I don't enjoy officials groveling before me."

Akitada flushed again, but he started to feel resentful, so he bit his lip and said nothing.

"Can you sit or do you prefer standing?"

"Either, your Excellency."

"Let us sit then."

They sat down on silk cushions on either side of the prime minister's desk. Akitada saw his report resting on it. The prime minister said, "I have read your report. You know, of course, that most of this is empty charges with no proof."

"Yes, sir."

"In other words, you merely wished to tell me that you had been forced to submit a false report by your superior."

Akitada swallowed. "No, sir. I began an investigation and found evidence of theft and misappropriation. When I reported these to Minister Morozane, he ordered me to submit a report that cleared all the persons involved. I obeyed because I was afraid of losing my position. I beg your pardon for this offense. I submitted the new report directly to your Excellency to share my concerns and to present the correct version of my investigations. I'm in hopes that my years of service might gain me a favorable hearing in spite of my offense."

The prime minister stroked his chin and was silent for a while. Then he said, "I see. It's an unlikely tale, but you never do things properly."

Akitada said nothing. Was he now going to be excused on the grounds that he was so inept and odd an official that this was just another example of erratic behavior? If so, he would accept the slight gratefully.

But the prime minister said, "I have brought you to this private meeting to get to the bottom of this matter." He tapped Akitada's report. "If your charges are correct, then it will be best not to announce them to the world too soon. I take it that was why you decided to bring your report to me directly in that irregular manner?"

Akitada felt himself flushing again. He bowed in response.

"Well then, let us start with the matter of Otsu. You seem to think that the newly appointed provincial chief is in some way involved in diverting tribute shipments at the harbor of Otsu?"

Akitada took a deep breath. "My retainers are skilled in observing people's behavior in crowded places like markets and harbors. I sent them to the Otsu harbor, and they reported seeing soldiers wearing the uniforms of the imperial guard supervising the unloading of a tribute ship. Their uniforms proved to be faked copies, and they returned later to the compound belonging to Minamoto Norisuke."

"It would be expected that imperial guard members would supervise imperial tribute. How certain are you that your men did not make a mistake. Not all guard uniforms are the same shade."

"One of my retainers has a son who serves in the guard. He is certain."

"Hmm. You go on to say that Norisuke's people guard his property and use violence against trespassers. What do you mean by that?"

"One of my men observed the capture of a boy who had climbed over the wall. He later found the boy dead inside the compound."

The prime minister frowned. "Was the death investigated?"

"No. There was little point in calling the police. The body would have disappeared by then. Apparently dead people wash up frequently in Otsu."

"Well, clearly you have no proof, just the word of your man, who appears to have entered the Minamoto residence illegally. I would caution you against bringing such shocking accusations against a man who has devoted his life and those of his followers to serving his emperor and this nation. The punishment for empty charges of this kind is death."

Akitada swallowed. It was true. He knew his report could be construed as a false accusation. As a collection of false charges. If it had fallen into the wrong hands, the story would have become known and he would surely have been arrested. He said, "My man did not expect to find evidence of a murder, most likely committed by servants or soldiers belonging to the place. He entered the compound to look for tribute goods intended for the court."

"Did he find them?"

"No. He was discovered and had to flee."

"Again, you have no proof and your methods of investigation are highly questionable. Let us move on to your observation of the transport of tribute goods on the highway between Otsu and the capital."

"The tribute goods that are unloaded in Otsu are hauled by local day laborers, some of them harbor workers. They are apparently supplied by authorities in Otsu and in the capital. Their loyalty is to whoever pays them. Some of them said they are employed by the left market. The goods I saw were to be delivered to the left market. This made it likely that goods are pilfered and diverted on a regular basis."

The prime minister nodded. "Probably. But it is not proof that they act on orders from the noblemen you accuse."

Akitada flinched at the word "accuse." He was beginning to fear that this conversation was headed directly toward an official charge of "false accusations." He said stiffly, "I reported on these matters because I was investigating rumors that corruption was present in the transport services of Otsu. It was a preliminary report. I did not have the staff or the powers to investigate fully and I was recalled before I could finish."

"Yes, yes. But all this is exceedingly flimsy. And that brings me to the charge that Fujiwara Yoshinari, the new director of the markets office, is not only not carrying out his duties but is building his new residence with stolen lumber. Can you really support that?"

"I visited the markets office, where a drunken clerk was the only one in charge. The clerk told me that Yoshinari does not come to the office and that their record keeping is minimal. As you know, I observed timbers that were marked for the imperial court at Yoshinari's construction site."

Silence.

Akitada glanced anxiously at the prime minister. He was grimacing and gazing into the distance. It was almost over. He was, no doubt, pondering how to phrase his decision.

Akitada had gambled everything to preserve his honor, his reputation, his face. Perhaps Akiko had been right. Perhaps he had been a fool.

As the silence lasted, Akitada shifted nervously and wished it were over.

Finally, the prime minister said, "I don't need to tell you that your actions in this matter have been extraordinary and quite shocking."

Akitada bowed his head again. "I know, your Excellency. I regret having had to report such problems."

"But you persist in your charges?"

Would they really try him for making false charges? Men like Norisuke and even Yoshinari would find it easy to deny them. His fate depended on the man who frowned at him. He took a deep breath and said, "Yes."

"I see. Well, I agree something must be done. Too many tribute and tax shipments have disappeared or arrived depleted. It causes problems. We accuse the provinces and their governors, and they bring witnesses that prove they are innocent. However, you are in no position to investigate the entire transport system. The Central Affairs Office will handle that together with the Bureau of Taxation." The prime minister paused.

The relief was dizzying. He was not being sacrificed to government interests and family ties. Instead, some good would come of this. He was filled with immense gratitude and with pride in his government.

The prime minister regarded Akitada thoughtfully. "There remains the matter of murder in Otsu. And clearly you're the man for that. You may not be able to lay the death of a vagrant boy at Norisuke's door, but I want you to look into his activities. Mind you, I don't want the Minamoto clan insulted, so step carefully. If Norisuke is in fact guilty of any outrages, I'll deal with it personally."

Akitada was deeply dismayed. How was he to enter the Minamoto stronghold to ask questions about a child's death without offending Norisuke?

The prime minister, who had apparently expected an enthusiastic answer, pursed his lips. "Are you well enough to start or not?"

"I'm well enough to travel," Akitada said.

A frown. "Hmm. You may rely on the current governor. I know him well. He's my cousin Sanenari. Well then, good luck!"

Akitada bowed and left the office in a daze.

37

Lucky Gods

They returned to Otsu two days later. The weather was clear and city and lake were unchanged, but nothing else seemed the same. Akitada mourned Kobe and had nearly lost his life, Tora had become frail and moody, and Saburo was the father of a son.

As their lives had undergone subtle but profound changes during the preceding month, each approached the return to Otsu with a very different attitude.

Tora caused Akitada new concerns. His moods alternated between a desperate desire to live or die by the sword and the conviction that he would never fight again and would die before year's end. His recent battle and old wounds were responsible for this, and Akitada had been so concerned that he had almost left him behind. Only the conviction that this would cast his old friend into utter despair had changed his mind.

Saburo was not enthusiastic about their new assignment. He longed to be at home with Masashi and did not relish dangerous spying missions involving the murderous Minamoto Norisuke.

And Akitada? He was nearly healed and had salvaged his career, but he was now faced with an impossible assignment.

As they paused to gaze down at the placid, blue lake stretching toward far distant blue shores, Tora said, "I wonder what Master Cricket is up to."

Saburo snorted. "Him again?"

Tora scowled. "We need luck."

Saburo said, "Pray to Ebisu. He has special powers in Otsu. They're having a big festival for him this week. Come to think of it, it was at Ebisu's shrine that I found Masashi. That was very lucky for me."

Akitada reminded him, "Ebisu brought no luck to Masashi's brother."

Saburo bit his lip. He had been responsible for Kai's ill-advised visit to the Minamoto compound. He said, "Kai believed in a Bishamonten who wasn't real. He was an evil human being, even if the boys thought of him as a god."

"And so what happens to your faith in the gods of good luck?" Akitada asked.

Tora said, "Better a wise man. They know what's what. They can tell the difference between a false god and a real one."

Saburo laughed. "That old man was just another fake. You said he looked like Jurojin with his long

314

beard and bald head. I bet he played a part, just like Lord Norisuke does."

It was strange to think how many times luck, both good and bad, had played part in their recent lives. Akitada thought of Norisuke and his large painting of Bishamonten. What did Norisuke believe in? Clearly martial strength and wealth mattered most to him. His position in Otsu and his reputation at court were both based on them. Martial strength, his control over warriors and allies, made him a desirable ally and good fortune was essential to maintaining his position. Norisuke's military talent was well attested, but his luck was not. Where did his alleged wealth come from? Maintaining armies was extraordinarily expensive. And without his armies he was no more than just another provincial lord. Akitada said, "There is no point in praying to the gods of luck. Fate is with heaven."

Tora agreed. "That's a fact. It's the Way of Heaven that brings Good Fortune. If you do what's right, heaven will help you. That's why we won and Heishiro lost."

Akitada smiled. Humans lived to create gods. It was the way they explained what happened to them. He wondered if one could destroy men like Norisuke by taking away what they believed in. Alas, wishful thinking would not help. What lay ahead would require an enormous amount of luck.

They stayed again with Yukiko's brother. Arihito's reception seemed cool. When they were alone, Akitada asked him, "Any news of Yukiko?"

"No! I told you, we have nothing to say to each other. And could you please inform Okura of it? The man shows up every week to ask for news."

"He's also been to see me. He's surprisingly attached to her."

Arihito snapped, "She brings shame on us all whether she's around or not. I think you would have more reason than anyone to resent her."

"Arihito, I accept that you're angry with your sister, but I think she may be in danger. Have you informed your father?"

Arihito snorted. "Nonsense. And I told you I don't want him bothered."

Arihito was becoming hostile. Akitada said, "Well, perhaps we'd better seek refuge elsewhere."

This brought instant apologies and the subject of Yukiko was dropped. They discussed Minamoto Norisuke instead.

"People admire him," Arihito said. "He's young and a fine soldier. The nation needs men like him. The people here look up to him."

"Do they? I came to find out just what he's been up to."

Arihito stared at him. "You think he's done something illegal? Who says so? You can't believe court gossip. What do those spoiled bureaucrats know of war?"

Akitada himself was part of the bureaucracy. What was more, he knew that Arihito had not excelled during his military service. Yet he was a capable landowner and managed his father's estates well. So he said nothing and changed the subject again.

The next day, Akitada paid the governor a visit. Fujiwara Sanenari, the prime minister's cousin and also a cousin of Akitada's friend Kosehira, was younger than both and a pleasant, smiling man who resembled the portly Kosehira more than he did the prime minister.

He received Akitada with such flattering enthusiasm, that he felt guilty for not having called on him before. It seemed the prime minister's letter had preceded Akitada, and Sanenari did not waste time.

"I'm glad you're here. Norisuke is a thorn in my side. So many complaints, so many charges, and my hands have been tied. I have twenty men at my disposal in the provincial guard; he has two hundred. And as there never is any proof and people refuse to testify against him, I haven't been able to confront him directly. I feel like a coward, Akitada, but I can't make war in Otsu. He'd win easily and the blood would run in the streets. Find me proof, and I'll investigate."

Akitada was mildly surprised. He had not expected to find an official with a conscience and a will to protect his people. He wished again that he had been less cynical, and had consulted Sanenari on his last visit. It would have been a courtesy and he might have learned more from him than from Arihito, whose mind had never been on matters of administration, and who had never had a desire to follow in his father's footsteps in administration.

He tried to make up for his oversight by sharing freely what he had learned and how he had come by the information. Sanenari's eyes grew round when he heard about Saburo's discovery of the dead boy in the Minamoto compound.

"A child!" he breathed in horror.

"To be fair, the boy was killed by Norisuke's guards."

"But he condoned it. And he didn't report it."

"And now we have no proof. I suspect that Saburo would not be believed. He had climbed the wall like a thief and his background as a discredited former spy in the service of the monks on Mount Hiei will not help either."

"Oh, no. They hate the Mount Hiei faction here. What to do?"

"What about other murders?"

Sanenari spread his hands. "Unsolved. No witnesses. Or people won't talk."

Akitada had expected it. "Well," he said, "I must go to see him again. Perhaps I'll think of something. Do you have any information about his place?"

"Ah! Yes, that I can do. We have the plans of the compound and you can talk to the man who supervised the construction." Sanenari smiled a little. "My father built the place and my brother sold it to Norisuke last year. He may have made some changes, but I think you'll find most of the information correct."

It was a little bit of luck, though Akitada had no idea how useful it would be. "Would it be possible to get Norisuke and his military contingent out of the compound?"

Sanenari chuckled. "For a little breaking and entering, you mean?"

Akitada flushed. "We are to produce evidence. The evidence is inside and well-guarded. I doubt we could get admission for an official investigation."

"True. Well, we have a holiday coming up. The local fishermen perform their annual rites praying for good fortune."

"Yes. To the god Ebisu."

"Well, him, too, but mainly the ceremony is in the Buddhist tradition and to the god of the lake."

"Is it a big occasion?"

"Oh, yes. The local people love it. There will be entertainments, and people come from everywhere."

"I suppose you could invite him and his followers? To keep order?"

"The police and the provincial guard do that, but Norisuke has been invited to join the procession and he's offered to perform feats of military skill with his men. He likes that sort of thing. It should empty the compound for an hour or so."

"He has no family here? His wives and children?"

"I believe they are at home in his province. I've wondered about it, but I think he finds enough courtesans in the capital."

"That will be helpful."

They smiled at each other.

In the tribunal archives, Akitada sat with Tora and Saburo bent over the plans of the Minamoto compound.

"There." Saburo pointed. "That's where Kai and I climbed over the wall, and that must be the warehouse I saw. Next to it is the stable. And this enclosure is where I found the poor boy's body. After that things got hazy. I was upset and mostly wanted to find a way out. Somehow I ended up in the garden. And back here is the small gate I climbed."

Akitada leaned closer. "I think we must try to get in that way."

Tora said, "Nothing to it. We'll force the lock. Why didn't you just unlock it and walk out, Saburo?"

"It's a lock with a key. There was no key." He paused. "Besides, they were after me and I didn't have time."

"It doesn't matter," Akitada said. "It will be the best way in or out. I'm not climbing any walls."

"Where is Bishamonten's treasure, do you think?" Tora asked.

"Most likely any gold is in the main house. Other goods will be in the storehouses. Saburo will look for those."

"And what will I do?" Tora asked.

"You'll stand guard. The compound won't be empty. Norisuke will leave some servants behind even if he takes his small army."

Over the next few days, they spent more time planning and refining their plan, but on the morning before the festival, Akitada paid Norisuke another visit.

He found him exercising some of his men. Akitada had been admitted by a servant, who had announced him and then taken him to a large space behind the stables. Norisuke clearly did not mind showing off. He waved and flashed Akitada a broad smile from horseback. He and his warriors were dressed in full armor as they circled a target at a full gallop while loosing arrows at it. Norisuke excelled at this sport, and his men were well-trained.

When they were done, Norisuke dismounted and walked to Akitada, smiling broadly. "Sorry, Sugawara. You caught me at my practice. I don't have the leisure you lucky officials enjoy. You're back for a visit to our beautiful lake, I see." There was something rather odd about the way Norisuke regarded Akitada, smiling a little as if amused by something.

Akitada bowed. "Too much good luck invites trouble we officials always think."

Norisuke laughed. "My thought also. You must be prepared to face your fortune or guard it. Let's go into the house. Exercise always makes me thirsty."

Servants came to take Norisuke's helmet, his purple-silk-trimmed armor, his bow, and quiver.

Norisuke, in his brocade hunting suit, strode energetically toward the main house. Akitada followed, both impressed and revolted by the man.

They sat again in the reception room under the large painting of Bishamonten. Akitada noticed that Norisuke's mustache was trimmed to match that of the god in the picture. The resemblance was striking.

He was in high good humor. "You admire my scroll? I commissioned it. My family prizes good luck in battle."

"So I hear. Do you expect to fight many battles here in Otsu?"

Norisuke's eyes narrowed. "Am I still a suspect? I was told by your superior the matter was settled."

Akitada nodded. "You have heard already? Indeed, Morozane signed off on the report himself."

Norisuke relaxed. "Ah. It's good of you to come and tell me. Well then, you'll be here for the festival tomorrow? You mustn't miss it. My men and I shall give a demonstration of our skills. You saw our practice earlier. You will come, won't you?"

"The governor was good enough to invite me. Will your family attend?"

"No. My wives and children remain at the family home in Izu Province. A warrior cannot be tied down by family."

So Sanenari had been right. It would make matters easier. With no small children to look after, most of the servants would attend the festival.

They exchanged a few more pleasantries, but Norisuke had lost interest in his visitor. Akitada glanced once more at the scroll of Bishamonten and took his leave.

38

The Festival

The day dawned clear, and when Akitada stepped out on the veranda to gaze at the lake and the distant horizon, he found that ships and boats were already gathering for the festival. Not only would there be religious services at the shore, but also on boats. And fishing contests took place on the waters while the military competitions and acrobatics entertained people in town.

He knew that Norisuke's warriors would demonstrate their skills right after the midday banquet. That was the time when he and his companions would break into Norisuke's compound to find evidence of crimes. But before and after he must make an appearance at the festival. The governor had invited him and other dignitaries to the banquet. Norisuke would be there and take note of his presence. Akitada planned to take his leave unobtrusively as soon as it was over.

As it turned out, it was Norisuke who left the banquet early to change into his armor. They had been seated on either side of the governor, and Sanenari now turned to Akitada with observations about the festival and Norisuke's role in it. Akitada was impatient but it was impossible to leave. The governor's comments shifted to Norisuke's enjoying a particular house of assignation in the capital. Sanenari clearly took an interest in such matters. The information was interesting, but Akitada was eager to leave. Tora and Saburo would already be waiting. He finally excused himself by claiming he needed some fresh air to clear the *sake* fumes from his head and hurried as quickly as he could to the Minamoto compound and its small rear gate.

Saburo and Tora were waiting in the quiet, empty side street. You could hear distant sounds of the festival from the direction of the town and the lake shore. Tora and Saburo wore dark clothes, and Akitada slipped off his outer robe of green brocade, leaving it in a bush, and then tucked his silk trousers into his boots. They all had short swords stuck through their belts. Saburo used a set of lock picks on the gate, and they walked in. The garden lay deserted. Tall trees hid most of the buildings with only the curved, tiled roof of the main house showing. It was silent except for festival noise and bird song.

"All seems well," Akitada said. "Saburo, you go and examine the storehouses. Be careful. There will be some people about."

Tora laughed. "I bet they're in the kitchen, stuffing themselves and guzzling Norisuke's wine."

"Maybe so, but we cannot risk discovery. I'm going to look into Norisuke's private study. Tora will watch from the front veranda. Report when you are done."

Saburo left, moving quickly and silently through the trees, and Akitada and Tora walked toward the main house. As they skirted a shuttered pavilion, Akitada stopped. He listened, then walked around the corner to look at the door.

"What's the matter?" Tora asked softly.

"These would be Norisuke's women's quarters."

"I thought you said he has no women here."

Akitada stared at the door. "I wonder." He shook his head. "Never mind. We're going to the main house first."

They walked cautiously, but the garden lay deserted and the only sounds were made by birds and the distant festivities. Somewhere people were shouting and applauding. When they reached the veranda, Akitada said, "You go around to the right. I'll go left. We'll make sure there are no guards on the veranda and have a look at the front courtyard."

Akitada moved silently along the veranda. He heard no sounds from inside. Before turning the corner, he looked around it, and when he reached the front, he was doubly careful, because a guard might have been posted there. But he saw no one until Tora's head appeared at the far corner. Tora pointed at the front gate and there, at a safe distance, sat a group of guards. They appeared to be shooting dice. Akitada gestured to Tora to return to the back of the house.

There they opened one of the doors and went inside, making a rapid search of the rooms. They were luxuriously furnished with thick, new *tatami* mats and hanging shades trimmed with brocade but otherwise held no interest. Norisuke's study was a businesslike room with a desk and writing utensils, as well as a desk for a scribe. Some silk cushions lay about for visitors. The most interesting object was an impressive chest of lacquered wood with ornamental iron bands and a large lock.

Tora's face lit up. "I bet that's where his gold is. We need Saburo to open it."

Akitada shook his head. "Gold is gold. Unless he stored it with identifying marks, it won't do us much good." He turned to a stack of ledgers. "This may be better." After a look, he selected some pages from the most recent one and put them inside his robe. "Come along! We don't have much time." They finished with the rest of the house quickly and emerged on the rear veranda just as Saburo appeared.

"I couldn't open the lock to the small storehouse," he said, "but the stables contain some contraband horses. I found saddles and bridles embroidered with the imperial chrysanthemum." He held up a bridle.

Akitada nodded. "Excellent. Anything else?"

"In the big storehouse behind the kitchen are bales of silk. Why would Norisuke need that much silk unless he plans to become a silk merchant? It was dark and I couldn't read the marks on them, but I think they are from tax shipments."

Taxes could be paid in rice, the most common form, or in other products of a province, such as silk, gold, horses, and other useful and negotiable items.

Akitada said, "Most likely this is part of what his people have unloaded in the harbor. Good work."

Tora grabbed his arm suddenly. "Hush! Listen!" They listened but heard nothing. Tora said, "It's too quiet. I think Norisuke's performance is over. We need to get out."

Akitada agreed. They should have been more careful. It might well be too late already. But there was one more thing he had to do and he preferred to do it alone. He said, "You two go ahead. I want to have a quick look at the women's pavilion. I'll meet you outside."

They resisted, but he was firm. "No. It won't take a moment to have a look."

As they were hurrying away, Tora protested again, "There's nothing there. It's shut up."

"They may have left some maids," Saburo said. "I thought I saw a female from a distance."

Akitada snapped, "You could have mentioned that earlier."

"I wasn't sure. It might have been a blue door curtain."

They parted on the gallery. Tora and Saburo went down into the garden and toward the back gate, while Akitada hurried along the open gallery that led to the shuttered pavilion. He had noticed earlier that its door was barred from the outside. All was still silent as he unbarred the door. It opened and he stepped into a dim interior. At first he saw only tumbled bedding and a clothes rack with women's robes draped over it. He was about to look behind it, when he heard a rustling and a soft moan. The sounds came from the far corner.

"Who is there?" he asked.

The answer was choking cry. He went toward it quickly and found a naked woman tied by her wrists to a hook in the wall above her head. Her back was toward him, and her long black hair was gathered with a white

327

silk ribbon stained with blood. Her back was lacerated with the stripes of a brutal whipping, and the blood-caked whip lay on the floor at her feet.

He gasped, recalling the ugly stories his friend had told him about Norisuke's treatment of prostitutes. Using his short sword, he quickly cut the thick ropes that held the woman's wrists. She collapsed to the floor with a whimper. Blood had spattered the wall and blood covered her back, hips, and thighs. It had run down her legs and dripped on the floor.

He asked, "Are you able to stand?"

She did not answer but curled into herself without turning her head.

He went to get one of the gowns from the clothes rack and covered her with it. "If you can walk," he said, "I'll take you out of here, away from this place, but we must hurry. They're coming back."

She still did not answer. A shudder ran over her and she pulled the gown closer. "It would have to be you," she finally said.

The voice was familiar. The bitter tone more so. But Akitada had already known. Had suspected for days now. It had been a logical explanation: she had met another man, a new lover; someone who was all the things neither Akitada nor Okura had been; someone who lived in or near Otsu, for that was where she had built her house for their secret meetings; someone who could have employed the servant couple to lie if her brother or anyone else asked questions about her.

Yukiko.

He had found the lost Yukiko— found her in the house of the heroic Bishamonten himself. And she had unwittingly become his latest victim.

He felt a great pity wash away the years of resentment and anger and gently put his arms around her to lift her up. "Oh, Yukiko!" he murmured and stroked her hair, breathing the remembered scent, holding the familiar body in his arms..

She burst into tears and clutched at him.

At that moment he heard quick, heavy steps approaching along the gallery that linked the pavilion to the main house. The door flew open.

Norisuke stood there, still in his magnificent display armor with the golden helmet he had worn for his performance at the festival. His clothes were red brocade and this armor was threaded with red silk. With the light behind him, he glowed, a figure at once strikingly beautiful and unreal.

But then his hand went to the long sword at his side, his eyes flashed, and the image disintegrated into fury.

Akitada released Yukiko and stood before her. His hand gripped his own sword, his pitifully short sword never intended to do battle with a man like Norisuke.

Norisuke raised his weapon, ready to slash at Akitada's head, then paused. His eyes went past Akitada to the cowering Yukiko. A nasty, sly look passed over his face.

"What's this?" he asked. "A reunion with a spouse? What are you doing in my women's quarters, Sugawara? What happened here?"

His attempt at innocent surprise failed. Akitada said coldly, "I came to release Lady Yukiko. I'm certain her family will demand satisfaction for your treatment of her."

"Yukiko?" Norisuke asked. "What happened to you, my love?"

She clutched at Akitada for support and spat, "You bastard! I'll see you dead!"

Norisuke chuckled. "Such language from a highborn lady! Well, what are we to do about this, Sugawara? You broke into my house. In fact, you look more like a robber than a nobleman with that little sword in your hand."

Akitada put his free arm around Yukiko to steady her. "We shall leave. I doubt you'll risk harming either one of us."

Yukiko freed herself. "No! Kill him, Akitada! He raped me and he beat me and kept me his prisoner here. He's treated me like a slave, like one of his whores, the animal. Kill him now!"

Akitada ignored her. He knew he had little chance of winning an unequal sword fight and killing Norisuke was definitely not part of his assignment, though he yearned to do so. His short sword was no match for the reach of Norisuke's long one and Norisuke was much younger and a trained soldier. His best hope was to bluff their way out. He asked Yukiko, "Can you walk or shall I carry you?"

She stepped away and glared at him, her face as unmarked and beautiful as ever, her voice filled with hate. "You're a coward, Akitada! You've always been a coward! Give me your sword!"

Norisuke laughed.

She snatched at Akitada's sword hand and the blue silk gown he had draped about her slipped from her shoulder and revealed a breast that was bruised, bloody and covered with teeth marks.

Sickened, Akitada turned to Norisuke. "I'll make you regret what you did! And you'd better be prepared to face the wrath of her family."

Norisuke laughed again. "Face it, Sugawara, your ex-wife is a whore at heart. I enjoyed breaking her in. You missed your chance there."

The confrontation had been inevitable all along and Yukiko was about to be the death of him. He gripped the sword more tightly and stepped away from her. "Let her go. This is between us."

Norisuke shook his head. "No. She's made her choice. And you'll die here. No one will know what happened to you."

Yukiko screamed, "I'll never be yours, you devil!"

Norisuke looked at her coldly. "You won't be missed either, Yukiko. Nobody else will look for you here. Your bodies will never be found."

Then he attacked.

Akitada gave Yukiko a hard push. She fell with a cry as he moved forward to meet Norisuke. The long sword hissed toward his head. He ducked and came up again to strike at Norisuke's wrist hoping to disarm him.

The only way to fight a man with a longer sword was to get close enough to use a short weapon. It was a deadly move. If Norisuke corrected quickly enough, it would all be over. As it was, Norisuke did not expect it, and Akitada might have succeeded, but his body had not had time to heal completely and the sudden extreme movement sent a searing pain across his chest and back that took the strength out of his arm. His blade did no more than brush the other man's gloved hand.

Norisuke jumped away, laughed, and came again, this time slashing at Akitada's waist to forestall another close encounter. Akitada jumped to one side, slashing at Norisuke's leg as the other man passed. He managed to draw blood, but his opponent seemed unaware of the wound, turned and came again, swinging his long sword back-handed. Akitada flung up his weapon to block the attack and moved in again. His own sword quickly sliced upward and severed the cord holding Norisuke's helmet. The helmet slipped forward, blinding his opponent briefly before he tore it off and tossed it away.

But Akitada had gained a moment and now struck Norisuke across the face with the flat side of his sword as hard as he could. Blood spurted, spraying Akitada's face, and Norisuke swayed and choked. Akitada kicked him in the crotch and Norisuke screamed as Akitada's left fist rammed into his temple. The great warrior fell.

Akitada picked up the long sword and bent over him. He was unconscious but breathing. Bubbles of blood popped from his nostrils and his face was a bloody mess. Akitada straightened slowly.

"Is he dead?" Yukiko asked.

"No."

She stamped her foot. "Kill him! Kill him now! Use his sword! Quick! Before someone comes."

Akitada pushed his own sword through his belt and wiped Norisuke's blood from his face. "You'll have to walk," he said coldly. "Cover yourself better!"

She stared at him. "You're not going to kill him after what he did to me?"

"No."

She dashed past him to reach for Norisuke's sword. He caught her and dragged her out of the pavilion and into the garden where he tossed Norisuke's sword into a shrub. She fought him, crying, "Coward! Let me go!"

He snarled, "Shut up, if you want to save your life!"

That silenced her, and they reached the rear gate safely. He opened it and pushed her through. Tora stood outside and caught her.

39

Resolutions

They walked as quickly as they could to the Fujiwara residence. Yukiko was shaky, but she took one glance at the crowded streets and stopped to slip the robe on properly and hold it closed about her. Her hair was still in a wild tangle, but her beautiful face was unmarked, and as Akitada walked with one arm around her, they attracted admiring and amused glances.

She held herself stiffly and was silent. Disapproval emanated from her and Akitada reflected that he had once again proved he was a coward.

They did not speak until she realized they were going to her father's house and stopped. "I will not see Arihito!" she said through clenched teeth.

Akitada asked, "What do you propose to do?"

"Take me to an inn or a temple."

"There are no rooms anywhere because of the festival."

Her face fell. "Then take me to the capital with you. Rent some horses."

"You're in no shape to ride a horse. And you forget I have a wife again."

She flinched, then raised her chin defiantly. "In that case, just leave me here. I don't need you. I can fend for myself."

"No." Akitada took her arm again, with a firm grip, and walked her to the gate of her father's home. Tora and Saburo followed, rolling their eyes.

Arihito came when they had already reached the reception room. By then his sister had sunk down on a cushion. She was pale but had not so much as whimpered though she must be in pain. They stood around her. Her brother's face was both shocked and disgusted. "Where was she?" he demanded.

Yukiko glared up at him. "A fine greeting, brother!"

"You don't deserve better. Akitada's been searching high and low for you and so has that Okura fellow. Where have you been?"

"What do you care?"

"You're right. I don't care. You've shamed us enough."

Akitada cleared his throat. "She was locked up in Norisuke's place. He had abused her."

Arihito paled and looked more closely at his sister. "Abused her?"

Akitada pulled Yukiko's gown off her shoulders, revealing the bloody stripes of the whip. She snatched it back up angrily. Her brother gasped. "Dear gods!" His voice broke. "He whipped her? Oh, Yukiko! What happened?" At his concern, her face crumpled and Arihito went to kneel before her with open arms. She crept into them and wept, murmuring and hiding her face against his chest.

They waited in silence while Arihito made soothing noises and she clutched at him, bawling. In the end, Arihito murmured something to her and then rose to call for servants. An elderly maid came and Yukiko meekly left with her.

When they had gone, a white-faced Arihito turned to Akitada. "Did you kill him?"

"No. It would have caused trouble."

"I don't understand you. Though it's true, she's not your concern any longer. I'll kill him. He cannot be allowed to live after this."

Akitada winced. "No. Leave him to his punishment. Norisuke will be dismissed and return to his home."

"How so? You cannot tell anyone what happened to my sister."

"The governor and the prime minister will have to know or Norisuke will make trouble."

Arihito clenched his fists. "It will shame us. It will shame her. No man will want her after this."

"Arihito, by now your sister has a certain reputation. This will not make things worse. It may make them better for her."

"But Father . . . it will kill him."

"No. It will not affect his reputation, and he knows his daughter by now."

"You're very hard."

This from the brother who had angrily rejected his sister for months. Akitada said nothing and Arihito thought about it. After a moment, he nodded. He glanced from Akitada to Tora and Saburo, who had been waiting stoically, and said, "I'm in your debt. How did you manage it?"

Tora said, "Norisuke was busy with the festival and he'd taken all his people. The master thought it a good time to find some evidence against him. But we weren't with him when he found Lady Yukiko. We don't know what happened."

Akitada had long since been aware of an increasing sticky wetness on his back. Surely the half-healed wounds from the cudgels would not bleed quite so much. The layers of festive silk and brocade clothing had apparently hidden any stains, but he was becoming slightly disoriented. He thought back to the fight with Norisuke. He had felt nothing then, though now his neck and left shoulder burned like fire and his arm felt numb.

Arihito was asking more questions, adding threats against Norisuke. Akitada heard only part of it. He wanted to go to his room and lie down to rest. He must think of what to say to the governor and prime minister. He wondered what Norisuke would do when he regained consciousness. What if he brought his warriors here?

Feeling very tired, he sat down abruptly and said, "Arihito, tell your people to close the gates and guard them."

Arihito's eyes widened with surprise. "Why? Wait. Does Norisuke know you freed her? Did he see you?"

"Yes. He tried to stop us leaving. I only wounded him." The room seemed to move and Akitada closed his eyes. "I wounded him. Left him unconscious . . . had to get Yukiko out. . . can we talk about it later?" He swayed.

Arihito's voice sounded far away. "You fought with him?"

Tora asked, "What's wrong, sir?"

Saburo said, "He's wounded. Why didn't you say anything, sir?"

Arihito asked again, "Why didn't you kill him?"

Akitada took a breath and said, "I didn't feel it before."

More questions. He did not bother with them. He tried to get up to go to his room, but passed out and fell.

The wound on his back was slight but long, a glancing cut made by Norisuke's sword. The blood had slowly but steadily soaked the back of the many layers of robes and run down to where his belt stopped its progress. The sword fight and their hurried escape had covered any pain, but Akitada had lost enough blood to become light-headed and eventually lose consciousness.

When he woke to his surroundings again, he was on his stomach and a doctor was probing the wound. It hurt and Akitada protested.

"Oh, you're back with us," said the physician, unimpressed, and continued his probing after instructing someone to hold him down.

"Stop that!" Akitada groaned.

"There," said the physician, holding up a tiny bit of bloody fabric before his face. "I hope that's all. Now to mop up and put on a bandage."

Eventually he was done and Akitada could sit up and glare balefully at Tora and Saburo. Tora said, "Sorry, sir. The wound had to be cleaned."

The doctor left and Tora said severely, "This wouldn't have happened, if you hadn't stopped at the women's pavilion and sent us away. How did you know Lady Yukiko was there?"

"I wasn't sure. But I saw the door was barred from the outside, and that meant someone was being held prisoner. And I'd been told that Norisuke did not bring any of his own women to Otsu and that he had a lover. I thought it likely that he had met Yukiko and she would have been attracted to him."

Saburo said accusingly, "Why did you send us away?"

"It seemed best to spare her embarrassment if she was there."

Tora snorted. "What was Lady Yukiko doing at that place?"

Akitada was becoming irritated. "Go away! I want to rest."

They left, and he thought about Yukiko. He should have realized sooner that she would find Norisuke to her taste. The man was everything her husband had not been. He was young, he was handsome, he was a warrior; and he had wealth and power. She would have found his dangerous reputation doubly tempting.

He had assumed all along that Yukiko had found a new lover. The little house on the mountain was a lovers' hideaway. But Norisuke had his own reasons to hide their affair. As their relationship progressed, she must have left her place to move to his house, perhaps hoping to become his wife. It would have made sense to her, because she was of higher rank than his other wives. It was unclear what Norisuke's intentions had been, but once she was with him,

Norisuke had returned to his old perversions. When Yukiko objected, she had become his prisoner. Akitada wondered how long she had suffered and how much of the appalling violence inflicted on her had been for sexual stimulation and how much had been due to angry frustration. Yukiko could make a saint angry, and Norisuke was no saint.

Akitada found no satisfaction in the fact that she had brought about her own punishment. Her situation had been terrible and likely to have ended with her death. Norisuke could hardly have left her alive to accuse him. She was no lowly prostitute or courtesan.

The next morning, Akitada gritted his teeth against pain and paid the overdue call on the governor. Sanenari was eager to find out what they had discovered. Akitada handed over the papers he had removed from Norisuke's study. When he reported about the horses and the silk Saburo had found in the stables and storehouses, Sanenari nodded but he still looked worried. Then Akitada told him about Yukiko and the condition he had found her in. The governor was aghast and jumped up to pace angrily.

"It's unbelievable!" he said. "It cannot be tolerated. I shall immediately order a thorough investigation. Norisuke shall not get away with this. We'll find enough to finish him, even if Lady Yukiko's story isn't enough."

Akitada nodded and mentioned the fact that he had wounded Norisuke.

Sanenari goggled at him. "You fought Norisuke? And you wounded him? And here you are? How absolutely wonderful!"

For a compliment it wasn't entirely flattering.

Akitada returned to the capital without telling anyone that he was feeling feverish. The wound had become infected after all. He was quite ill for days and when he started feeling better, he fretted about his report to the prime minister.

As it was, the prime minister came to see him.

Akitada, having been warned of the visit, had left his bed and sat, leaning on an armrest near the open door to his garden. There was still some spring bloom, but it would soon be summer. When the prime minister was shown in, he tried to get up, but his Excellency, who had come alone, said quickly, "No, don't get up. How pleasant to sit and admire your garden."

He made himself comfortable, accepted some wine, and said, "I heard a strange story and had to come myself to hear it from you."

Akitada, feeling awkward and still very uncomfortable, said, "I'm sorry I haven't reported yet."

"No, no. You did report to Sanenari and he gave me an outline of what happened. I came to hear the details about Lady Yukiko's tribulations and your battle with Norisuke. How is your wound?"

"Healing. I had been concerned about Lady Yukiko for several weeks when I heard she had disappeared. Rumor had it that Norisuke had a female guest, though he had not brought any of his wives with him. It could of course have been a courtesan, and, having heard about his behavior with women, I hoped it was, but when my retainers and I explored his compound and I saw his women's pavilion barred from the outside, I decided to take a look." Akitada paused and grimaced at the memory of what he had found.

The prime minister shook his head. "It must have been shocking. Your former wife in such circumstances! Lady Yukiko is a high-ranking court lady. We met occasionally. She is a well-known beauty."

"She would prefer that the incident not become known too widely."

The prime minister nodded. "They won't find out from me or Sanenari. But you must know that such a story cannot be suppressed completely. Was she there against her will?"

Akitada found this difficult to answer. He said, "No woman would willingly submit to such torment. I believe she knows how rumor will deal with her. So does her family."

"There's the problem. What do they intend to do?"

Akitada thought of Kosehira who loved Yukiko with an extraordinary attachment. How would he bear this latest shameful event? The prime minister's curiosity suddenly irritated him. He asked, "What do *you* intend to do?"

"Ah, yes. That would depend on circumstances. As I said, Norisuke is, alas, a valuable ally."

"Surely not!"

Akitada's shock was clear in his tone, and the prime minister smiled a little. "Well, politics and the needs of the country make for unpleasant associations at times. But that is not your affair." He sighed. "Get well quickly. I have more work for you. A new assignment is long overdue." He got up, gave Akitada another smile, and walked out.

40

Twisted Strands of Fate

Akitada did heal quickly this time. Physically, he was soon well enough to return to work. Not much had changed there, but Akitada had not expected it. The prime minister had been quite clear about it. Morozane was secure in his position. Fortunately, his manner toward Akitada was no longer as hostile as it had been, and he left his senior secretary pretty much alone.

This rather dull and quiet period was welcome at first. It gave Akitada time to mourn Kobe and ponder his own future. Kobe's family had apparently accepted their losses, and Kobe's peasants were content working under the temple's supervision.

Lord Okura called on him at home. He came shyly and with apologies, but for once Akitada received him gladly.

"You've heard?" he asked.

Okura blushed. "Yes, I heard. Such joy! I came to thank you. They said you were wounded. How are you? I feel responsible."

"No need. I was glad to have the chance to release Yukiko. How is she? Or do you know?"

Okura blushed more deeply. "Yes. I've seen her. Oh, I was so happy to see her again. She is getting better. It was painful to know that such a dreadful thing happened to her! But she was very kind, thanked me even. She said I'd saved her life. I told her that was nonsense, that you were the one who found her and fought for her."

Akitada was aghast. "No, no! You mustn't tell her that. It's not true. It was a mere accident. I was on a different assignment when I found her." He had no wish to have Yukiko convinced that she owed him anything, or worse, that he was indeed the hero who had rescued her.

Okura did not altogether believe his disclaimer but he changed the subject to tell Akitada that he had hopes she would become his wife after all, that he had proposed marriage, and that her father and older brother both approved of the match. He practically glowed with happiness. Akitada expressed his heartfelt congratulations and hoped that Okura's devotion would survive any future abuse Yukiko might feel inclined to shower him with.

Kosehira, returned from his provincial assignment, also came to see Akitada. He looked older and his hair had turned gray. Seeing him getting old was painful to Akitada. They were nearly the same age. His friend had also lost his habitual cheerfulness and for once came into the room without smiling, so that Akitada was afraid for a moment that he would be blamed for what had happened to Yukiko.

But Kosehira said merely, "Forgive me, Akitada, for delaying so long, but my journey back was long and difficult. And I found my home in disarray, with my son threatening to raise an army against Norisuke and a daughter who had once again shamed me by taking up with such a man."

"She could not have known what he would do," Akitada said. "I believe he courted her. Probably first in the capital and later in Otsu. It was only when she put her trust in him and came to live with him that he started to mistreat her."

Kosehira merely humphed. "It's still unbelievable. And you've once again stood by my family. I shall always be in your debt."

"There is no debt. You stood by me many times when I was in trouble. When I was young, you were the only friend I had. Our friendship is mutual and strong. I was glad I could help Yukiko, for her sake as well as yours."

Kosehira brushed away a tear and finally smiled a little. "I trust she's learned a lesson. She'll marry Okura," he said. "I shall make sure this time that she behaves properly. He's the father of my granddaughter." He paused, embarrassed. "Okura told me that he begged for your help. Did you not find it unbearable to have the man who seduced your wife appeal to you?"

Akitada, who had long since come to like Okura, laughed. "A little at first, but his devotion overcame my reluctance."

Kosehira chuckled also. "Yes. He does seem completely besotted. I hope she honors his feelings."

They parted on the old comfortable terms with promises to meet again when their lives were more settled.

That summer, Akitada lost his daughter. Yasuko, eighteen years old, tall, slender, and more beautiful than her mother, married Minamoto Michiyasu, the twenty-five-year-old son of an imperial prince. The wedding festivities were memorable, though bride and groom were oblivious in their happiness and Akitada felt lost among so many illustrious guests. He withdrew into tearful melancholy, feeling his loss because his child had joined a world alien to him. Fortunately, such sentimentality by a father was expected and approved by the guests.

Akitada's grief was eased not only because he really liked Michiyasu and his family, but also by the prospect of a new assignment. He was once again to serve as a governor, an extraordinary appointment outside the normal court calendar of appointments. The previous official had died suddenly, and Akitada was to finish what remained of the man's tenure and then stay on for his own four-year term. He had long wished for such an opportunity. It would take him away from the dreary ministry job and the detestable Morozane and offer new challenges and surroundings. He was considered lucky beyond all expectations.

The news of his good fortune—and the marriage of a daughter into a family with imperial blood was also counted as lucky—reached the ministry within hours after he had been told himself. Morozane sent for him the moment he arrived for work.

"My dear Akitada," Morozane cried, coming with open arms to embrace him. "What excellent news! I've never been so gratified."

A startled Akitada retreated a step. He had been ignored for weeks and had daily expected recriminations for giving the ministry a bad name with his report. "I beg your pardon, sir?" he said, mystified.

"Oh, call me Morozane. Why such formality between friends? I just heard of your fine appointment. First the very good news of your daughter's marriage, and now this. You played the game well, Akitada, very well indeed."

Akitada swallowed. He almost repeated, "I beg your pardon!" in a tone of outrage. How dared the man suggest that he had blackened the reputations of several officials, including Morozane's, in order to benefit himself? He put more distance between himself and the other man and asked coldly, "You sent for me, sir?"

Morozane still smiled, but a little uncertainly now. "Yes, Akitada. I wanted to inform you of the results of our investigation."

"*Our* investigation, sir?"

Morozane shuffled. "Yes. I always thought there was something we could do to stop those thieves. They were much too greedy. One expects to lose a few things in transport across the country, but I felt enough was enough when the director of the Markets Office built his new house with stolen lumber. Still, I couldn't have done it without your help. Good work, Akitada."

Akitada was speechless. So Morozane had decided to turn Akitada's investigation into his own and take the credit. He should have expected it.

Morozane waited a beat for Akitada's "Thank you," and when it did not come, continued, "Needless to say Yoshinaro not only lost his position but is being sent to Kyushu to serve as assistant to the governor there. His career is over. As for Otsu, Minamoto Norisuke has resigned. He's gone back home. A local man has been appointed. I was a little surprised by that. What exactly did you accuse Norisuke of?"

"Nothing, sir. Governor Sanenari asked for the reassignment. I believe there was a raid on Norisuke's warehouses."

Morozane digested that. He frowned. "There's a rumor that Norisuke was injured during a festival. They say his face is disfigured. Do you know anything about that?"

"Not much. An accident during a military drill, I believe."

"Ah! Yes. That makes sense. Bad luck! He was a very handsome man."

Luck again, good and bad. The good luck of the complacent Morozane who had survived Akitada's charge of falsifying an official's report, and bad luck for Minamoto Norisuke, who had not only lost the favor of the court but his godlike good looks. Morozane would not hold a grudge, but a man like Norisuke would never forgive Akitada. The threat would always be there, remote perhaps but lasting. Our actions come back to haunt us, if not in this life, then in the next.

Akitada shook off these fancies. He had no time for them. New ventures waited, bringing perhaps fresh risks, but just as likely fortuitous events.

Historical Note

The year of this novel is 1040 AD. The events take place in the capital, Heian-kyo, and its surroundings, especially in the port city Otsu. Much of the novel deals with problems in the administration of the country. This was in the hands of one ruling family, a branch of the Fujiwara clan. It had established its preeminence via marriage politics by furnishing imperial wives and controlling young emperors. The control of the government now rested primarily with senior Fujiwara nobles, plus a few families descended from ancient clans, and the more recent Minamoto clan. The Minamoto clan came about when the name was adopted by younger imperial princes unlikely to succeed to the throne. They lost imperial powers, but close connection to a recent emperor bestowed special privileges.

The government maintained an elaborate rank system for its noble members. Only the top six ranks could hold senior positions in ministries, bureaus, and the central council. Only they had access to the emperor. The lower ranks staffed the ministries or served as governors in the provinces. It was through appointing court nobles to the administration of these provinces that the central government controlled the rest of the nation. The pay of all these officials was based on their rank. Essentially, there was little opportunity to gain wealth except through promotion, and governors became notorious in enriching themselves at the expense of their subjects once they gained sufficient distance from the capital.

Originally this bureaucracy was a meritocracy as in China. Rank and income were covered by precise laws governing officials. They were annually evaluated, and the Taiho code of 701 spelled out rules and punishments for both the administrative and the penal systems. It quickly became too restricting for the Fujiwara administration and was revised into the Yoro code in 757. Many positions had, by then, become hereditary, and corruption of officials became common.

In the article "Traffic between the Capital and Countryside in Ritsuryo Japan," Hotate Michihisa deals not only with the massive problems of tax shipments from the provinces to the capital and the multiple ways in which all types of goods moved, but also with the many ways they could be stolen. These included raids by gangs of robbers who sold the goods in the markets of the capital, as well as corrupt nobles and officials in port cities and along the major highways who served as overseers but maintained their residence in the capital. They sold barrier passes, dressed their attendants as imperial guards, and maintained armed bands to plunder tax goods.

Otsu, only ten miles from the capital, was one of the major transportation centers. It is located at the south-western tip of Lake Biwa. Three major highways ran through Otsu toward the capital. They are the Tosando, linking the middle provinces to Heiankyo, the *Tokaido* reaching into the far eastern provinces, and the *Hokurikudo,* which leads into the eastern mountain provinces. In addition, shipping along the coast of the Japan Sea and on Lake Biwa carried goods which passed through Otsu on their way to the capital.

The city is quite ancient and once served as one of the nation's capitals. It is home to two great Buddhist establishments, the *Enryakuji* on *Mount Hiei* overlooking the city and *Miidera (Onjoji)* below. The two temples are notorious for their fierce battles against each other.

A few explanations about life in a noble family may be useful. Noblemen usually took more than one wife to assure the succession. First marriages occurred very early, while the pair were barely teens. Subsequent marriages generally involved wives who were younger than the man. Secondary wives might live in the same house or elsewhere. Most likely, first marriages were carefully planned between families to bring benefits to the husband and to future children. Both wealth and influence could assure secure futures. Husbands as well as wives could divorce by simply announcing the wish. Wives could and did own property which they controlled, though customarily this passed to their children. In a family with multiple wives, ranks were assigned to the women, much as in the imperial marriages. There was always a senior wife, who had usually gained her position through the power and influence of her family. Her male children rose higher in the official hierarchy than the sons of other wives. Hence, Akitada's panic over his daughter's betrothal is entirely reasonable for his culture.

The noble couple might start life in the bride's family home, a reasonable arrangement when both were still very young. They might later move into a house belonging to her husband. Their home was likely a *shinden*, a main house connected by galleries to additional pavilions and additions. This house would occupy a large city lot that also contained service buildings and gardens. The buildings were rectangular, single-story, post-and-beam constructions. They were elevated a few feet above the ground and surrounded by verandas. Roofed galleries linked additional dwellings to the main house. Inside, the spaces were open but could be divided with movable walls. Louvered or latticed doors led to verandas and reed screens could cover the openings when the doors were open. It would have been very cold in winter, and they had little to protect them beyond braziers, screens, many-layered gowns, and quilts and comforters to sleep under.

Strict customs surrounded a death. In Shinto—and the emperor was most strongly associated with this faith—contact with the dead made a person ritually unclean. Thus funerals were conducted by Buddhist clerics. Usually they took place at night and involved cremation, the ashes to be placed in Buddhist cemeteries.

To conclude, we come to the matter of the lucky gods. There are generally seven of these deities in Japanese tradition. Six of them are Buddhist in origin and came from India and China; the seventh is a native Shinto god. This one is Ebisu, the fisherman, commonly depicted with a fishing rod and a fish. Of the rest, there is Bishamonten, the warrior with his spear; Daikokuten, with a rice bale; Hotei, the fat little Buddha of happiness; Fukuroju and Jurojin, both associated with learning and virtue; and the only female, Benzaiten, representing the arts. All seven are worshipped because they bestow wealth and good fortune. All of them are quite ancient and would have been popular in Heian times. They have been depicted many times in Japanese art.

About the Author

I. J. Parker was born and educated in Europe and turned to mystery writing after an academic career in the U.S. She has published her Akitada stories in *Alfred Hitchcock's Mystery Magazine,* winning the Shamus award in 2000. Several stories have also appeared in collections, such as *Fifty Years of Crime and Suspense* and *Shaken.* The award-winning "Akitada's First Case" is available as a podcast.

Many of the stories have been collected in *Akitada and the Way of Justice.*

The Akitada series of crime novels features the same protagonist, an eleventh century Japanese nobleman/detective. *The Lucky Gods of Otsu* is number twenty-one. The books are available as e-books, in print, and in audio format, and have been translated into twelve languages. The early novels are published by Penguin.

I. J. Parker

Books by I. J. Parker

The Akitada series in chronological order

The Dragon Scroll

Rashomon Gate

Black Arrow

Island of Exiles

The Hell Screen

The Convict's Sword

The Masuda Affair

The Fires of the Gods

Death on an Autumn River

The Emperor's Woman

Death of a Doll Maker

The Crane Pavilion

The Old Men of Omi

The Shrine Virgin

The Assassin's Daughter

The Island of the Gods

Ikiryo: Revenge and Justice

Contact Information

Please visit I.J.Parker's web site at http://www.ijparker.com. You may contact her via e-mail from there. (This way you will be informed when new books come out.)

Trade paperbacks of the novels are available on Amazon. There are electronic versions of all the works. Please do post reviews. They help sell books and keep Akitada novels coming.

Thank you for your support.

Made in United States
North Haven, CT
15 November 2024